TEACH ME TONIGHT

Nor could he come into Dashwood as Juan and not kiss her senseless again—the thought set Ewan back on his heels.

The mask had made him do what he had done. It had to be the mask and the freedom it had given him.

What other explanation could there be? Only one remained: he found Miss Lucy Bowes attractive, an object of his desire.

Kissing her had driven all other thoughts from his head. She had tasted sweet, but a spiciness underlay the sweet. That spiciness had driven him on. He needed it, craved it, realized that within it he had found someone who could match him fiber by fiber, step by step, desire by desire. She was unschooled, but if he had learned anything about Miss Bowes, he had learned that she was a quick study.

Her Other Thief

Glenda Garland

ZEBRA BOOKS
Kensington Publishing Corp.
www.kensingtonbooks.com

ZEBRA BOOKS are published by

Kensington Publishing Corp.
850 Third Avenue
New York, NY 10022

All Kensington titles, imprints and distributed lines are available at special quantity discounts for bulk purchases for sales promotion, premiums, fund-raising, educational or institutional use.

Special book excerpts or customized printings can also be created to fit specific needs. For details, write or phone the office of the Kensington Special Sales Manager: Kensington Publishing Corp., 850 Third Avenue, New York, NY 10022. Attn. Special Sales Department. Phone: 1-800-221-2647.

Zebra and the Z logo Reg. U.S. Pat. & TM Off.

First Printing: December 2004
10 9 8 7 6 5 4 3 2 1

Printed in the United States of America

To my dear family—
Jared, Sammy, and Scott—
for all the love and support
you have given me the last year.

Right back at you guys!

ACKNOWLEDGMENTS

Her Other Thief takes place a year after *The Unexpected Sister* (Zebra Books, March 2004) ends. *The Unexpected Sister* tells the story of Caroline Norcrest and Lord Thomas Dashley. Jennifer Ashley, a fellow writer and friend, suggested that Caroline's good friend Lucy Bowes deserved her own story. Thank you, Jennifer, for the excellent suggestion, for editing drafts whenever I sent up an SOS, and for saying, "I love Lucy."

Chapter 1

August, 1815

"Will you not speculate at all upon Dashwood?" Miss Lucy Bowes asked her best friend Caroline, newly Marchioness of Dash. "We have been traveling to it for two days now, and you have studiously avoided the subject."

"You are tired of traveling, Lucy?"

"In your well-sprung carriage, with your company, changing views of lush hills and shady woodland, and a fine inn last night? No, I am not tired of traveling. Are you?"

"Since Thomas is yet detained in France with Wellington," Caroline replied, slanting sunlight illuminating her blond hair, and the carriage's motion causing the fine ribbons decorating her exquisitely detailed sky blue dress to sway, "the only pleasure I take in opening his family house after his older brother's death is from your presence. If I have not said thank you for coming with me, thank you."

"You have said so about twenty times," Lucy replied. Lucy was still amazed that Caroline had invited her to accompany her to Dashwood, home of the marquesses of Dash, for she judged herself perpetually bad company these days. "And it is my pleasure. What would I be doing with myself otherwise?"

Caroline merely looked at Lucy, ready sympathy warming her beautiful features. Of all the people in the world, Caroline knew her best. Caroline had stood by her, as Lucy's brother Jack embarrassed her by escaping the law after being discovered to be a thief. Since he had yet been a commissioned officer, the Army had taken his flight as desertion, compounding his shame.

And hers. Lucy tried to pretend she had not accepted Caroline's invitation as an excuse to escape from the many people who knew her shame. But what was the point? Just sitting in Caroline's well-sprung carriage, admiring her dress, led Lucy inexorably down to the same dismal, self-pitying conclusion. Jack had stolen Lucy's future, too, for no one would want a plain, outspoken woman whose only funds were tied up while she waited six more years to declare her brother legally dead.

Their carriage abruptly slowed. Both of them looked out the window. There was only countryside about them, no sign of Dashwood yet. They were almost up a broad, grassy hill and would come to a stop at its very crest.

Lucy shared a frown with Caroline, then pulled a pistol from her bandbox, settled it in her lap, and placed her blue- and green-patterned Norwich shawl over it. Caroline goggled.

"Desperate times demand desperate measures," Lucy said.

The carriage stopped. A dark-haired man appeared at the window. "My lady Dash?" he asked.

Caroline gestured to the man to open the door, and Lucy took fresh appreciation of her friend's mettle because Caroline did not need to be told she should sit back immediately should Lucy need a clear line of shot.

The man wore a forest green uniform, much frogged with black over silver buttons, with red facings and an officer's deep red sash. In addition to the dark hair, he possessed alert brown eyes, a jutting chin, and highly chiseled cheekbones. An overall symmetry to his face managed to render these strong features curiously patrician.

"Sir?" inquired Caroline in her best marchioness voice.

The officer bowed. "My lady, I am Captain Sandeford, a new neighbor of yours. Your husband Colonel Lord Dash wrote to me and asked me to render you any assistance you may require."

"Good God, sir," Lucy said, quietly uncocking the pistol. "And you thought scaring us half to death the way to do it?"

"I beg your pardon?"

"My friend hides a pistol under her shawl in case you should have been joined by masked highwaymen," Caroline said.

Captain Sandeford started satisfactorily.

Lucy drew the weapon from beneath her shawl.

"It is not cocked," Captain Sandeford said, relief and something like disdain in his voice. He seemed to Lucy to be measuring her, as though wondering whether she might yet turn out to be an intelligent woman. She felt distinctly out of sorts. She did not like surprises on the best of days, and she had had to endure many of them this last year.

"Not anymore," Lucy said. "I heard no warning from the coachman."

"May I have it, please?"

"Why?"

"I have a long history of disliking guns pointed at me," he said.

"Then are you not in the wrong profession?" Lucy asked. "But if the pistol bothers you, I shall put it away."

"Are we far from Dashwood, Captain?" Caroline asked.

"It is about four miles off."

"Then since you have ridden out this way, do join us."

"Very good, my lady. Thank you. With your coachman's permission, I shall tie my horse behind the carriage."

He disappeared.

"Did you know about this?" Lucy asked in a low voice.

"No," Caroline replied. "But it is like Thomas. Although he thought it proper to open Dashwood, he was quite reluctant to send me up here by myself."

"I do not like this Captain Sandeford. However did Dash choose him?"

Caroline shook her head. "Maybe his options were limited. I must say being stopped alarmed me."

"So you do not like him, either?"

"My lady," said the captain at the door. He climbed into the carriage and sat down opposite Lucy and Caroline. Instantly the well-sprung carriage felt small to Lucy, and off balance.

Caroline, however, betrayed no nervousness. She said, "May I present my dear friend Miss Bowes to you, Captain."

Captain Sandeford inclined his head with all correctness. "Miss Bowes, the pleasure is mine."

Lucy could tell he liked nothing of her. Her pistol had annoyed him, she had nothing of beauty to make him reconsider, and her serviceable dark blue dress did not proclaim her as someone who had interesting connections. But for Caroline's sake she forced her lips into a slight smile. "Sir. You are all kindness."

"Do you know my husband well, sir?"

"I met Colonel Lord Dash but a few times."

"It speaks very well of you, sir," said Caroline, "that

you would accept such an office on so slight an acquaintance."

"You, my lady," he said, "are not hardship duty." Then he glanced at Lucy, one brow raised.

Caroline might not be hardship duty, Lucy deduced, a peculiar combination of perverse satisfaction, pride, and bone-deep disappointment swirling through her.

Lucy left them to make non-hardship conversation during the remaining short distance to Dashwood, an imposing house, mostly of red brick, although like other English mansions, it had been built up here and there, in higgledy-piggledy fashion. One wing to the left was of a much lighter brick and stuck out at an odd angle. Still, it looked prosperous and cared for.

The Dashwood servants had lined up in regulation form on the graveled drive. A host of men in black and white headed by a stiff, balding man of about fifty years preceded a blank-faced woman with her equivalent in maids. The stables and gardening staff stood a rank behind the household staff. To a person, they were straightening collars, cuffs, aprons, and caps.

The balding man stepped forward. "I am Walters, my lady. Welcome to Dashwood."

"Thank you, Walters," Caroline replied. "This is my dear friend, Miss Bowes, who will be staying with me some time. And this is Captain Sandeford, who may be known to you. Lord Dash asked him to escort me."

"Very good, my lady. Permit me to introduce you to Mrs. Walters, who is housekeeper here."

They all looked very nervous, Lucy thought, although that was not to be wondered at. Caroline would reassure them with a kind, deceptively firm hand. It would be a kindness on Lucy's part, though, if she let Caroline have a little time with them to work her magic.

Coward, she mocked herself. The truth was that Lucy

wanted to put some distance between herself and Captain Sandeford, who continued to regard her with the same ill-concealed fascination one reserves for messy accidents.

Lucy spied a path leading off the drive that likely went toward the stables and around the back of the house. She caught Caroline's eye, then tipped her head toward the path. Caroline nodded, still listening to Mrs. Walters introduce the lesser chambermaids.

As Lucy set off, though, a stolid, steady-looking man from the back ranks loped toward her and touched his cap.

"Ma'am. You want to see the garden, ma'am?"

"Just to walk about a little bit. It is not necessary for you to follow me. I shall not stray from the path."

"Ma'am," he said, but showed no sign of leaving her be.

"I shall come with you," Captain Sandeford said.

"I am sure that—" she looked to the gardener.

He touched his cap. "Fletcher, ma'am."

"That Fletcher here will be suitable escort."

"It would give me pleasure," Captain Sandeford said.

"Very well," Lucy replied, seething that he could not take a hint. In light of the staff's nerves, Fletcher's insistence made sense, but Captain Sandeford's? Explanations defeated Lucy.

She concentrated on Dashwood and tried to ignore both Captain Sandeford and Fletcher, who walked behind them. The gardens were lovely, a fine balance of textures and blooming summer colors, with enough shade to make the warm summer day quite tolerable.

"Tell me, Miss Bowes," Captain Sandeford said in a voice of grim resolution as they progressed past the stables and toward the back of the house, "why did you assume I was a highwayman?"

Fletcher gasped behind them.

"What is it, man?" Captain Sandeford asked.

Fletcher shook his head. "Nothing, sir. Sorry, ma'am."

"These are hazardous times," Lucy said. "But now that I have thought on it, I realize you could not very well have showed up here to meet us."

"Your consideration means much to me," he replied, with a resolute politeness to his tone that made Lucy again think of herself as hardship duty and wonder why he had come with her.

In chilly silence they proceeded around the back, where the initial regularity of the house's shape revealed itself. Each upper-floor room had its own balcony, encased by a stone balustrade. Ivy covered the entire wall and twined around the balustrades' spindles.

Except for one very irregular patch to the right of a balcony, second room from the left. About a yard or more of warm red brick showed. At first Lucy wondered what it was about that patch that the ivy deigned not to grow there. Then she realized that broken strands of ivy hung down erratically from the sides.

"Fletcher, what caused that gouge in the ivy?"

Fletcher looked distinctly uncomfortable. "We think it was a polecat, ma'am."

"A polecat, you say? That would be an exceptionally large polecat. Did it get into the house?"

"No one saw him, ma'am," Fletcher said, but he ducked his head, making Lucy suspicious. Had someone *heard* something?

"I am sure the Dashwood staff has the matter well in hand, ma'am," Captain Sandeford said, checking a pocket watch. "Should we not be rejoining Lady Dash?"

Lucy recalled her earlier impression of Captain Sandeford as looking patrician. A patrician who believed such a gouge could be caused by a polecat! It was no wonder Rome finally fell. Indeed, it was amazing Britain had stopped Napoleon with such officers.

But if she lingered, no doubt Captain Sandeford would begin to comment on women who could not leave well enough alone. Lucy nodded for answer, resisting a last look at the ivy.

They found Caroline inside in the main hall. Walters and Mrs. Walters followed in her wake. Walters looked stoic, Mrs. Walters's thin face considerably less than.

A polecat indeed! No foot-and-a-half-long polecat could cause a three-foot gouge. If Mrs. Walters knew a "polecat" that could cause a three-foot gouge in the ivy was getting into Dashwood, she certainly had a right to be worried.

"What do you think, Lucy?" Caroline asked.

"It has, as my father would have said, 'good bones.' The walls and floors are exquisite. Only look at how attractive the grain is in the oak paneling, and how superb the marble. I dare one to match the main stair for grandeur. I would not presume to hazard a guess on the quality of the paintings, though, Caro, not while you are here. I think it must be the furnishings that make me feel less than comfortable."

"That is just what I was thinking," Caroline said. "They are . . . not to my taste. Starting tomorrow we will take a thorough inventory of this house and decide what to put into storage."

"That is a very ambitious undertaking, Lady Dash," Captain Sandeford said.

"Do you mean to imply, sir," Lucy asked, "that we are not equal to such a task?"

"I mean to imply no such thing, Miss Bowes," he replied stiffly. "It is merely that this is a very big place, and Lady Dash only just arrived."

"I am certain you meant kindly, sir," Caroline said with a warning look to Lucy.

Lucy finished counting to twenty, found it did not calm her as much as it usually did. "I am sorry, Captain Sandeford. Shall we start tomorrow, Caroline?"

"Best to get started before I find other matters to distract me," Caroline said.

"I will let you rest after your long journey. Perhaps, Lady Dash, I may call on you tomorrow?"

"Thank you, sir, that would be very considerate of you. I am glad to know that there is a respectable gentleman such as yourself in the neighborhood."

He bowed and took his leave of them.

"You are very up in arms, Lucy," Caroline said.

"Do not be making such jests, Caroline."

Caroline laughed. "Come, admit it was clever."

Lucy had to smile, too. "I am convinced the only way one earns Captain Sandeford's respect is with a pistol."

"Why do you not like him?"

"Do you? Like him, that is?"

"I am not sure."

"For you, that must be a strange place. Dash has been a fine influence on you, Caro."

Caroline blushed, as Lucy knew she would. "You will tell me what to think, won't you?"

"No, I have no need to do that. I like your idea of going through this place right away, and not just because Captain Sandeford counseled to wait."

"Why do you not like him?"

"I am not certain," Lucy replied. "He seems sharp to me, like every one of those buttons could cut one to ribbons."

"A hedgehog in regimentals?"

Lucy winced. Hedgehogs and polecats within a quarter hour of each other were too much native fauna for her. "Something like that. When he is not being sharp, he seems curiously aloof. I do not like that in an escort."

"Nor would I," said Caroline, amused.

"Nor do you, then," Lucy said, "for he has pledged himself to be your guide, Lady Dash. I am merely here for the entertainment."

"And *you* always accused *me* of speaking fustian."

"Whatever can you mean?"

"You know very well what I mean," said Caroline as they walked toward the staircase. "I am going to tell Walters to arrange for baths for us and dinners on trays in my room, if you would like. I do not wish the estate dinner today."

"Let them impress you tomorrow."

"Just so. Lucy, I really do want to thank you for coming here with me."

"As always, the pleasure is mine," Lucy said.

"I asked Mrs. Walters to prepare a room for you near mine."

"Perfect," Lucy said.

"Do you wish to rest?"

"No, not yet. Since both Fletcher and Captain Sandeford insisted on joining my walk, I do not feel like I have had it. Would you excuse me for a bit?"

Caroline hugged Lucy. "Go. Walk."

Lucy headed for the back of the house, studied the gouge in the ivy again. Some of the dangling tendrils looked about to fall down on the loose broom shrubs beneath them that lined the back of the house. Lucy felt around their tops and on the ground beneath them for any other downed ivy, but it appeared the garden staff had cleaned it up.

Her head stuck almost inside one of the brooms to explore its far side, she glimpsed two objects missed, and teased them out of the broom. The first object was a two-inch piece of brick. Lucy backed up to look at the wall again. Now that she knew what she looked for, she could see where this piece had come from. Every so often, a brick had been inserted into the wall length side out, for texture. One such brick within the gouge was missing its corner.

The second object was a black leather strap such as might have decorated a boot. Lucy doubted, given the soft suppleness of the leather, that it had been long subjected to the elements. Had the gardening staff, in its desire to make all ready for Caroline's arrival, cleaned up the ivy and not had either time or imagination to fish around in the brooms?

Something—no, someone—had tried to come into Dashwood, and recently. Why this stealthy person had chosen to scale the ivy to the second floor instead of breaking in downstairs, Lucy did not know. Doubtless he had his reasons, however arrived at.

Would he try again? Lucy did not know, but the debt of gratitude she owed Caroline itched her sorely. It seemed that neither the staff nor Captain Sandeford wanted to admit the possibility that someone was stealing into Dashwood. It was up to Lucy to find out the truth if she could and let Caroline know if there was a problem.

Lucy considered the ivy-covered wall. Under the ivy the next balcony over, there was a delightfully regular outcropping of brick. Any self-respecting "polecat" that could not easily climb in the other balcony might find its way up there.

Right then and there, Lucy resolved to sit up in the room next to that balcony and see whether any kind of polecat climbed in. Quite likely her proposed vigil was absurd. Until she knew for certain, she would not alarm Caroline.

But she would need to set up precautions, certainly.

Lucy smiled, making plans.

Chapter 2

Ewan hid in Dashwood's far gardens and watched for the lights in Lady Dash's rooms to extinguish. No other room on that floor showed light. Miss Bowes was either around front or had gone to sleep before she needed to light candles. It was hard to imagine such a dragon sleeping, and early.

She was an odd creature. Ewan did not like either her unnatural propensity to point a weapon at him or her judgmental gaze, which had disliked him on sight. A surprise, that, since most women tended to flatter him. Perhaps Miss Bowes had grown used to men disregarding her and had stopped trying. While Ewan admitted that her hazel eyes sparkled with some brilliance, they did so only when she was being acerbic. Although her chestnut hair curled nicely, its color was unremarkable. She had no spots, but then, neither did Ewan, or many a prettier woman.

Miss Bowes had shown no sign of relenting her poor opinion of him. Indeed, her lip had positively curled when he had presented himself as being of use to her friend. She had also considered him either a fool or far too nice for believing the gardener's story about a pole-cat climbing up Dashwood's walls.

Ewan, however, was grateful that the gardener had invented a story, no matter how implausible. A gouge in the ivy, while odd, would not lead someone to believe conclusively that someone was coming into the house.

And Ewan needed to keep sneaking into Dashwood, a task severely complicated both by the random movements of the Dashwood staff on the lower floor—late last night Ewan had knocked down a surprised, red-haired footman on God-knows-what business—and the arrival of Lady Dash and Miss Bowes.

Why did women always feel the need to reorganize everything? That would add a further complication.

At least the ladies' arrival had given him an excuse to get closer to Dashwood in the light of day. During his walk with Miss Bowes, he had observed a regular out-cropping of stone that ran up close to a balcony.

Now he located it again in the dark and began to climb, congratulating himself on how this ascent to the upper stories resembled a smooth, easy ascent upon a ladder, rather than his previous, haphazard scramble that had left him suspended from a balcony railing fifteen feet above the ground and kicking out against the wall.

He was keen to creep down to the drawing room where Lady Dash and Miss Bowes wished to start their reorganization. The room contained any number of pictures, but interspersed between these were shelves of ornamental boxes. Any of those boxes could contain the late Lord Dash's supply of vowels, including the strange IOU he had induced Ewan's brother Charles to sign. Ewan would search all of them tonight.

Cautiously Ewan crept into the room, looking into its shadows and listening for footsteps in the hall. Just as he headed to the door leading to the hallway, a sudden voice, low but clear, said from his left, "Yes, you *are* an exceptionally large polecat."

Ewan spun toward the voice. A pistol cocked in deliberate warning.

"Stay where you are, sir, or I shall certainly shoot you." Very still Miss Bowes sat in a wing chair far back in the shadows. She wore a dress almost as dark as Ewan's own black shirt, pants, boots, and the bandanna he had used to cover his hair and help hold his mask in place. Her pistol balanced neatly on her lap.

Ewan swallowed a curse. He was caught, well and for certain. He had not wanted to be caught, naturally. This was only his second entry into Dashwood.

Being caught was bad enough. But allow plain, pushy, pistol-toting Miss Bowes to delight in his chagrin and shame? No, Ewan could not stomach that.

She must not know that the masked man she had trapped with her wretched pistol—and Ewan took deep exception to being on the wrong end of that pistol for the second time that day—was Captain Ewan Sandeford.

Although the mask covered his face, she might recognize his voice. How to free himself from this predicament?

Ewan bowed with a flourish and spoke in the Spanish he had perfected while in the Peninsula. "*Hola, señorita.*"

"Spanish," Miss Bowes said in English, as though spitting the word from her mouth. "Why would it *have* to be Spanish?" Then she continued in heavily accented, but passable Spanish herself. "Do not be polite with me, *señor*. You are a thief, and here I hold a pistol. You would do best to go right back down the ivy."

"You speak my language," he replied. "How charming." How utterly provoking! How very much like her.

"I speak your language," she retorted, "with an atrocious accent, so I am told, since I but recently learned the language, and my vocabulary lacks some of the color you may employ."

"Your accent *may* lack something in melody, but you cannot convince me you would misunderstand any colorful expression I might use."

"It never matters. I am convinced you also speak some English, so if a word or two fails me, we may handily complete this, our one conversation, before you leave by that window."

"Do you not worry, *señorita,*" Ewan said with all seriousness, "that I could overpower you and take your pistol?"

"Not before I blew a sizable hole in you. Did we have all the time in the world, I would prove it to you. Now you shall have to take my word for it."

He tried to distract her by pointing toward the window. "I had no intention of leaving in such a rude way."

She was not distracted, blast her. "That, *señor*, is not my problem. Do go now, before I think you are trying to trick me and I raise the house. Do you see here?" She nodded to her left hand. "I have attached a line to the bell pull. I need only give it a little tug . . ."

"I take your point."

"Good."

"But if I may, why must you assume I am a thief?"

She chuckled, a surprisingly pleasant and unlooked-for sound. "Do you mean to tell me that your mother dressed you this evening?" she asked. "Or that this is the new fashion for Spaniards deep within England?"

"No," he answered, amused despite himself. It had been an absurd question. Was he stalling for time, thinking to catch her off balance? No, he thought, he was enjoying sparring with her, despite her great pistol that pointed unwaveringly at him.

"What have you come to steal, then?"

That blunt question put him right back out of humor. "None of your business, *señorita.*"

"None of my business? Really? I would have thought that you would have no compunctions about saying jewels or gold, even artwork." Here her mouth tightened alarmingly. "The house is filled with art, and were you to steal that, I am certain you *would* want to leave by a downstairs window instead of this balcony."

"You do think ahead."

"I anticipate many things," she replied. "As you see."

"Are there perchance those who accuse you of being downright incapable of being led, too?"

"Of course," she replied, somewhat smugly. "They are the ones who also prefer a firm hand on the reins."

"Or a firm hand to your pretty . . ." Ewan rolled his finger.

"No man will ever take his hand to me and keep it."

"That is a shame."

"Are you being ironic, *señor*?"

"Indeed, I meant nothing but to flatter you."

"Do not, for we both know that you cannot possibly see my pretty, ahem, nor am I like to stand and turn so you may discover whether you are correct in your guess as to its beauty or lack thereof."

"You wound me, *señorita,* truly you do."

"I will, of course, if you take one more step in my direction." Her tone, although light, was deadly serious.

Ewan spread his arms. "We find ourselves at an impasse. Much as I have enjoyed our conversation, I do need to be about my business. Put the pistol down. I shall be quickly gone."

"Your rapidity in stripping this house of valuables does in no way recommend my letting go of them."

"The house belongs to you, then?" Ewan asked, all innocence. "Should I then be calling you '*señora*'?"

"The house does not belong to me, but that never matters. It belongs to my dearest friend."

"She must be a dearest friend if you would fight so hard to prevent a poor thief such as myself from his task."

"I am likely the last person you will meet who has any love or sympathy for a thief." She spoke so vehemently that the pistol dropped a fraction. It now pointed toward Ewan's belly rather than his heart, though, so he could not boast of being in a much better position.

He did not doubt her sincerity. She would likely shoot *at* him. The most pressing question in his mind was whether she had ever shot anyone before. If not, the slight hesitation she would feel—every soldier Ewan had ever seen hesitated the first time—might work to his advantage. Then again, it might not.

Following that important question came another, distracting, but there nonetheless. Why was she the last person likely to have any sympathy for a thief? What had happened to this sharp-tongued, cool-headed young woman to make her say such a thing?

"And if stealing meant the difference between having a roof over my head or not?" he asked.

"I would be very sorry for you."

"But otherwise unmoved?"

"Still as a statue made of stone."

"But only the finest marble," he said.

Her mouth moved, but he could not make out her expression. "I have figured out a way around our impasse."

He tipped his head. Any other movement would alarm her, and, more importantly, take his eyes from her pistol. "I tremble with anticipation."

"Do not, I beg you."

"Why not?"

"You would make me miss your heart should I need

to shoot you, *señor*. I am told that wounds to the stomach are excessively painful and must be endured for some time before the sufferer finally dies."

Good Lord. "You do not take relish in such an eventuality?"

"You have not harmed me or mine," she said. "Not yet."

That was a straightforward answer, he thought. "What is your plan?"

"I shall count to ten. Then I shall pull this bell. If you are yet here, you will be caught. If you are not here, you will get away."

"Why not just pull the bell now and have me run?"

"Call it . . . compassion," she said.

"You believe I should trip over the ivy going down."

"And if I did? One, by the way."

Ewan heard the smile in her tone, but he did not think her amusement would prevent her from shooting him. He said, "I should take it very ill for you to have such a low opinion of my dexterity."

"*Destreza*?" she asked.

Well, that was one word she did not know. Ewan said, "How accomplished I am, how well I work with my hands." The moment the words were from his mouth, Ewan wished he could have rephrased.

Her head tipped to one side. "Getting up is one matter. Going down quite another, and you are going down, *señor*. Two."

"I certainly am, am I not," he said.

"You certainly are. Three."

"Tell me, did you climb many trees as a girl?"

"When I could, *señor*." She wiggled forward on her chair.

"Do take care. I would hate to be shot by mistake."

She stood, carefully, never taking her eyes from him, never letting her pistol waver or the cord drop from her hand. "Do not trouble a hair upon your head, *señor*—if you have hair, that is."

"I protest."

"What?"

"I am not bald, *señorita.*"

"I am happy to learn it. Four."

He would have no opportunity to grab either pistol or cord. Ewan bowed to the inevitable. "I see I must invest in a rope."

"Five. Why?"

"That the next time I might be assured of being down the wall before you get to ten, *señorita,* for I have so enjoyed our conversation I can barely force myself to leave." He had. He hated to admit such a thing, having disliked her so well this afternoon, but it was true. He had enjoyed sparring with her.

"There will be no next time."

He cautiously backed up toward the window and balcony, as she edged toward the center of the room, keeping the distance between them. "Oh, my dear *señorita,* but there will. And you forgot to count six."

"Six, seven—"

"I am gone. I am gone." Lightly he leaped over to the other side of the balcony railing. He tried to be as light in his finding the first brick outcropping, but they lay under a moon shadow from the balcony. He stumbled, causing an abysmally embarrassing hissing in the ivy.

Then he heard her chuckle and say, "Eight, nine, and ten. Run quickly, *Señor* Polecat, and do not come back."

"Good night, *señorita,*" he called softly in reply. "I will run, but I make no promises."

Chapter 3

Firmly now on the outcropping steps, Ewan managed the ground in half a minute and loped into the gardens. He did not stop until he reached the woods, where he had hidden his dark mare Bella. Speaking quietly to Bella, he tore off his mask and the bandanna he covered his hair with, stuffed them in the sack he carried for the purpose, and pulled on a gray coat.

Thus restored to some degree to being Captain Sandeford, he rode the three miles to his home, Barberry Lodge, a well-proportioned, eight-room house that in no way resembled Dashwood's size or ramshackle reputation.

He quietly stabled Bella himself and slipped through an open window into the library, where his younger brother Charles turned the chessboard to play Ewan's side.

"You are back quickly," Charles said. "Did you find it?"

"No. I was stopped. Lady Dash's friend Miss Bowes sat in wait for me."

"How did she know?"

"She must have seen the same brick steps up the house."

And to think Ewan had congratulated himself on how easily he had been able to climb up Dashwood. Martinet-eyed Miss Bowes had obviously made much of that tear in the ivy.

Still, he could not prevent some grudging admiration for her. She was certainly no milquetoast miss. And maybe, just maybe, he had stoked her suspicions by not calling the gardener on his story.

"Why did you not just overpower her?" Charles asked.

Ewan stripped off his dark shirt, folded it precisely, and slipped it into a desk drawer they used for the purpose, saying, "Miss Bowes possesses a fine pistol and the ability to use it."

"Ewan! A pistol? In the hands of a female?"

"I must have neglected to mention that she also turned it on me this afternoon, when I met her and Lady Dash on the road."

"Good God. Never say she thought you were a highwayman."

"As good as. Fortunately, she has very steady hands."

Charles considered that, and said, "Did she recognize you? Just now, I mean."

"No. We were in the near dark, and I spoke Spanish, so she would not recognize my voice. She did not."

"What does this mean for us?"

"It means, dear brother, that I shall have to find another way in tomorrow night. Hand me the white shirt, will you?"

"Here. Ewan, you have to let me go—"

"No. We decided this already. Navy life has not made you suited to scaling fortresses." *Nor,* Ewan thought, *would your temperament have permitted you to fence with Miss Bowes. You she would have shot as you attempted to jump back out the window. Or she would have called down the house upon you.*

So a retreat must be considered a stalemate, not a loss. There was tomorrow. Ewan would find other ways into Dashwood. Riskier ways, perhaps, but ways. He promised himself that. Given the number of fortresses he had scaled, he would not believe that one English country mansion would defeat him indefinitely. No one was shooting down at him, even. At least, not yet.

"This does not have to be a referendum on the relative merits of the Army and the Navy," Charles said.

"Of course not," Ewan said, while he pulled the shirt over his head and buttoned it. "The Army is by far superior."

Charles shook his head in resignation. "I do not like your insisting on taking all the risk and responsibility."

"It is my privilege as older brother."

"Maybe this is that occasion when you should not prevent bad things from happening to me," Charles said.

"You don't even know why this happened. Or how. You don't remember all of that night, and it's been a year and a half since, besides."

"Thanks for reminding me. I am not one to drink to excess, Ewan, you know that. I hate feeling sick the next day, and the next day, I felt especially sick."

Ewan brushed aside Charles's self-pity. "I can tell you that you are not the only one who thinks there was something very odd about blasted Dash having you sign an IOU to a house he knew you didn't own. Run through what Dash said the next day."

Charles twisted his lips. "He showed me the IOU, laughed in that quiet, nasty way he had, and said he would collect on it when he would. We have been over and over it."

They had, ever since Charles had gotten off his ship three days ago, fresh from a stint in the West Indies, and told Ewan the story of the night he had met the late Marquess of Dash eighteen months ago in London.

"Sometimes you can remember something, even when you've been over and over it," Ewan said.

Charles just shook his head.

"He could have asked me to be your proxy and settled it," Ewan said. "I have been back from the Peninsula for a year. He had nine months from when I came back to when he died. He resisted the impulse. He knew that IOU was worthless, although embarrassing."

Potentially litigious, too, Ewan thought, depending on the temperament of Lord Thomas Dashley, who had succeeded his brother as Marquess of Dash. Ewan wished he knew whether the brothers and Lords Dash were indeed cut from the same disreputable cloth. He had seen Lord Thomas—now Colonel Lord Dash—briefly last summer, looking excessively drawn and unsteady. Had he reverted to dissipation on being home from the Peninsula, or had his ghastly appearance been caused by the war?

God knew the war had changed Ewan enough to make him grateful for his house, when before he had wanted only to escape it and find adventure. Now life's little details had aligned themselves in a fine, prioritized order, and he had been plowing through them with relish. Should that all be put on hold while he waited for the matter to be discovered and sorted out? No. He would find that IOU himself, claim the high ground, Dashwood or no Dashwood, Miss Bowes or no Miss Bowes.

Hm, he thought, wondering if the stirring within him could be attributed to anticipation of meeting her again by moonlight, or to getting this troublesome job done.

"Dash, the late Dash that is, would never have asked you about the IOU, Ewan. He never gave *you* any trouble, but you know that there were stories . . ."

"Would to God you had never sat down with him."

"Would to God I could merely have you horsewhip me, like you did that time I spied on the barmaids down at the Rook and Ram. A horsewhipping would heal and be done with. This," Charles waved his hand toward outside, "just keeps getting worse. Why does everything always seem to happen all at once? Why couldn't Colonel Lord Dash have waited a little while longer before sending his wife to open Dashwood?"

Ewan said, "His brother's been dead three months. He's waited that long. You and I both know what it's like to be under orders, and not your own man."

"But Wellington does trust him." It was half question, and a backhanded plea. They had discussed Colonel Lord Dash's singular military career when Charles first told Ewan of the IOU three brief days ago. Charles had hoped they might go to Colonel Lord Dash, present the whole business, but Ewan had refused. Breaking into Dashwood carried its risks, but they were more the kind of risks Ewan tolerated taking.

"Wellington has trusted many a scoundrel," Ewan said. "Primarily because he can be a scoundrel himself. No, Charles, you and I both know that a man can win battles and turn around and punish the men who won them for him."

"Colonel Lord Dash's letter to you asking you to look after his wife seemed most genial."

Ewan winced. "And her friend. He asked me also to look after Miss Bowes. Do not forget her."

"It seems you may not. But can a scoundrel write such a letter?"

Ewan had debated that very question himself, for Colonel Lord Dash's letter appealing to him as a respected fellow officer had suggested a man of a much different character than the late Dash. Explaining that he had all confidence in Ewan, Colonel Lord Dash had even written, *You earned your reputation for daring, but I never thought you reckless.*

Dash had seen through the façade so many others had taken as Ewan's entire description. Ewan still felt warmed by the praise, and uncomfortable underneath it. No one could deny Colonel Lord Dash's acumen as a soldier. Ewan could appreciate the recognition did he not also believe it stemmed from Dash's own ability to dissemble. Dash could not have been an exploring officer—charting out territory and local sentiment in uniform behind French lines—were he not able to be as winning, threatening, or deprecating as the situation demanded.

There was no way to tell what sort of reaction Colonel Lord Dash would have to the IOU Charles had signed. He was yet in France, held by Wellington to conduct peace negotiations. From his brief meeting with Lady Dash, Ewan suspected she would defer to her husband.

Would life were simpler. Would one not have to take the bad with the good. Ewan knew in his head that such would always be the case. His heart still rebelling, he sighed and said, "Yes, even a scoundrel can write such a letter."

Charles frowned.

"For all we know," Ewan said, "Colonel Lord Dash knows about the IOU, knows my reputation within the Army, and sent me that letter thinking to tie my hands with honor and obligation. Certainly with her friend Miss Bowes about, Lady Dash needs little protection from any foe."

"You think he could be that subtle?"

"I put nothing past anyone I do not control."

"That includes pistol-pointing dragonish spinsters, eh?"

"She does belong to those ranks, yes." Ewan paused but a beat. "But I am working on that, and you are going to help me. I hereby propose a difficult assignment for you tomorrow."

Charles sat up. "Do tell."

"The ladies told me that they will start inventorying

the furniture tomorrow, and let me tell you, it is typical Dash."

"Done in late Hellfire Club?"

"It does not seem as bad as all that, but from what I saw, it varies between ribald and distasteful. We will be sitting next to them while they do it. Your job, Charles, will be to turn the ladies up sweet while they pretend to ignore the more outré pieces. Do not blush, I beg you." Ewan tucked the white shirt into his trousers, took a cravat, and tied it neatly, if not intricately.

Charles grinned. "What will your job be?"

"Keeping my eyes open and trying not to murder Miss Bowes. I do not like her by day."

"You liked her by night?" Charles asked, astonished.

"No," Ewan said, tugging the bell pull and marveling that he could do so with equanimity when the last bell pull he had seen had been connected by a thin cord to Miss Bowes's hand and had held his fate so precariously. "Not exactly."

"Not exactly?"

"Don't worry about it." Ewan shook his head and sat at the chessboard opposite Charles. "You have had yourself winning."

Charles made a mock salute, then poured Ewan a brandy from a table at his left. "Why not?"

"No one on my staff will believe I would lose a chess game."

"Then you've been playing the wrong people, haven't you? I could have explained it as you having a temporary setback."

"Here I give you a temporary setback," Ewan said, and moved his bishop.

Charles frowned and hunched over the board.

Ewan's manservant James scratched on the door and came in.

"A small plate of bread and fruit and cheese, if you would," Ewan said. He did not feel particularly hungry, but he had to convince the servants he was about his own house.

"Very good, sir," the man said.

While Charles continued to study the chessboard, Ewan drummed his fingers lightly on the arm of his chair, consigning the late Lord Dash to a circle of hell and wondering how he would come up with a plausible reason for a Spaniard to be running in and out of an English mansion. If he met Miss Bowes again by moonlight, he did not think she would be fobbed off so easily.

In fact, he half hoped she would not.

Chapter 4

"That is the third time you have yawned," Caroline said as they donned aprons in the main drawing room off Dashwood's foyer. They planned to begin inventorying the furniture there. "Did you not sleep well last night?"

"I am sorry," Lucy said, taking her hand away from her mouth. "I slept well, but did not get to sleep until after midnight."

Make that well after midnight. Meeting with the thief had awakened Lucy in ways she had never experienced. She could not sleep for another hour or more for thinking about it.

So often she had heard people talk about dangerous experiences as exciting. She had never appreciated such stories, or the ability to feel such things. Above all, Lucy liked order. Or at least she thought she did. Thieves represented all disorder.

Certainly her thieving brother had fractured Lucy's life into uncertainty, insecurity, and, possibly, eventual poverty.

But this thief, with his broad shoulders, teasing manner, and deep, liquid Spanish, had made her heart beat faster, her senses feel more keen. Now she had a glimpse of how others could find danger exciting.

"My goodness, this piece is uglier than the settee,"

Caroline said, pointing to a battered-looking chair that had once been painted white and gilded.

"It does look like a woman who has gone a week without a maid's attention," Lucy said, recalling herself with a guilty start to the task at hand.

Like the Red Salon in Caroline's childhood home of Norcrest Manor, Dashwood's main drawing room boasted a wealth of artwork on the walls and equally opulent decorative boxes, statuettes, and vases on shelves. Beyond that structural similarity, however, it diverged greatly in tone. Where Norcrest Manor did not pretend to be a poor cottage, it made one feel at home. Impressed, certainly, but at home.

Dashwood, Lucy thought, was sharing some sort of private joke with itself. The people in the portraits leered, or maybe Lucy's eyes suggested the impression since the furniture that was not hopelessly ugly could only be called outré.

"You did not anticipate this task when you agreed to come with me," Caroline said.

"No, indeed. I am not showing my hand, dear Caro, by saying that if I anticipated anything, it was having to reassure you that it is all right if you displace the Local Arbiter of Taste and Elegance. It is, in fact, quite inevitable."

"You are absurd," Caroline said.

"Why? How am I absurd? Your taste is exquisite, or you would not desire to put a period to so many of the pieces in this room. Besides, would you have me pity someone who has doubtless been ruling the countryside with an iron fist, large frown lines running down her disapproving face? No indeed. I will not pity such a one, and you cannot make me. I prefer your method of cajoling. No dragons for me, thank you.

"But," Lucy continued, as though making a concession,

"if you will have me pity someone, I shall pity the woman you displace as Reigning Local Beauty."

"Lucy, stop!" Caroline said, gasping from trying to contain her laughter.

"You are right. I am become quite too pleased with myself. But is it not a far better act of charity on my part to pity the poor thing who has been petted and stroked all her life, and will now have to make allowances that the Marchioness of Dash cut a very lovely figure at the assembly or Mrs. So-and-so's house?"

"Mayhap she will be prettier."

Lucy screwed up her lips. "Maybe as, but no matter what this poor chit has in her favor, she will not have the Marquess of Dash hanging from her every word."

"The Marquess of Dash is not here."

Lucy cursed herself for reminding Caroline of that very fact. "Buck up, old thing," she said. "He survived the Peninsula. He survived Waterloo. He will survive the peace."

"The last peace nearly killed him," Caroline said, but she was rallying.

"You will say so, but he found you in the process, so all in all, I think he came out ahead."

"I just wish Wellington would send him home."

"Yes, it will be hard to show the Reigning Local Beauty how he hangs on your arm when he is not actually hanging."

"You are a beast."

"True," Lucy replied with satisfaction.

Caroline laughed, and Lucy laughed with her. Then Caroline said, "No, *I* am a beast to be complaining of my troubles, when you suffer much more than I."

"Suffer? How do I suffer?"

Caroline gave her another one of her looks, and Lucy relented under it. "Very well," Lucy said. "You have seen me avoid the post even as you rush toward it. But you will not have seen me avoid it since coming here, nor will you. I anticipate it will take any party who needs to contact me about Jack several days to track me down. In the meantime, I get to enjoy the delights of Dashwood, such as . . ."

Lucy indicated an ornately carved circular side table whose stem consisted of a nude mermaid.

"Thank God it has a tail, Lucy," said Caroline, covering her mouth with one hand. "I should not be subjecting you to such hideous, indecent—"

"Do give over, Caro."

They laughed.

"Mark this piece, John," Caroline said to the footman.

"Yes, milady."

"And I shall enter it on my list here," Lucy said, settling down at the escritoire in the far corner. "For which duty you have suitably primed me."

"I should not like to disappoint Thomas by appearing an indiscriminate manager."

"Despite this being an indiscriminate house?"

That brought a nervous twitch from John the footman.

Caroline smiled her just-humor-me smile, and Lucy subsided into her list and her thoughts. The midnight thief had awakened her, true, but he had also stirred up regrets she had hoped to leave behind in Oxfordshire for a little while.

Where are you now, Jack? The last time she had seen him, he had been standing unhappily between the two imposing forms of Lord Thomas Dashley and his sergeant-major, John Rowan, while the Spaniard that Jack had injured, Don Alessandro de Almarez y Santiago, accused Jack of stealing artwork from his father's holdings.

Lucy could not blame Jack for his unhappiness or for resenting being caught. Nor did Lucy wish him caught, and likely shot. Not quite. But there was no denying his being outside the law had placed her in an awkward position. The money to run their house belonged to him. To him went the ability to draft the notes to pay for all the necessities of life.

Lucy knew how the midnight thief paid for his necessities of life. He stole for them. But how had he, who was likely a Spanish gentleman, come to be in Somersetshire?

Lucy spun private stories while she took down descriptions of furniture, knickknacks, lamps, and bric-a-brac. She would, she decided, have the pleasure of asking him the next time he came into Dashwood attempting to rob it. The thought gave her a wicked anticipatory pleasure, like watching someone mix a cake, smelling it baking, and then helping to spread the icing before being given a large piece all to one's own.

Lucy retreated from this tasty, dizzying daydream to register that Walters, the butler, had come into the drawing room and was hovering next to Caroline. He summoned up his courage and asked, "What would your ladyship like to do with these pieces?"

"I should like to burn them, but I will settle instead for permitting you to dispose of them as you see fit. The pictures, however, will be stored in the attics. In my family, we never throw away a picture."

"Very good, my lady." Another footman handed Walters a note. "Are you home to Captain Sandeford and Lieutenant Sandeford?"

"Lieutenant Sandeford?" Lucy asked. "There are two of them?"

"His younger brother, ma'am, who is in the Navy."

"Please show them in here, Walters," said Caroline, "and bring refreshments."

"My lady."

"Hm," said Lucy, "I wonder if the younger brother is cast in the same mold."

"Perhaps this one will appeal to you."

"I will be content not to be annoyed," Lucy muttered. Caroline chuckled.

"Really, why ever did Dash choose him?" Lucy asked.

"Maybe his options were limited."

"So you do not like him, either?"

Caroline raised her shoulders, about to make some remark, but then stopped, seeing Walters about to announce the two callers. Both men bowed deeply. Although she did not like to, Lucy admitted that Captain Sandeford looked as handsome in his country apparel of brown coat and breeches as he had in his regimentals. A shame his manner did not match his looks.

"Lady Dash, Miss Bowes, may I present my brother, Lieutenant Charles Sandeford, of His Majesty's ship *Midnight*?"

"Lieutenant," Caroline said, extending her hand, "I am very pleased to meet Captain Sandeford's brother."

"The pleasure, my lady, is all mine. He has spoken of little else but meeting you."

"Such consideration, sir," Caroline said, blushing.

"And Miss Bowes," the lieutenant said, taking Lucy's hand and bowing over it. Lucy could have picked him out as Captain Sandeford's younger brother at twilight, for they shared not only the same dark hair and snapping dark eyes, but also their other features.

But he was also clearly an entirely different species. It was not so much, Lucy thought, the depth of his tan that differentiated them, or the allowance for about seven years of age. The difference lay in degree, the older brother's features sharper, more pronounced, reflecting his grim and taciturn nature, while the younger's were softer, leading Lucy to believe him easy and good-humored.

She was disposed to like him on this contrast alone. "Lieutenant Sandeford, my pleasure," Lucy said.

"Mine, truly. For you also occupied no few speeches by my brother."

Lucy forced herself to smile. "I do not doubt it." She found Captain Sandeford watching her, and the expression on his face reflected intense speculation, not the barely concealed dislike she had seen yesterday. His look made her feel oddly warm and uncomfortable. "Peace, Captain Sandeford, I shall mention no particulars you may not have already spoken of to your brother."

"I doubt you could embarrass me, Miss Bowes," he said, a smile playing about one corner of his mouth.

"Are you impervious to embarrassment, sir?"

"Not impervious, ma'am."

"Oh?"

Lieutenant Sandeford said, "Like some people can tolerate more pain than others, Ewan can shrug off as a mere nuisance what would render many a man a stuttering chucklewit."

"Did Captain Sandeford imply that speaking to me would reduce you to a stuttering chucklewit?" Lucy asked.

"Not at all, ma'am. No, not at all."

Lucy eyed the silent Captain Sandeford, wondering if the mouse watched the snake with much the same fascination. "I should not dare try to embarrass you, sir, even if I wanted to. I must admit I have never appreciated those conversations where I am invited to admit my most embarrassing moment."

"You cannot choose?" Lieutenant Sandeford said.

"She must make up a story," Captain Sandeford said. "Miss Bowes would neither feel comfortable relating something trivial, nor something too sensitive to be joked about."

Although impressed by his discernment, Lucy resented any feeling they might have in familiar. Her opinion must have shown, for Captain Sandeford tipped a brow at her and relaxed his stance, pronouncing himself the winner of that skirmish.

Caroline invited the gentlemen to be seated.

"We would not take you too long from your cataloging?" asked Lieutenant Sandeford. "Ewan mentioned you had planned to do some redecorating."

"Do not trouble yourself, sir. The thing will get done in good time," Caroline said.

Lieutenant Sandeford glanced at his brother, who shook his head slightly. What was the significance of such a look?

They sat in a small grouping of chairs and divans before the marble fireplace that could not quite contain Captain Sandeford, Lucy judged, although it would be a near thing.

"You never mentioned your regiment yesterday, Captain," Caroline said.

"Fifth Battalion of the Sixtieth Foot, my lady. The Royal American Rifles."

"You were not recently at Waterloo, then," Lucy said.

"Correct. We were not called up."

"You remember what regiments were and were not called up for France?" Lieutenant Sandeford asked. "That is impressive."

"We had little else to occupy ourselves," Caroline said. She forced a too-brilliant smile, and Lucy squeezed her hand.

"Now we are here," Lieutenant Sandeford said, "and will liven things up for you."

"I am certain that is true, sir," Caroline said.

Lieutenant Sandeford wiggled to the edge of his chair. "Do tell me, Miss Bowes, who taught you to use your pistol. Ewan here has spoken of little else since he came back from Dashwood yesterday."

Captain Sandeford appeared almost lazy in his regard of her, but Lucy sensed that the answer mattered to him. Perhaps he could be embarrassed more readily than he let on. "Captain Sandeford is too kind," she said.

"I did state that you had skill with it," Captain Sandeford said.

"I would never imply that you would do anything less than compliment," Lucy said.

Captain Sandeford's smile challenged her. "You have not answered the question."

"My brother taught me."

"What regiment is he?"

"He has no regiment," Lucy said. It was the truth, too. A deserter had no regiment.

Caroline said, "Would you, Lieutenant Sandeford, tell me about life in the Navy. For," and here she addressed Captain Sandeford artlessly, "I have heard much about the Army from Dash, but I know so little about the Navy."

Captain Sandeford nodded politely, content it seemed to drop the subject and let Caroline charm his brother.

Lucy often forgot that almost five years separated her from her friend. It came back to her to watch Caroline and the young man. So warmed and yet disconcerted by her thought, she glanced at Captain Sandeford, as the other older person there with whom to share her amused rue.

Leaning back against his chair, arms folded, head

tipped, he was already studying her enigmatically. Lucy flushed. Captain Sandeford smiled.

Lucy fumed. A small statuette depicting a slender lighthouse rising from two boulders stood on the table next to her. She pictured herself picking it up and throwing it at him. She thought of him ducking and hearing the delicious crashing of the marble. Or maybe she could surprise him and it would connect with his forehead. He had a good amount of forehead to hit. There, right above his brows, where his hair waved down from an off-center part.

"Miss Bowes, did you have any return of your polecat last night?"

It was all Lucy could do not to start or give some exclamation.

"Polecat? Why, what is there to do with a polecat?" Caroline asked.

"One of the gardeners, Fletcher, I think his name was, told us some faradiddle yesterday, when we walked about the house, about a polecat climbing up the walls around back."

"Faradiddle?" Captain Sandeford asked. "What do you think caused the damage to the ivy if not a polecat?"

"Why, how large is the damage?" Caroline asked.

"It could as easily have been from a ladder placed inauspiciously," Lucy said. "And the damage is only to the ivy, Caroline. But it never matters. The ivy will recover in a month or two."

"Well, then. But I do not like the idea of the staff making excuses."

Lucy shook her head. "I think Fletcher is done telling such tales."

"Why?" Captain Sandeford asked.

"Because, sir, they are patently ridiculous. That is

why. He appears a sensible man. He knew I believed it
to be a faraddidle. And so do you, sir."

"Do I? I know that it is patently ridiculous?"

"Yes," Lucy said with the exaggerated patience one
assumes when one is explaining something to a child.
"Your average polecat is a foot and a half long." She
measured out the distance between her hands, extended
it to three feet, then drew it back again and shook her
head.

Caroline chuckled.

Lucy put her hands down. "Besides, anyone who
cannot figure out how to discourage a polecat from returning . . ." She shrugged.

"But you were quite concerned about it yesterday,"
Captain Sandeford said.

Lucy quite thoroughly disliked him for keeping this
subject alive. Did he exist for the sole purpose of argu-
ing with her? "It is only a matter of thinking the matter
through, sir, and planning accordingly." He still looked
about to argue, so Lucy turned to his brother. "What is
your opinion, sir?"

"On these sorts of questions, ma'am, I defer to my
brother. I have not half the strategic brain as Ewan here.
Why, he beats me every night at chess."

"You, sir, are no help to me," Lucy said, forcing a
light, teasing note into her voice. She did not like the
captain, but the lieutenant seemed harmless enough. He
did not deserve her opinion of his brother to taint him.
Besides, Lucy resented feeling so combative. She had
had quite enough of *that* over her own brother.

"Lucy adores chess," Caroline said. "Usually she and
Dash play, for I cannot pretend to remember how the
pieces move. Since he is away, perhaps you will oblige
her some evening, Captain Sandeford."

Lucy stared hard at her friend, but Caroline sat looking

as if butter would not melt in her mouth. Marchioness of Dash or not, Lucy promised herself she would have things to say to Caroline later. "Do not feel yourself obliged, sir," Lucy said with what she considered no little restraint.

"To the contrary, Miss Bowes, it would be my pleasure. Do you not enjoy a challenge?"

"Usually."

"Good. That has settled the matter then," Captain Sandeford said.

"Tomorrow night, possibly, gentlemen?" Caroline asked. "Would you first join us for dinner?"

"I think I may accept that gladly for both of us," Captain Sandeford said.

Lucy thought dark thoughts in his direction. He was enjoying himself too much for her taste, and at her expense.

He stood, and his brother did likewise, signaling their intention to end their call, but Walters at the door prevented him from saying so. "My lady, Lady Grayson, Mrs. Lansing, and Miss Alton have come to call."

Caroline looked down at the apron she had pinned on to do her inspecting, making Lucy realize she had been wearing a like one in *his* presence the last half hour. Lucy began removing the pins.

"Lady Grayson is the new wife to Viscount Grayson, who is your next-nearest neighbor, of Graywoods, my lady," Captain Sandeford said. "Mrs. Lansing is her mother, who is visiting, and Miss Alton Lord Grayson's sister."

"Then I shall receive them," Caroline said. "Please show them in here, Walters."

"Very good, my lady."

Caroline likewise removed the pins from her apron and handed it to Lucy, who stuffed them both in a window-seat box. "You will stay while we are introduced, sir?"

"Our pleasure."

Walters ushered in the three ladies.

Plump like a ripe peach, Lady Grayson beamed good health and good nature. Her blond hair permitted her to wear yellow in the latest fashion. She curtsied properly, but with no awe. Lucy thought she could like her. Her mother Mrs. Lansing Lucy likewise approved of. A handsome woman in her late forties, her countenance and air suggested a character at home with itself.

Miss Alton had strawberry blond hair, fine gray eyes, and a pleasing figure dressed to advantage in white muslin figured with red. She looked all about her, and her greedy eyes took in the mermaid table and battered, gilded chair.

Here was the person Lucy must feel sorry for. Doubtless Miss Alton qualified as the Reigning Local Beauty, for the neighborhood could not support three such women, once Lucy counted Caroline and Miss Alton as two.

Miss Alton smiled and curtsied, then assessed Caroline feature by feature as she had assessed the room. Lucy determined, by the frozen aspect to her otherwise perfect smile, that she did not like the way her assessment came out.

Lucy grinned inwardly to think that Miss Alton had barely noticed her. Miss Alton would be one of those women who believed herself in the exalted club of the well endowed, and the door closely guarded. Lucy shuddered in amused horror, though, to think of what went on behind those doors.

Caroline welcomed the ladies to Dashwood, introduced Lucy, and determined that Lady Grayson and Mrs. Lansing did not know the Sandefords. They both bowed with military precision, and Mrs. Lansing began questioning Lieutenant Sandeford about a ship that her nephew had been assigned to.

Miss Alton stepped forward, separating herself, Lucy, and Captain Sandeford into their own group. She said to him in a sugary tone, "How nice to see you again, sir. I had wondered whether you were visiting, or if business had taken you to town."

Her speech amused Lucy. She suspected Miss Alton tried to boast of how often she could claim Captain Sandeford's company. Instead she had admitted how little she knew of him and his plans. Lucy would not have made such a speech. She could not tell, however, whether Captain Sandeford appreciated it.

He said, "My brother came in only four days ago. We have been catching up."

"It has been a very long time since I saw your brother."

"It has been a very long time since almost anyone around here did."

"Well, I am glad you are now moving about again in society."

"Thank you," he replied.

When he volunteered no other information, Lucy witnessed all the symptoms of frustration and disappointment cross Miss Alton's face, although with a rapidity that suggested she was learning to keep such feelings in check. Lucy recognized, too, that Captain Sandeford had been deliberately opaque, which made her wonder to what degree he found Miss Alton interesting.

Despite this ambiguity in his feelings, Lucy found herself resenting Miss Alton's notion that Captain Sandeford belonged to her and her alone. It was not that she desired Captain Sandeford's good opinion. She merely disliked beautiful people who thought they could lay claim to anyone anytime. The way he, for instance, had stopped their carriage yesterday and arranged tomorrow's game of chess came readily to mind.

"Perhaps you could invite Captain Sandeford over for chess," Lucy said.

"Chess?" Miss Alton said in astonishment.

Captain Sandeford's sardonic gaze provoked Lucy to continue. "Yes. Chess."

Miss Alton recovered. "I am sorry. I have no idea how to play. I have always considered it a very inappropriate game for a lady. Why, only bluestockings play chess, I am sure."

Content to let this mark of difference between her and Miss Alton speak for itself, Lucy said nothing.

For whatever reason of his own, however, Captain Sandeford said, "Miss Bowes has agreed to play with me tomorrow evening. I look forward to the challenge."

Miss Alton turned an unfriendly but considering gaze upon Lucy.

"You do not know, sir, whether I shall provide any challenge at all."

"I have every confidence, ma'am, that you will comport yourself readily."

To this provocative statement, Lucy could think of no suitable reply. Fortunately Caroline approached them, saying, "Miss Alton, your sister-in-law and her mother have agreed to join us for dinner tomorrow evening. It will be a nice little party."

Miss Alton curtsied. "Thank you for the invitation, my lady."

"It is time for us to take our leave of you, my lady," Captain Sandeford said, summoning his brother with a look. He bowed over Caroline's hand, then, to her surprise, took Lucy's. "Miss Bowes, I look forward to our next encounter."

Though decidedly uncomfortable to be so detained and singled out, Lucy rose to the challenge by saying, calmly, "Thank you, Captain Sandeford."

His smirk told her plainly he understood she did not return the compliment, if compliment it was. He and his brother left, and the ladies from Graywoods followed soon after.

"You are about to upbraid me for suggesting you play chess with Captain Sandeford," Caroline said. "Have at it."

Lucy laughed. "How can I, against such a frontal assault?"

"I did not think he would take up my suggestion with such relish, nor to frame the matter as a challenge. I had thought, since the gentlemen seem to think we are in dire need of assistance, to provide them with some diversion."

"He is a frustrated soldier."

Caroline's expression clouded, and she nodded slowly. "You are likely right."

"There will be a letter from Dash tomorrow."

"Do you think so?"

"He writes with the regularity of a clock."

"And you cheer me up with the same regularity." She linked arms with Lucy, and they passed out of the drawing room and into the foyer, by tacit consent done with their inventorying that day. "So, what did you think of the Graywoods ladies?"

Lucy told her, then added, "Do be excessively gracious to Miss Alton, Caro, so she has to contain all her complaints of you."

Caroline laughed. "You are absurd."

"I live for these little amusements." But, Lucy reflected, that no longer quite held true. She also anticipated with some excitement the prospect of meeting her bandit again.

Chapter 5

That night Ewan decided to risk encountering one of Dashwood's servants. He entered the house through a small room off the main drawing room by the simple expedient of forcing a weak lock on a large window. He opened and closed the window several times, making certain it would quickly slide open for him without noise when he desired a retreat.

There was nothing to search in here. The room might once have functioned as a lady's study. Now it contained only a chaise lounge and a small side table. Ewan wondered, as he passed them, whether the late Dash had used the room as a convenient trysting place during his famous orgies.

Ewan passed into the drawing room where Lady Dash and Miss Bowes had entertained him and his brother that afternoon.

Moonlight rendered the portraits bizarre, as though each and every one of them was staring at him. If they had had real mouths, would they have giggled to see him sneaking about the place? Or would they have screamed "Thief!" at the top of their lungs?

You are safe from me, Ewan thought. He could not imagine wanting to steal any of Dashwood's paintings. He found portraits chiefly of interest to those who remembered the person portrayed or who took family

pride in some ancestor. He preferred either the passionate storytelling of Reynolds or the picturesque
landscapes that had become so popular.

Ewan's first goal tonight lay at the far end of the
room, a not-so-large rolltop desk. He had spied it only
that afternoon. It fit with the décor in that it looked both
expensive and overdone. It stood out, however, for being
the only desk Ewan had seen in the house. It amazed
him that the late Lord Dash could have run an estate this
size from such a small desk. He required something
much larger to run his own Barberry Lodge.

He doubted Dash had put Charles's IOU in the desk.
It was such an obvious choice, Ewan believed it would
have been discovered long ago by some executor. Still,
he felt conscious of not overlooking the obvious. Sometimes the rustling in the underbrush had really been a
French patrol, and not squirrels.

He looked through it, found nothing of interest, and
went on to pick up a small porcelain box that gleamed
whitely.

"*Buenas noches, señor,*" said Miss Bowes softly behind him.

Ewan did not startle, but he did curse silently. He
turned around. She stood near the large mantel, her pistol in a steady hand. "*Buenas noches, señorita,*" he
replied. "You have the silent feet of a cat."

"Thank you."

"Where did you acquire such a skill, if I may ask?"

"Only recently, and from incentive."

"I see," Ewan said, and promised himself to ask Miss
Bowes on the morrow, when he spoke to her as himself,
why she had accompanied her friend to Dashwood. He
knew of no other young lady who would practice walking silently so as to protect her friend's house. Miss
Bowes must be considered unique.

"I thought I might find you here," she said.

"Indeed. Why?"

"You yourself said there would be a next time, and you gave me the impression you would come downstairs. Please put that back."

"Did I?"

"*Señor,* I must insist."

Ewan put the box back.

"Thank you."

He bowed.

"Let me escort you out."

"I would prefer not showing you where I came in."

She pursed her mouth. "Very well, *señor.*"

She had not thought of that, Ewan surmised. "Are we again at an impasse?" he asked.

"I will let you judge."

"You are not sure. You see the furniture I may jump behind. That divan there, for instance. There is no call bell near you, nor could you have known just which room I would head for and set up your trap. No, *señorita,* this evening we are not quite at an impasse."

"What purpose your hiding behind a divan if a shot has roused the house?"

"Only this: I may escape out a window before anyone could get here."

"The windows are locked. You would jump through glass?"

"If I had to, to prevent my being caught."

She considered him. "I do not understand you."

"What is not to understand? There are penalties for being caught."

"Why do you invite such penalties in the first place?"

"Is that your very polite, English way of asking me why I am a thief?"

In the moonlight, he could not tell if she blushed, nor

did he expect such a reaction from her. What surprised him, however, was how attractive she appeared by moonlight. He did not know why, or how to account for it, but he could not fail to appreciate it.

"Yes," she said.

"For that, *señorita,* I must insist we sit down." He grandly illustrated the opposing divans they had been sitting at that very afternoon. He hoped that while she seated herself, he could jump behind one of them. He counted on her shooting at the divan and his being able to undo the simple lock on the windows and get out. Although he had debated several wild stories, he thought them all too incredible. Any delay would aid him.

"Very well. You first."

Ewan cursed inwardly and held his hand over his heart. "I may be a thief, but I am yet a gentleman. Can I sit before a lady does?"

"You may consider my pistol as the cancellation of any scruples you have on that score."

"You are a strange creature for a lady."

"A thief is a strange creature for a gentleman."

"We are neither of us perfect, are we?" he asked.

"Do sit down, *señor,* or permit me to escort you from the house."

He considered ways of overpowering her, if he could not run suddenly. The trouble, he decided reluctantly, lay in the necessity of sacrificing his bandanna to gag her. Otherwise he would have to lock her up some place as yet unknown instead of merely tying her with curtain cords. Having her out of his way but able to identify him served no purpose.

Ewan sat down, although it went against every instinct. She again displayed the remarkable control he had witnessed the night before. Her pistol never wavered, nor did she look behind her, while she sat. She reached to one side, plucked up a cushion, and propped her pistol hand upon it. The muzzle pointed at his chest.

"Why do you wish to know my story?" he asked.

"Likely for the same reason you insist on coming in here."

"That is?"

"It gives you pleasure."

"Speaking to you, *señorita,* gives me pleasure. Coming into this house does not." Speaking to her like this did please him. He enjoyed the ready give-and-take she could support as easily as breathing. He had accepted playing chess with her tomorrow evening because he had admired her quick wits.

Her pistol, however, continued to annoy him. He would need to come up with some way to avoid her tomorrow, although for the life of him he did not know how. She had as much as admitted patrolling the house for him.

"I will regard that statement as *fustian,* and give you leave to begin."

"Fustian?" he asked, as she had used the word in English.

"Oh, give over, do," she said, also in English.

Ewan merely tipped his head at her.

She sighed and went back to Spanish. "Fustian is nonsense."

"Nonsense? But why nonsense? Why may I not enjoy speaking to you?"

"Because I am holding a pistol on you and preventing you from doing what you came here to do."

"It is possible to separate the eagerness to continue my work from the enjoyment of this interlude."

Her lips quirked. "Possible maybe, but not likely. You are even now wondering how you may distract me and escape."

"You know me so well?"

"I know you so little. Hence my desire for this tête-à-tête. But what I suggested is undoubtedly what I would do if I were in your position."

"How would you go about it?"

"No, no," she said, wagging a finger at him. "That would be cheating you of your challenge."

He spread his arms. "I had to try."

"Naturally. Should you find a way to escape, *señor,* may I say now that I beg you not to come back again."

"Why?"

"You are preventing me from my beauty sleep, and lest you protest quite gallantly that I have no need of it, do permit me to remind you that you have not yet seen me during the day."

"Your modesty becomes you."

"Modesty has nothing to do with it. I insist on honesty. I am no beauty, not even when I was but a girl of eighteen and had youth to recommend me."

Ewan was struck by her seriousness. "You are not old, *señorita.*"

"No, but I am on the shelf."

"The friend of the lady of such a house must possess certain advantages."

"Yes, of entertaining gentlemen thieves in the middle of the night."

"Do not ring for refreshments on my account," he said.

She chuckled quietly.

"Very well," he said. "Let us suppose, for a moment, that I am a poor sailor, cast adrift on the shores of your fair isle when your fairer navy sank my ship."

"Were you aboard a ship, *señor,* you would be an officer. You *are* a gentleman."

"I continue to admire your discernment."

"You said so yourself, so there is no need to laugh at me again."

"You do say amusing things, though."

"How amusing is it to say that our countries have been allies these six years?"

"It would be very amusing. I did not say, *señorita,* that I was on a Spanish ship."

"I stand corrected." But she looked grave. "Did you join the French willingly?"

"The French had nothing to do with it," Ewan said, harshly, and not as he had intended. He took a breath. "It was an American ship."

"You do have a confusing history."

"Confusing understates the matter, I assure you."

She considered that. "Why did you not present yourself to the Government and ask for transport home?"

Ewan put a hand over his heart and resorted to vagueness. "I had my reasons."

A sharp crack sounded behind her, most likely the result of the house settling, but it startled her as nothing else had startled her. It startled Ewan as well, but battle-honed training allowed him to recover more quickly than she did. He bounded up and over the back of the divan and crouched on the balls of his feet, heart thumping.

But she surprised him by not shooting at the divan. "*Señor,* do please come out from behind there."

Ewan estimated the distance to the next grouping of chairs closer to the windows. He had a knife in a scabbard for forcing windows and opening things if necessary. He took it from the sash he wore about his waist and pushed it along the floor toward the other chairs, hoping that Miss Bowes would believe he had made it that far.

She did walk slowly toward the divan he hid behind.

He had to admire her caution, even as he deplored his position. In the daylight, it would have been no hiding place at all. She rounded the divan, pistol out, but he had time to spring at her and wrest the pistol from her hand.

In one fluid motion he dropped the pistol onto the divan cushions and pulled her wrist behind her back. At her squeak, he clapped his other hand over her mouth, also pinning her left arm to her body. She smelled of violets, which was odd, he thought fleetingly, since the only thing she and such a small, delicate flower might have in common was an intensity of tone.

"Not a sound, *señorita,* not a sound."

She stiffened, no doubt feeling the pain in her arm, and then nodded. The movement of her hair against his chin and cheek caused a strange sensation. It mimicked desire. But how could he desire Miss Bowes, and in such a predicament?

"If you promise not to scream, I will let go your mouth."

Again she nodded. He let go and pinioned her arms across her chest. With the length of her back and round derrière against him, he found himself far too aware of how his own heart beat quickly within his chest in unison with hers.

He began shuffling them toward the windows, with her feet reluctant. She guessed his intention of going out the window. When he took one arm from her to unlock the sash, she stomped at his feet and tried to twist away from him. Ewan, however, had expected something and altered his grip on the rest of her accordingly. Even so, had he not been wearing his boots, she could have broken his foot.

She gasped at her failure.

"I am sorry, *señorita*," he said against her ear, "but I am much stronger than you. Hold still now."

"I wish I had shot you last night," she hissed.

"On that point, shall we agree to disagree?"

She did not deign to reply, and he found himself admiring her spirit as well as her earlier caution.

Ewan flipped open the sash and raised the window. Its width would allow him to jump through it, and there was nothing but grass and graveled walkway outside this section of the house.

"Do not let me stop you," she said.

"One moment," he replied, and shuffled them back toward the closest grouping of chairs. There on the floor, against a patterned rug, he spied his knife. Without planning to, he lifted her hand, which he had held pressed against her body, to his lips and kissed it. She gasped again.

"I *am* sorry," he said, and pushed her hard away from him, toward the divan. He scooped up the knife, jumped out the window, and ran for the cover of the gardens. Ewan would not have blamed her if she shot him in the back. Indeed, he expected that if she had the chance, she would take it.

Lucy recovered herself quickly, retrieved the pistol, and ran to the open window. He was running toward the taller hedges of the gardens. She aimed her pistol at his broad back, but something within her stayed her hand.

She tried to tell herself she did not shoot because her hands were shaking. She would fire wild and rouse the house, and to what purpose? To claim she had seen a masked bandit with whom she had spent a good quarter hour in conversation? To claim he was the same one she had let go the night before? Absurd.

She lowered her pistol, made sure it was no longer cocked, and set it down on a table. Then, as though someone had blown out a candle, she felt her knees weaken. A chair behind her served the important function of standing between her and the floor.

The scorpion had shown its stinger. She should not be surprised, she thought, fuming. To be a thief, one must be corrupt in one's soul. Besides, she had known from the sheer breadth of him, and from hearing him climb up the ivy the night before, that her masked bandit could overpower her. She had tried to keep her pistol out of reach to guard against just such a possibility.

She had not guarded against the possibility of his arousing such decadent feelings in her. Her back pressed against the hard, muscled length of him roused an undeniable wanting for *more,* although she did not quite know what she wanted *more* of. The feeling had worsened when he had kissed her hand. The courteous gesture made feelings bloom within her that were anything but polite.

How were his lips different from any other man's lips? Were they at all, or did the difference lie within her? What did that say about her?

Important questions, for which she had no answer.

Gradually her furious heartbeat calmed, and a night breeze from the open window cooled her heated forehead. She collected her pistol and closed the window with a thud.

As she exited the room, though, a sudden light forced her to shield her eyes with the hand not holding the pistol. "Who is it?"

"Walters, ma'am," he said, and lowered the lantern he carried. He had hastily thrown on pants and shirt. "What has happened?"

"What do you mean?"

"We heard noises, ma'am."

"What noises?"

Walters's gaze was riveted to Lucy's pistol. He licked his lips and said, "Banging about, and something rustling outside."

"I wonder at your being the only one sent to investigate."

Walters shrugged. "Am I not back within ten minutes, someone else will come."

"Is that your normal practice?"

"Yes, ma'am," he answered promptly, then frowned.

He had not expected or wanted to make that admission. Nerves stretched thin could cause any amount of mischief, including the blurting of things usually left unsaid. How long had strange things been going on in Dashwood?

"I am sorry you had to get out of bed, Walters. You heard me down here. I opened a window for some fresh air and tripped coming back from closing it."

"Very good, ma'am." He pointedly ignored her pistol.

"I do not always carry this," she said, holding up her pistol, "in the middle of the night, but you should be careful approaching me if you see me."

"Very reasonable, ma'am. Should I so inform the rest of the staff?"

"Yes, that would be a good idea. Good night, Walters."

"Good night, ma'am."

Lucy turned away and felt her way up the main staircase. Upstairs in her room, the single candle she had left burning on her dressing table had gone halfway down. She tossed her dress over her dressing-table chair. But as she turned to her bed, she gasped. A single red rose lay across the white coverlet and pillow.

With shaking fingers, she picked it up, felt the dew that had begun to form, and inhaled its rich scent. Then, remembering she should be careful of thorns, she looked for them. He had taken them all off.

"I shall accept your apology," she murmured, and stroked the rose against her cheek. "For now. But there will come a reckoning between us."

Chapter 6

Lady Dash oversaw an excellent table, Ewan thought. All details attended to. And the staff had exhaled collectively when she had nodded to Walters at the end of the meal.

Viscount Grayson had accepted Lady Dash's invitation, too. He was a fine gentlemanly soul of some two-score years, not given to swaggering, expansive with the ladies, and eager to listen to others' opinions on various subjects, mostly, Ewan thought, because he did not believe in exercising his mind sufficiently to entertain his own.

Although there had been no talk of Ewan and Miss Bowes's chess match over dinner, it had dominated conversation over preprandial sherry. The break had done nothing to alleviate Ewan's anticipation. He suspected Miss Bowes had similar feelings, although whether her anticipation mixed with dread or annoyance, who could tell.

Ewan wondered what she had thought when she had seen the rose on her pillow. Had she taken it as the apology it had been intended, or had she shredded its petals and dropped its corpse over her balcony?

Lord Grayson ran out of questions, and they were able to rejoin the ladies. Miss Bowes was sipping tea, hazel gaze uplifted over the rim of her cup.

Lady Dash indicated that she had had the chess table set up in the corner of the room, near the windows. "For some of us will want to converse, and I know how Lucy and Dash appreciate a bit of quiet when playing."

After this gentle reminder to any spectators of their manners, the party separated itself into two groups of four. Lady Dash, Lord and Lady Grayson, and Mrs. Lansing stayed together and played cards. Miss Bowes, Ewan, Charles, and, surprisingly, Miss Alton retired to the chessboard.

Miss Bowes glanced toward the open windows and settled herself where she could see out of them. Ewan did not believe she thought for a moment that the bandit would risk coming in with all this light and noise. Still, her impulse provided him with a certain grim amusement.

"What unusual pieces," Charles said.

The pieces were large and heavy, of finely grained marble, the black with specks of white, the white with streaks of pink and red.

"Lady Dash and I agreed we should keep these," Miss Bowes said.

"Whatever do you mean, Miss Bowes?" Miss Alton asked.

"We are sorting out Dashwood. Lady Dash is sensitive to atmosphere, and her taste is exquisite. The décor here seems . . . eclectic."

"What will you do with the pieces you eliminate?" Charles asked.

"I am not sure what she has planned, sir," Miss Bowes said with a bright, inquiring look.

"Charles, would you do the honors?" Ewan asked, to distract her and remind Charles of his earlier warning not to try any verbal probing with Miss Bowes. If she could become suspicious over a gouge in the ivy, what would she make of continued interest in her friend's furniture?

Charles picked up a white pawn and a black, put them behind his back, then drew his two closed fists out. Ewan nodded to Miss Bowes, who selected the right. Black. She tipped her head a little, indicating that she accepted going second. They had to turn the board, and then Charles and Miss Alton settled in on either side to watch.

"Is there a timer?" Miss Bowes asked.

"Do you think we will need one?" Ewan replied.

"Should it become an issue," she said sweetly, "I am sure we may alternate taking turns about the room. Your move, sir."

They began cautiously, feeling each other out. But they had not exchanged more than seven moves apiece before Ewan realized he had indeed met a fine player. He moved his bishop in a feint. Miss Bowes met his gaze, ignored his feint, and brought her rook across the board to attack his king. She had to retreat, but she had answered his question. Miss Bowes would take risks.

The time between moves began to lengthen, although Ewan did not really notice until Miss Alton stood up to get some more tea. Candles had been lit. A glance at the clock confirmed that they had been battling for the better part of an hour and a half. Charles's brow quirked.

"Would you like a break, Miss Bowes?" Ewan asked.

"Do be silent, sir," she replied, studying the board.

Ewan had to smile. He folded his arms and leaned back in his chair, observing how Lady Dash engaged Lady Grayson in conversation and kept the rest of the party amused. Lady Dash, Ewan suspected, could likely get any information Lady Grayson had on any member of their neighborhood community with her delicate probing. She had an easy touch, Lady Dash did.

Ewan would not admit he distrusted women with an

easy touch, but he would never willingly link himself to someone he thought could manipulate him.

Watching Lady Dash made Ewan wonder again what sort of man Colonel Lord Thomas Dashley, Marquess of Dash, was. From all accounts of their wedding last autumn, Ewan gathered his marriage to Lady Dash had been a love match. Did she love him in return, or had she succumbed to that very female desire to be married for better or for worse?

Ewan could not square her gentle amiability with Dash's afflicted appearance last summer. Perhaps she had cured him of any desire to stray or to overindulge. But who really knew who held the reins in a marriage? How many people suspected that Ewan's mother had ruled his father with the tip of an eyebrow, or the curl of a lip?

Miss Bowes leaned forward, regaining Ewan's attention. She pushed a pawn. Then she gasped and covered her mouth with her hand.

"What is it, ma'am?" Ewan asked. Charles, too, looked at her with alarm.

"Nothing," she said and frowned.

"Nothing?"

She shook her head. "A momentary illusion. You have experienced them, I am sure, sir. When, for example, one looks down a street and sees someone one is convinced is a particular friend. Then, when that person comes closer, one realizes there is only a resemblance in the turn of the countenance or the shape of the body."

"That happens often aboard ship," Charles said easily. "It is very disconcerting, because one knows that no one new has come on or off."

Ewan wondered who Miss Bowes had thought she had seen. Had she a sweetheart at some point? Or did she look for that brother she had mentioned with such an obvious effort at controlling her feelings?

"It is your move, sir. I shall join Miss Alton for a moment in obtaining a cup of tea."

"If you are tired, Miss Bowes, we may pause our game."

"No, sir," she said, rising. "It is just that Dashwood does make some noises at night that are strange to me. I have been sleeping but indifferently since coming here."

Ewan wondered if she realized she was rubbing her right wrist, where he had twisted it behind her back. As he sat down to study the board, he wondered again how she had taken his peace offering, and the thought so distracted him he almost dismissed her moving the pawn as a throwaway move. He had his hand on his bishop to take the pawn, but drew it back suddenly.

"Miss Bowes is more subtle than I gave her credit for," he said to Charles.

"Her deployment seems rather random," Charles said, shrugging.

"That is its genius," Ewan said and smiled.

"What do you mean?"

Ewan shook his head. "I am learning much of Miss Bowes this evening. She will take risks, she can apply the hammer resoundingly or with the barest tap . . . But can she maintain her nerve? That is an important question indeed."

"You have spoken of Miss Bowes as you have spoken of no other woman."

This statement wrested Ewan's attention from the board. "What the devil do you mean by that?"

"Precisely what I said," Charles said, but a stiffness to his jaw belied his easy tone.

"Do not worry, I harbor no *tendre* for Miss Bowes. She interests me as someone to elude."

"You do not resent her for these last two unsuccessful nights?"

"One has to admire determination. Otherwise she reminds me far too strongly of our mother."

"Yes, that comparison would discompose you."

"I maintain I would not have this ridiculous Scottish name had our Grandmother Sandeford been present at my birth to support our father's backbone, as she was at yours."

Charles laughed, then said, soberly, "There are worse things than ridiculous Scottish names."

"Let me think, would you?"

Miss Bowes returned a few minutes later, having drunk her tea. She elected not to comment on his not having moved yet, allowed the barest rise of her brow to mark his eventual move. He had ignored her pawn gambit and begun to address the larger problem of her encircling his king.

Two moves later she took his queen in another cross-board move that rocked Ewan back on mental heels. He felt vulnerable in the extreme to lose the queen, and surprised altogether. No one had beaten him at chess for longer than he cared to think.

Another three inevitable moves and Ewan tipped over his king. Miss Bowes was sitting back in her chair, tapping her finger against her slightly smiling mouth. She deserved to be satisfied by such a victory, Ewan thought, and his question was answered. Miss Bowes had the nerve to carry out her plans. He wondered why, then, she had not shot him either of two nights running.

So although she deserved to be satisfied, he could not succumb to the desire to give her the fulsome praise he would have otherwise bestowed on so capable a partner if he were to carry on his masquerade.

He stood and bowed. "Very nicely acquitted, ma'am."

She blushed, although whether from embarrassment at the praise or vexation at the lack of warmth in his tone, Ewan could not tell. Whatever the cause, the color brought a definition to her face and eyes that could only be considered attractive. Ewan recalled the feeling of her back against his body and chided himself for thinking of Miss Bowes as he would another woman.

He had bedded women who were far less attractive than she. It was not her looks that made him reluctant. No, Ewan had to remember that Miss Bowes possessed two very important checks against his desire. She was the friend of Lady Dash, and she would not be the sort of woman who would take pleasure in her body without also engaging her mind, and his obligation.

"Do you mean she has won?" Miss Alton asked.

"You have it precisely," Ewan said.

Miss Bowes's lips twitched.

"But how did that happen?"

Charles opened his mouth, but Ewan said, "One move at a time."

"I cannot believe it," Miss Alton said. She regarded Miss Bowes as if she were a Bedlamite, then picked up her skirts and swept off toward the other group.

"I appreciated your feint within a feint, Miss Bowes," Charles said.

"Thank you," Miss Bowes said simply. To Ewan, she said, "I enjoyed our game, sir."

"I as well. Tell me, how often do you beat Dash?"

"Enough to make it interesting, sir."

Cheeky woman, Ewan thought with admiration.

Lady Dash and the others joined them. "You have finished your game, I understand?" Lady Dash said.

"Yes," Ewan said, "and the victory goes to Miss Bowes."

Since Miss Bowes would have suspected Miss Alton

to have apprised the others of this point, Ewan had not expected her to blush again. But blush she did. "Captain Sandeford is an excellent player."

"You should have a rematch sometime, then, eh?" Lord Grayson asked.

"It would be my pleasure," Ewan said. "Miss Bowes?"

"That would be fine," she replied.

"In the meantime, though," Lady Dash said, "Lord and Lady Grayson have invited us to a picnic tomorrow, and I have accepted for us."

"That is very kind of you," Miss Bowes said to the Graysons.

"The invitation extends to you both, too," Lady Grayson said to Ewan and Charles.

Ewan answered that they would be pleased to attend, and their party began to break up. Miss Bowes seemed quiet, and she glanced out the window more than once. She was calculating the odds, Ewan thought, of whether her thief would dare to come after seeing lights downstairs for such a time into the already late summer night. He could have told her she could safely go to bed. He had no intention of coming back here tonight.

"I am glad you enjoyed your game," Caroline said to Lucy when they had said good-bye to their guests and climbed the grand staircase to their bedrooms. "He is a good opponent, I take it."

"Yes, but much different from Dash."

"Indeed? How?"

"He plays more by intuition than steadiness," Lucy said.

"Dash said he had a reputation in the Army for being neck-or-nothing."

"Then he runs true to form."

"You do not trust intuition," Caroline said, smiling.

"Intuition has its place," Lucy replied, "but for the most part, I prefer something well thought out in advance."

"You are lucky, Lucy, to have the kind of mind that can think things out well in advance."

Lucy pursed her lips, both at her friend's self-deprecation and because it was not always true. Sometimes the desire of her intuition did distract her from her planning. It certainly had when she had discovered her brother's theft of artwork. Her impulsive act had led to her brother's eventual arrest, his flight, and her having to host a Spaniard in her house for two months.

Hence her atrocious Spanish accent.

Tonight, another incident had triggered a bout of intuition. For a second, when she had looked up from the chessboard and seen Captain Sandeford's outline, lit from behind by the candles, she could have sworn her masked thief had come to play chess. Lucy had tried to dismiss the notion by telling herself that one man's form looked very like another's. Two men having the same breadth of shoulder was not to be wondered at.

After all, it was ridiculous to imagine that an English gentleman—even one with a reputation in the Army for being neck-or-nothing—would pose as a Spanish thief and attempt to rob his own neighbors.

It was beyond ridiculous. It was insane.

But the notion had teased her, so she had gone for a cup of tea, watched him speak to his brother, and finally accounted for her disconcerting impression. Instead of his regimentals, Captain Sandeford wore a charcoal gray coat. Its dark line had been what had acted on her imagination.

"You are kind to compliment me, Caro, but do not

impugn advance planning into everything I do, I beg you."

"Promise. Now do you go on to bed. You really have not been sleeping well, have you? Is there anything I can do?"

"No. Tonight I shall go right to sleep. I suspect nothing will disturb me until morning."

"What will there be to disturb you in the morning?"

"Captain Sandeford over a picnic blanket instead of across a chessboard," said Lucy, meaning it. She appreciated him as an opponent. There were rules there, and not much conversation.

Caroline laughed, gave her a hug, and sent her to bed. Lucy went willingly, wondering if there would be a rose on her pillow the next morning when she woke.

Chapter 7

No rose graced her pillow in the morning, just streaks of sunshine that crept along either side of her dull gold bed hangings. Lucy regarded the lack of rose with satisfaction and growled at the sunshine to go away before falling back asleep for another hour. Consequently, she felt marvelous when she arose and dressed for the picnic.

The Graysons' picnic spot delighted Caroline and Lucy. No mere picnic blanket for the Graysons. Their picnic spot consisted of a large stone gazebo complete with table and benches nestled against the side of a meadow, half in the forest. Flower-encrusted vines grew up the gazebo's columns, and, if one could still one's exclamations over the prettiness of the sight, one could hear a nearby stream trip and gurgle over rocks.

Lucy and Caroline found the others already enjoying fruit, cheese, and other delicacies set upon a table.

As Captain Sandeford politely stood, his outline broad and true against the blue sky, Lucy again dismissed her strange notion of the night before. He and her midnight thief did share a breadth of shoulder, and they did both move fluidly, but their similarity ended there. Certainly there was nothing, well, playful, about Captain Sandeford.

Captain Sandeford bid her a courteous good day and passed her a glass of lemonade, but otherwise did not address her during the first half hour of conversation.

Instead, Lucy found herself between Lady Grayson and Mrs. Lansing, discussing, of all things inane, whether the pattern of cloud cover could be considered handsome or not.

Instead, she thought. Instead! Instead of *what*? Conversing with someone who seemed to appreciate her only as a rival?

"It is dreadfully unkind of the weather to be so variable," Lady Grayson was saying. "One moment the sun is warm, the next, these big clouds cover it, and I do not know how to feel."

Perhaps Captain Sandeford and her midnight thief did share a similarity besides shape. They both enjoyed sparring with her until they had no further need of her. Then they were cheerfully indifferent.

Such sour thoughts, Lucy reflected. Maybe her full night's sleep had done less good than she had thought.

No, it *had* done her good. She felt better, and not just from being more rested. She had anticipated her thief three days in a row.

"One should take the good with the bad, daughter. Have I not always said so to you?"

But did "indifferent" state the case too strongly? Standing beside Caroline, Captain Sandeford glanced at her frequently. Did he do so because they had shared some connection over chess—as rivals, if nothing else—or because he wished to know where she was so he could avoid her?

"What is your opinion, Miss Bowes?"

"I like variety, ma'am."

Caroline had looked severe. Now she was biting her lip. Caroline severe with Captain Sandeford suited Lucy just fine. Caroline biting her lip while conversing with Captain Sandeford could not be considered a good thing.

"Excuse me, ma'am, I think Lady Dash has need of me."

Ewan had considered it a stroke of good fortune to have Charles distract Miss Alton so that he might have Lady Dash to himself for a few minutes. He had much to ask her away from Miss Bowes. He began by expressing his concern over Miss Bowes's fatigue over the past couple of days.

"You are kind to ask, sir, and even kinder to ask me, rather than my friend."

Ewan wondered if he was experiencing one of Lady Dash's gentle reprimands. "My lady?"

"Miss Bowes has never appreciated being reminded that she is human like the rest of us. She would have me believe she may continue to do whatever she was called upon to do far past the point of normal endurance. Any remark that she is not capable quite puts up her back."

Ewan had to smile. "You would have me believe *you* protect *her*?"

"We protect each other, sir. You may think of us as a regiment of two." She looked over his shoulder, toward the trees on the other side of the meadow.

Ewan realized she looked east. Toward France? "You said a regiment of two, but you have your husband, and Miss Bowes her brother. Do you not include them in your reckoning?"

"Neither Dash nor Mr. Bowes are here right now. We are . . . reduced in complement?"

Ewan smiled. "You could put it that way." But Lady Dash's mention of regimental loyalty, in conjunction with her saying "Mr. Bowes," reminded Ewan of more details of Dash's troubles in Spain, troubles that could not be mentioned with a smile on one's face. "There was a Captain Bowes in the Fifty-second, as I recall, was there not? Your pardon if I inquire about such a delicate subject as Colonel Lord Dash's own inquiry, but do I not remember thinking it interesting that he would be called up for inquiry after he had served as witness in another one?"

"You have a fine mind for details," Lady Dash said.

So . . . "Is Captain Bowes any relation to Miss Bowes?"

"Her brother," said Lady Dash, trying to appear nonchalant, but coming off as reluctant.

Ewan could not help but glance at Miss Bowes, who stood with Lady Grayson and Mrs. Lansing, looking alternately cagey and bored. "I heard something else about Captain Bowes, my lady, more recently."

"You may have, sir."

A fellow captain in the Sixtieth had written him of the story, of how Jack Bowes, who had barely survived a board of inquiry in the Peninsula for cowardice under fire, had fled arrest here in England for stealing artwork from Spain.

Spain, Ewan thought. No wonder Miss Bowes had expostulated when he had spoken in Spanish. A thief would have been bad enough for her, but to combine thievery with Spain not only opened a wound, but rubbed salt on it. The situation would have been humorous if it were not so sad.

Lady Dash was biting her lip. "I will ask you not to tease my friend over this matter."

Ewan put his hand over his heart and bowed. "I would not do anything so cruel."

"I am sorry. I did not mean to imply that you would be cruel about it, sir, only that any mention of the matter would amount to cruelty. Miss Bowes does not take it lightly."

"I can well understand why." But Ewan understood from the remark that Lady Dash's opinion of the relationship between himself and Miss Bowes would not include positive adjectives. The assessment struck him most unpleasantly.

Miss Bowes approached them and linked arms with Lady Dash. "I am collecting opinions on the weather. Lady Grayson dislikes its variability—the sun peeking in and out of the clouds. Mrs. Lansing says one must be stoic no matter how things present themselves."

They might look dissimilar, Ewan thought, with Lady Dash all blond elegance and Miss Bowes plain and simply dressed. But a regiment of two understated the matter. "What is your opinion, Miss Bowes?"

"No, sir. I was asking you."

He tried to think of a good answer, but his disbelief momentarily confounded him. This young woman could not be sister to that bounder Jack Bowes. Although Bowes had narrowly survived his board of inquiry, no one in Ewan's regiment had been convinced Bowes was entirely innocent of misconduct. Ewan could recall his own disgust over the matter as freshly as if it had happened yesterday.

The Army could be a large place, or a very small one. Some regiments never met, but Ewan remembered meeting Jack Bowes once or twice, chiefly because he had already gained his notoriety for—allegedly—fleeing pitched battle and leaving his lieutenants to fend for themselves and his company.

Now that Ewan took the time to look, he could see the Bowes family resemblance. Jack Bowes was a handsome man, but it appeared that when nature had put his features into making a female, it had tried to put more in her slight frame and delicately shaped face than they could comfortably allow.

As far as courage went, however, nature had handily given Miss Bowes a double helping, where her brother had only been called for hors d'oeuvres. Who could doubt that, when she had sat in wait for a thief two nights in a row?

Ewan had long prized courage and decency. They had made Miss Bowes more attractive to him over the course of the last few nights. Perhaps, some day, after he was done sneaking into Dashwood, he could hope to win her friendship.

"My perspective on weather may be different from the ladies', ma'am, since I have been campaigning, and not so long ago. I appreciate mildness in whatever form it takes. Mildness tends to keep my boots dry."

"I am certain Dash would make the same comment, do you not, Lucy?"

"Yes." Miss Bowes spied Charles and Grayson moving in their direction and spoke up. "Lieutenant, tell me, what is your opinion of the weather today?"

"Fine, very fine," Charles answered. "Nothing compares to a good, steady sou'wester of eight knots or so." He smiled deprecatingly at Ewan's look of amused disgust.

"Excellent. The Navy and the Army have weighed in, and appropriately, too. And you, my lord?"

Grayson's servant refilled his wineglass. He sipped, then said, "I would be feeling more in charity with the weather today did it not follow the weather last night."

"My lord," said Miss Bowes, "such a statement provokes a question."

Grayson raised his brows, puzzled.

"Miss Bowes wishes to know what it was about the weather last night that disconcerted you," Ewan said.

"Oh, well, as to that," he said and cleared his throat,

looking uneasy. "Not sure if it is fit conversation for ladies."

"My dear Grayson," said his wife, drawing near, "you told Mama and me and Althea this morning over breakfast."

Althea looked none too pleased to have to discuss the subject again.

After some more harrumphing—which Ewan took for Grayson's thought processes—Grayson said, "It rained some last night, as you know."

Ewan had not known. He had been fast asleep. From Miss Bowes's expression, she had not known, either. He had to admire her ability to correctly read her midnight thief's intentions toward her friend's house.

"A highwayman held up a carriage last night, about three miles from my holdings."

"Indeed, my lord," Miss Bowes said, surprised and wary.

"Was anyone hurt?" Lady Dash asked.

"No, my lady. Nor anything taken, although not for want of trying."

"What happened?" Ewan asked.

"Well, stand and deliver and all that, sir," Grayson said. "But the thief did not see the extra outrider and was nearly shot. He wheeled away at the gallop."

"Could the carriage driver or passengers describe this highwayman?" Miss Bowes asked.

"Only that he was dressed all in black."

"Complete with black scarves about his head," Lady Grayson added.

"Eminently practical for someone sneaking about at night," Mrs. Lansing said.

"You praise applying common sense to thievery?" Miss Bowes said. Ewan thought she intended her remark to be light in tone, but she did not quite carry it off. The others shifted in their stances, even Charles, who should have been prepared to endure such remarks with complacency.

"Why not?" Mrs. Lansing asked, with a gentle but condescending tone. "If I were a thief, would I not want to be the best thief I could be, so as not to get caught?"

Miss Bowes grimaced. "I do agree with that sentiment, ma'am. I am merely of the opinion that if one has decided to become a thief, one has already left common sense behind."

"Very nicely stated, Miss Bowes," Mrs. Lansing said, her condescension deepening so that Ewan could easily imagine her patting Miss Bowes on the head like a child who has learned her lessons.

Lady Dash was glancing significantly at Ewan, who tamped down his annoyance with Mrs. Lansing and took the hint. He said, "We began speaking of this because of the weather, my lord. Specifically, the rain last night."

"Hm, yes, the rain. Washed out the tracks behind the man, so no one could follow him."

"A lucky happenstance," Miss Bowes said, "for a thief."

"Even a thief must come into luck from time to time," Mrs. Lansing said.

Miss Bowes responded only with a polite smile and nod. Ewan tried to imagine what she was feeling, but she had herself well in hand. Highwaymen were not art thieves, he reflected. Perhaps having expressed her disgust of thieves in general, she had decided that this one deserved no more of her attention.

"Has this man been seen before?" Lady Dash asked. "Or is he an entirely new contention?"

"He has been seen here once before that I know of, my lady," Grayson said. "About a week back, and there have been stories of his being seen in the neighboring communities."

"A revolving highwayman?" Miss Bowes asked. "Or should we call him circuitous?"

"You would have them all eccentric, ma'am," Ewan said.

"True," she replied, lifting her chin. "But not for their poor sense of geography, sir."

"That is right. You have them bereft of moral focus."

"Just so, sir."

Ewan was tempted to ask her if she could ever see an instance where one might steal from some moral purpose, but refrained. Now that he knew what her brother was, he suspected she had either become an absolutist or felt she must present herself to the world as one.

Miss Alton said, "Brother, shall we not eat now?"

"Indeed," Mrs. Lansing added, "all this discussion of galloping and exertion . . ."

They turned their attention to the round table and sat, allowing Grayson's servants to delight them with cold roasted meats, vegetable salads, delicious fruits, and pungent cheeses. Miss Bowes, however, did not eat much. She did not gaze east, as Lady Dash did occasionally, but remained fixed on her plate.

The meal concluded, Miss Bowes went to stand at the gazebo's balustrade. Ewan joined her. She had not put her gloves on after eating, and her hand rested on the gray stone. Ewan had not noticed how delicate her hands were; not surprising, since most of the times he had seen them had been by moonlight, with them holding her decidedly wicked pistol.

She did not look welcoming and went right on the offensive. "I am amusing myself by deciding what some of these dreadfully variable clouds look like."

"Is it a sport that can allow company?" he asked,

placing his hands next to hers on the stone and leaning forward.

"Company, perhaps, but not collaboration. Do not frown at me, sir. You look very forbidding when you frown."

"You are not frightened of me, and you will not convince me that you are."

"You are correct. I am not frightened of you." She paused long enough to make him think he had won a point, then said, "But your expression does tend to direct my imagination into darker channels. I have always disliked circumstances that curb the limits of my imagination."

"I see," he replied. "Your pardon."

"Now you are laughing at me."

"I shall remove all expression from my face."

"Do not be ridiculous."

"Then would you please explain what you meant by no collaboration?" Ewan asked. "That was why I frowned to begin with."

"You may choose a cloud and proclaim your opinion of it, but do we choose the same cloud, you may not try to convince me that your opinion holds more than mine."

"My dear Miss Bowes, you can no more convince me that I could bully you than you could convince me that I frighten you."

"It does not follow, sir, that my ability to withstand your bullying implies that I must enjoy the process of withstanding it."

"Touché, ma'am."

She turned her gaze back to the clouds, so that the brim of her bonnet hid some of her face. She might have blushed.

Miss Alton joined them. "Whatever are you two talking of?"

"Miss Bowes is giving me instruction on the proper procedure to observe clouds."

"Captain Sandeford is laughing at me," Miss Bowes said, addressing him, rather than Miss Alton.

Miss Alton lay a gloved hand near Ewan's and said, "That one looks like a large wedge of cheese. What do you think, sir?"

Miss Bowes glanced at the stone rail, where her hands, then his, then Miss Alton's lay in a neat row. She folded her arms.

"A wedge of cheese it may be," Ewan replied. He thought of it as a tent, toppled by excessive wind, opening its owner to rain and sun and a host of biting insects.

"And what of that one, over there?" Miss Alton asked. "Is it not very like the crescent moon on its side? Come, sir, does it not look like a crescent moon? I would have your opinion."

Miss Bowes studiously looked toward the sky. Ewan thought she might even be edging away. Damn. He had wanted to draw her out. Should he allow her retreat from himself and Miss Alton, or should he risk Miss Alton making a unpleasant fuss by forcing Miss Bowes to stay by him?

"To me," he said, stalling, "it looks like a scythe. There is a handle to the right, there, see?"

"A hangman's noose," Miss Bowes said.

Startled by her macabre impression, Ewan said, "Did you not say there was to be no collaboration?"

"I am not trying to convince you of the rightness of my choice, sir, so there is no collaboration."

"You are splitting hairs, Miss Bowes."

"Indeed. How so?"

"Your image is a powerful one. I will not be able to

look at that cloud again without thinking of the hangman."

"Nor I," Miss Alton said, with asperity.

"I am sorry for that, then," Miss Bowes replied. "Perhaps cloud watching does not bear company any easier than it does collaboration. Pray excuse me."

Over his shoulder he watched her go to the shadier side of the gazebo, by the woods, and accept a glass of water from a footman.

"She is quite the strange creature," Miss Alton said. "She never speaks but she wants to amaze. I find her very hard company."

Ewan nodded, letting Miss Alton interpret that as she would.

"To whom do you refer?" Charles asked, joining them.

"Miss Bowes," Miss Alton replied, looking stormily in Miss Bowes's direction.

"I see," Charles said.

Miss Alton correctly interpreted this comment as a signal to put off conversation about Miss Bowes, and instead began trying to convince Charles that another cloud looked like a wedge of cheese.

"Nay, 'tis a sail," Charles said and laughed.

Ewan let them argue it out, noticing that Miss Bowes glanced over at them with barely veiled disdain. He could not help but think how successfully she had anticipated this difficulty. Truly she was a remarkable woman.

Miss Alton finally gave up both the argument and trying to include Ewan in it, and went to seek out her sister-in-law.

"You have had a decidedly odd expression on your face, Ewan."

"That is because I am thinking novel thoughts, little brother."

Chapter 8

The waxing moon rode higher earlier each night. Its clear, clean bluish light filtered through the windows of Dashwood's large foyer and traveled slowly across the marble checkerboard floor.

The curving spot on the great stair near the bottom where Lucy sat, however, remained deep in shadow. She had her back comfortably propped against the banister, her feet upon the broad step, her knees bowed. Since she had dressed in dark blue, she could barely see them.

She had waited in this fashion for an hour, sounded by the grandfather clock in the main drawing room. She expected her thief to come again, since she and Caroline had gone early to their rooms. If he did come, and had not been the man trying to rob a carriage last night, he would again head for the main drawing room. However subtly he had tried to do it, she had noticed how he examined the room. He had not finished his perusal when she had come upon him.

Lucy had chosen to wait on the stairs to put him off his balance. He might anticipate her in a room that had a convenient stepping ladder of outcropping stone and bypass the upper floors altogether. He might suspect her again in the main drawing room and try coming in through some other door or window. But unless he came in through one of its windows, or the windows in the small adjunct room, which locks Lucy had checked twice, he had to come through the foyer.

Then Lucy would surprise him.

She turned over all the possibilities in her mind again and tried to find some flaw in her reasoning. Only the obvious one remained: she was unbalanced to wait for him at all.

True, she had been the one holding the pistol on him. True, he did not carry a pistol himself, not even the second night. True, he had not hurt her as he could have. True, he had apologized for having laid hands on her.

But it was nonetheless true that did she continue to provoke him, he might not continue to forbear.

The sound of a booted foot treading softly upon the stairs above her made her instantly alert, although she had the sense not to move. The steps came toward her, and by looking from the far corner of her eye, she beheld her midnight thief. He was coming down the left side of the stair, his black-gloved hand skimming the banister. The fabric of his mask and the hilt and tip of his knife scabbard gleamed darkly in the moonlight.

Lucy held her breath as he came to within three steps of her, her heart racing.

Then of a sudden he stopped. "Would you have tripped me, fair *señorita,*" he said softly in Spanish, "despite my apology?"

His deep, liquid voice sent thrilling shivers through Lucy. But she had to answer as though sitting on staircases in the moonlight was as natural as breathing. "That would be a churlish trick," she said calmly, "and we are beyond churlish tricks, you and I, are we not?"

"Would you do me the honor of rising?"

"Why should I?"

"It would please me."

"I am all that is obliging," Lucy said, and stood. She

knew she would have to sooner or later, so she did not feel as if she had conceded anything.

"Ah," he said, folding his arms and bracing his chin on his hand. "I would never have said otherwise."

"I would never call a gentleman such as yourself a liar."

"Indeed?"

"No. Deluded, most likely, either as a result of your recent foray into criminal activity, or . . ."

"Or what?" he asked, so gently Lucy could not help but remember the strong, hard feel of him as he had held her two nights ago.

She swallowed. "Or from whatever happened to you that made you turn from your principles."

"I will delay any discussion of my principles to ask you where your pistol might be?"

"I do not carry it this evening," she replied.

"Why?"

"When something no longer serves as a deterrent, would I not look the fool to continue using it?"

He appeared much struck by this notion, for he pursed his mouth and tipped his head. "You are very wise, *señorita*." He came down the last few steps between them. "And surprising. Indeed I shudder to imagine the persuasion you might use to prevent me from taking what I have come here to take."

"What is that, *señor*?"

"No, no. That is my secret. So, what persuasion do you use? Do you have a throng of servants clustered behind the door, ready for your merest call? If so, I shall dash away immediately, if that is all right with you. I am not armed so fiercely as you, friend of the lady of the house."

"That has perplexed me, I must admit."

He shrugged powerful shoulders, creating a large ripple of moonshadow against the stair's corners. "I have never liked pistols and stealth in an enclosed space. The margin for mistake is too great."

"You have experience with such things."

"Am I confirming a theory of yours?" he asked, amused. "Do you spread out your suppositions as one might play at cards? Come, what is your favorite game?"

"I never play cards," she replied. "I prefer chess."

"Of course you would," he said, "although you are missing some keen opportunities for observing your fellow creatures by not playing cards. So, friend of the lady of the house who plays chess, you have not answered my question about the servants."

Lucy tipped up her chin. "For God's sake, my name is Miss Bowes."

"Yes, *Señorita* Bowes, I know that."

"How could you possibly?"

"People who live in rich houses are not the only people capable of talking."

Lucy flushed. "I am merely surprised you thought to ask."

"And why would I not?" he asked, his voice washing over her with the same lush feel of the deep shade she had enjoyed at the picnic that afternoon.

Her mouth felt out of all countenance dry. "I do not know your name, *señor.*"

"That is entirely right. Whom would you ask?"

"I ask you."

"You may call me Juan."

"*Don* Juan?" Lucy asked, incredulously.

He shrugged. "You would have me a gentleman. It does not follow that I aspire to more than that. Nor is every Juan a *Don Juan.*"

Lucy suppressed a smile.

"There, now that that business is behind us—you will

forgo more formal introductions, I trust?—would you please answer my question about the servants?"

"You have not impressed me as an impatient man."

"*Señorita,* I am usually the very soul of impatience. I make so many meals of impatience, that were impatience butter, I should resemble the Prince Regent. But these are unusual times, are they not?"

"Very well, then. I have not asked any member of the household to do what I do. Indeed, I hope none of them are restless and decide to wander about the house."

"That would be unfortunate," he said. "So, then, I now return to another question I have asked already. If you have no pistol and no servants ready to pounce, how do you propose to stop me from my business?"

"I do not."

"I beg your pardon?"

"What I propose to do is to follow you about."

All pretense of playfulness vanished. "Follow me?"

"Indeed," she said, striving for insouciance, or at least not trembling fear.

"And why would you want to do that? Are you fancying taking up a second occupation beside friend of the lady of the house?"

Lucy resented the implication of her relative worth and tried not to show it. "No, *señor.* Pray do not be ridiculous."

He smirked.

"You must understand that I am well known in my own neighborhood for my keen observations."

"An old bromide about a horn occurs," he replied, "but perhaps you English do not know it."

"Do be quiet and listen. I knew which window you were going to come in that first night because I saw the damage you did trying to come in the other way, and I found a strap from your boot in the bushes. See," she said, pointing to his right leg, "the one missing there? Does that not speak to my powers of observation? I have since observed that you have made twice for this floor, likely for the drawing room over there. I am fairly convinced you are not an art thief." Thank God, too.

He bowed.

"Were you, I trust you would be carrying something better to cut the pictures from their frames than that long knife, and quite possibly tubes to roll them into to prevent damage during your escapes. Nor are you a jewel thief, for you have passed over the more likely places where jewels might be found."

"How do you know I have not already looked there? You know only the last four nights."

"The mark in the ivy was fresh, *señor,* which indicated to me that you had not found your best point of entry. Climbing up ivied walls is no easy task, I am convinced, and—"

"Are we back to the subject of my dexterity?"

"No, and do attend."

He bowed.

"Where was I?"

"Your deductions about—what, exactly?"

"Oh, yes. I went back and looked at the mark again the day after our first meeting. Now that I know your height, I surmise you had necessity to cling to the balustrade, and caused the damage by kicking out. You were in some peril, I do imagine."

He did not answer.

"Speaking of peril, where were you last night? Were you on the road, about three miles from Viscount Grayson's manor, holding up a carriage?"

He smiled and settled the booted foot missing the leather strap upon the stair above. "So you heard about that, did you?"

"It is no laughing matter."

"What does that have to do with your observations and deductions?"

"I will get to it. I heard you got away only by the veriest chance." To her dismay, her voice trembled. She pressed her lips together and glared at him.

Again a stillness settled over him, which Lucy interpreted as the male's dislike of being reprimanded. His words, however, dispelled that notion. "You would have some sympathy for the poor wretch being shot at, even if it was you doing the shooting, would you not?"

Lucy could only look at him and wonder at his gentle tone.

"It was not me out there on the road. I may be a thief, but I am no highwayman to be robbing little old ladies at gunpoint."

"Well. Good, then."

"It bothered you, my dear *señorita,* did it not, to think of me taking to the High Toby." He rendered the last word in Spanish-accented English.

"It seemed unlikely, although I know very little of your background except for what you have condescended to tell me."

"At gunpoint, let us add."

"Were it not for my pistol, I would know considerably less," Lucy said repressively. "Do not think, however, that I merely take your word on the subject."

"Not for a moment, *señorita.*"

"Most of what I know of you I know from my own observations. They I may trust to be reasoned and accurate."

But even as she spoke, she realized how wrong she was. She was not anything approaching reasoned when it came to this man. Something about him stirred her senses, made their midnight blue meetings filled with more color than the picnic she had attended that afternoon.

If she could not be reasoned, how could she possibly be accurate?

"So, it *seemed* unlikely?" he asked.

He had seen her hesitation, Lucy realized. She had to press her point or look the fool before him. "Yes, that is what my observations told me, and behold, I am pleased to know I was correct. What gentleman takes to the High Toby?"

"A desperate one," he answered in a clipped tone.

"How desperate are *you*?" she asked softly.

"Desperate enough," he replied, "to understand what could drive a man." He reached out, and when she did not flinch away, he ran his fingers along her cheek, then over her lips. His touch felt like it tightened and loosened every fiber in her being, a confusing, but certainly heady, sensation.

"Are they the same things that drive a woman?" she asked. "The desire to be secure in one's home, to be able to do what one wants to do when one wants to do it, to be esteemed, indeed, to be esteemed when one is being oneself?"

"All those," he replied, "and one more."

"What?"

"Honor, *señorita*."

Lucy bit back the retort that women had honor, too. Nor would she here debate the common misapprehension that women's honor needed to be men's honor. "What here compromises your honor?"

"It is interesting that you choose to put that interpretation on my presence here."

"What other interpretation could there be?"

"I could be here because someone challenged me to do it."

"Fustian," Lucy replied. "You would not do this on a bet."

"Perhaps you underestimate the lengths to which a man will go to fulfill a bet."

"Perhaps I overestimate the sense I have of you that tells me for such a reason you would not put others at risk, or cause them undue pain. But I do not think so."

"You are correct in thinking I do not volunteer anyone who has not himself volunteered. Or herself."

"There, then," Lucy said. "You are not here to resolve some bet. It was a silly notion of you to offer. How would a Spaniard, far from home and who must avoid the Government, mix with the kind of people who could provoke such a bet? No, there is something here that compromises your honor. What other explanation could there be?"

"You are a very dangerous woman," he said, his tone poised on a knife-edge between admiration and pique.

Lucy chose to ignore the pique, or at least pretend to ignore it. "If you will have it that way, *señor,* it must be so."

His lips twisted. "And tenacious."

"That is why I am determined to follow you. You have proved I cannot stop you, so instead I shall take satisfaction in finding out what there could be in Dashwood that would so compromise the honor of a Spaniard accidentally deposited upon these shores."

"And if my honor does not allow such a thing?" he asked.

"Then I shall have recourse to alerting Lady Dash and the rest of the staff to be ready for you tomorrow. You are looking for something, and you have not found it yet."

"You would deprive your curiosity?"

"One must sometimes take the bad with the good," Lucy replied.

"What prevents me from stuffing you in a closet right now and looking?"

"Nothing, really, except . . . You cannot guarantee you will find the object of your quest tonight. Dashwood is a large place, and tomorrow the staff would be waiting for you."

"You must be quite an excellent chess player."

Lucy smiled, but her smile turned rapidly to alarm as he stepped closer to her.

"Why do you not want me to be caught, *señorita*?"

"I have said—"

"I know what you have said. I no more believe you than you believe me."

"Will you believe me when I tell you I hate vibrant, beautiful things to be trapped in ugly places? Will you believe that I hate waste?" she asked, and flushed, embarrassed by the passion in her voice.

"Yes," he said thoughtfully, "I will believe that." He bowed. "Your sentiments bring much credit to you. I will now bid you good night. I neither wish to have you see the fruition of my quest, as you will have it, nor to stuff you in a closet."

"And tomorrow night?" Lucy asked.

"Maybe we will play our game again. Maybe we will not. Who can tell?"

"You do delight in equivocation, *señor*."

"Please do not trouble yourself seeing me out." He kissed her hand, and, before she could react, sprang up the stairs.

An interesting evening, she thought, her mind aglow with an excitement she had only come close to when playing chess or listening to beautiful music.

She had not believed his story two nights ago. Tonight she believed only that he was searching for something within Dashwood and that he would use any means in his power to search with impunity. He could not have failed to see how she had reacted to his touch.

Indeed, from what she saw of the shape of his face beneath his taut masks, she suspected he was a handsome man well used to taking his pleasure of whatever woman he crooked his finger at. Even if her impression of him as handsome turned out not to be true, what woman could resist his voice, whether teasing or deadly earnest, or the tempting stimulation promised by his lean, rugged body?

Lucy had not been able to forget how he had felt against her. Every time he had touched her this evening, she had more sensations to remember. "*Buenas noches, mi Don Juan.*" She chuckled softly and heard the shaky note within it.

You are a fool, Lucy Bowes. You are an addlepated fool.

Chapter 9

Damn, Ewan thought as he rode home in the moonlight, the night air soft and refreshing on his unmasked face. *Damn, damn, and damn.*

Four nights and he had searched only one room. How did he hope to make any progress?

He shook his head, gritted his teeth, and faced up to the notion that he could not account his swearing solely on his lack of progress. Miss Bowes was making him swear for another reason altogether.

He had seen precious little mercy in the world. His mother had ruled his father pitilessly, worse, with a mailed fist within a soft glove of smiles and cajoling. The children with whom he had attended school had quickly taught him that one shut up and got along until one had developed either sufficient brawn, clout, or pure daring to deter future incursions.

Incursions. Yes, Ewan knew all about incursions. During his Army years, he had taken the incursion and raised it to a high art form. Even Black Bob Craufurd, who had formed the same Light Division Colonel Lord Dash belonged to, had praised Ewan's ability to take his riflemen across French lines and flush them out.

Some of these incursions had shown him a side of the war he had never expected. Atrocities committed by both Spanish and French to each other in a way neither side would have treated the English. Until the one day . . . No, Ewan would not think of that.

His horse whinnied and tossed its head.

Ewan realized he had pulled the reins tight. He loosened them, patted her neck, said, "Steady, girl. Sorry."

Accepting that there was little mercy in the world, Ewan had taken what he could from it, as quickly and as ably as he could. His Army friends called him reckless. But he had never thought of himself as reckless. Daring, perhaps.

Miss Bowes's mercy toward him made him wonder, however, whether he had deluded himself all these years. He had not anticipated anyone showing him or Charles any pity. He would not have expected it of the late Dash. He had not expected it of Colonel Lord Dash. He had not expected it of Lady Dash. He had certainly not expected it of Miss Bowes, who had shown every indication of being Lady Dash's dragon in waiting.

Had he chosen the wrong tactic? Ewan turned the matter around in his mind, recalling Miss Bowes's logic, and decided he had not. He suspected he knew how Lady Dash would react to learning of Charles's strange IOU, but her opinion did not end the matter. There was still Colonel Lord Dash.

But Ewan continued feeling unsettled. He turned Bella into his own yard, quietly rubbed her down, and headed toward the library window, which glowed brightly welcoming.

And in the light of that window, knowing that it meant Charles was waiting for him, continued to depend on him, Ewan understood the source of his disquiet. No one other than Charles had ever appeared to care about Ewan for himself. And Charles, Ewan believed, despite military service, had one of those temperaments that cared for many people for whatever they were. Charles possessed a tolerance of his fellow creatures Ewan had never developed.

It began with his parents, who had treated him with indifference. Fond indifference, he amended, but indifference nonetheless. As an adult he could comprehend that they had spent most of their energy battling each other. The women he had bedded treated him either as a fine playmate or a property owner. His company had treated him as one treats a fickle demigod, with equal measures of caution and admiration. Although they never knew what Ewan would lead them into next, they could count on its hazards, and most often, its successes. His friends, likewise, rarely became personal with him. They talked of things—politics, their shared military history, sports—not personal perspectives or family matters.

Then along came Miss Bowes, who spoke of being esteemed even when one was not putting on any sort of face. Who seemed to care about what happened to him, knowing nothing good of him other than that he had apologized to her for being so abominable as to lay hands on her. Who, whether she knew it or not, pierced the defenses he had so long put around himself, even when he wore a mask!

The truth was that with Miss Bowes, he expressed his own self most naturally. Ewan winced from the strange irony. He had found someone he could really talk to, but only because the odd circumstances of their meetings had him wearing a mask and speaking in Spanish about a problem that would exist fleetingly in his regular life.

He could not deny, however, the sheer enjoyment he derived from the way he directed arguments, the way he could exchange repartee for repartee, and the way he could tease her and provoke her. He had never met anyone who inspired him and challenged him as Miss Bowes did.

But Ewan would figure out some way to get around Miss Bowes and find that damnable note. Then he could forgo his secret identity as a Spanish thief.

Then what?

Ewan stopped short before he got to the brightly shining window and sat down on a large, broad rock that his father had never ordered moved from the garden, claiming one took one's ease the easiest way one could.

Would he have much contact with Miss Bowes when he was no longer her Spanish thief? Would he ever be able to have the same kind of interaction with her as plain Ewan Sandeford? Would it make a difference to him? Would he regret this phase of his life being finished?

Ewan could not decide.

He should have been able to decide. He considered his ability to look at a problem in its entirety and decide what was to be done quickly—and more to the point, accurately—as the hallmark of his character. He considered himself an intelligent man first and foremost. It had only happened that circumstances had directed him into the Army. Once there, though, he had found himself applying his wits to it as he would to any other game.

He had been thinking of Miss Bowes as a game, too.

How exactly did she think of him? That she cared what happened to him did in no way preclude her feeling as if their moonlight conversations were some strange, otherworldly game. She certainly played it to the hilt. She had taken his story and cheerfully picked apart its poorly sewn seams to show each irregularity. Then she had hazarded guesses about what he might do, and been far too close to the mark for Ewan's comfort. He did not like feeling open to her.

She, on the other hand, lay almost closed to him. She kept so much of herself private. He could not tell how much of her caring for him he could ascribe to her delicate feelings over her brother's actions, as opposed to just attraction to him. Lady Dash, the other member of her "regiment of two," had said only that Miss Bowes did not take her brother's situation lightly. Since only a completely selfish, self-centered person would take it any differently, Ewan considered the information less than illustrative.

Ewan nodded to himself. He would find out more about Captain Jack Bowes, lately deserted from the Fifty-second Foot and charged with theft. He would find out how Miss Bowes felt about him. And he would find some way to get into Dashwood that did not involve Miss Bowes. He enjoyed himself too much not doing what he had set out to do, and the clock was ticking. Soon Lady Dash would go back to inventorying her holdings. For all her sweetness of manner, she had the look of someone not long deflected from her course.

Ewan went to the bright window, raised it, and climbed inside.

Charles smiled. "You are later than last time. How did it go? Did you run into trouble?"

"No trouble," Ewan replied, "but I found nothing."

Charles sighed, although good-naturedly, and waved his hand over the chessboard. "Well, you haven't played any better here, that I can tell you. I almost beat you."

"Did the pigs grow wings?"

"No," Charles said, amused, "but clouds that should be shaped like sails are wedges of cheese."

"Or hangmen's nooses."

"I beg your pardon."

"Do not mind me."

"More novel thoughts?"

Ewan nodded. Novel understated the matter. "Good night, Charles. We'll finish this game tomorrow."

"It will be my pleasure," his brother replied.

The next morning, Lucy found Caroline in the breakfast room. "Fancy seeing you here," she said in an attempt at cheerfulness. She felt tired and befuddled, even though she had, for some mysterious reason, fallen asleep almost as soon as she had put herself to bed and slept hard and long.

"We have not breakfasted together since being here, it's true," Caroline replied.

"You have been rising far earlier than I have."

"Well, today was the day I decided to sleep in."

"The amount of food the Dashwood staff cooks to feed two women breakfast continues to astonish me," said Lucy. "Do you know, I told Walters two days ago that I intend to try everything before settling on a few favorites, and he seemed very surprised by the notion. Yum, blueberry muffins."

She carried a cup of tea and two muffins to the long mahogany refectory table and sat down next to Caroline. "You look pale, Caro. What's amiss?"

"I slept poorly, that's all. You are right. This house does make some odd noises."

Lucy studied her friend without trying to appear as if she were studying her friend.

But Caroline caught her at it and blushed as rosily as her morning dress. "You will think me a ninny, but I woke up last night wondering if I had fallen into one of my late brother-in-law's orgies. If, that is, I really knew what an orgy sounds like. It was a silly—"

"You do not really mean orgies?"

"Have I not told you about Thomas's older brother?"

"Not much," Lucy replied, suddenly feeling much more awake. "But I thought that was because you never knew him." It occurred to her that she had, in her fascination with her Spaniard and her desire to prevent him from actually stealing from Dashwood, not given as much consideration to what he might truly be after. He had said his honor was at stake, but she had partially dismissed the notion.

"I never met him, but I managed to get Thomas to speak of him once or twice, mostly because I pestered him excessively to explain why we did not invite his brother, the head of his family, to our wedding. Thomas wrote to him of it, that much I know, but Dash wrote back that he was too ill to travel. That may have been correct, too. Thomas was relieved. The rest that I know I know from Sergeant-Major Rowan."

"Who is a veritable fount of information," Lucy said, thinking that she had never heard the tall, bulky man who had been Lord Thomas Dashley's shadow utter more than a few stolid "yessirs."

"If you belong to Thomas, you belong to Rowan," Caroline said, smiling. "Then it is more a matter of getting him to stop giving his opinion."

Lucy sipped her tea, considering this. Then she put her cup down with a clink. "Enough anticipation. Tell all."

"It is not a pretty tale, and will not be long in the telling, because neither of them would give me more than the most cursory of details. I have had to fill in piecemeal."

"Caroline!"

"This is what I know. Thomas's father was one of those types of men who believe their heir should not be curbed. He thought it better for his first son to explore what was possible to the limit it was possible."

"Your Dash is certainly not like that," Lucy said, much surprised.

"Thomas was the spare," Caroline said, with a hardness Lucy had never before heard from her friend in the twenty years she had known her. "He was expected to know his limits and take responsibility for his transgressions. He took his role too much to heart. When he came to us, he was taking responsibility for everybody else's transgressions, too."

"What do you mean?" Then realization hit Lucy. "My God," she said. "In truth?"

Caroline nodded, grim. "But we will not speak today of what happened to my brother. Thomas joined the Army in '05, directly out of university. He could do nothing here. Every time he came here, Dash was throwing a party, and they were not for Thomas's benefit. Indeed, these parties were a normal routine for this house. Thomas will not speak of them to me beyond saying they were horrible and degrading to everyone involved, but he spoke of them to Rowan."

"And the sergeant-major told you."

"Hinted, more. I had to read in between the lines a little. There would be gentlemen invited down, the requisite amount of strong spirits and wine and *opium!*—opium, can you imagine?—at all hours, loose women, and young girls, sometimes even of good family. There were also, usually, boys, plucked from the fields, and cleaned up and told they were going to be able to better themselves. But first . . ." Caroline gestured helplessly.

"That is shocking."

"It is, and is it any wonder that Mrs. Walters goes around looking pinch faced and nervous? Have you not noticed the dearth of maids under fifty years of age?"

Now that Caroline had mentioned it, Lucy noticed. She had ascribed that, and Walters's patrolling, to nerves over the "polecat." But if there were such parties in the house's history, the "polecat" was only the most recent worry. "Oh."

"Just so."

Lucy read the resolution on her friend's face. "And what are you doing about it?"

"What I can, but I suspect it will be a slow process, requiring more than removing furniture of questionable taste. I was greatly encouraged by the Graysons coming over here. Miss Alton let slip that she had never been inside Dashwood before."

"That must say something of Lord Grayson's native wit," Lucy replied. She and Caroline shared a smile.

Then Caroline said, "I cannot tell the Walterses that I am not going to plan any bawdy parties. Nor can I drop every bottle of wine from the third floor, or inquire whether any stocks of opium remain in the house. Thomas would not like my speaking of such things. Besides, Dashwood has a good cellar." A smile flitted over her face. "No, I must instead let my actions speak for me."

"I had no idea you were wrestling with such issues," Lucy said. "My God."

"We have both had our distractions," Caroline replied gently. "I am glad we are talking of it now, though, for I would like to have your opinion, knowing what you know, about whether I should hold a masquerade ball in eight days' time. Dashwood used to host such a party every year on that date in Thomas's parents' time, and I would like to continue the tradition to show the neighborhood that the house has altered its course dramatically."

"I think it a very fine idea, typical of my friend Caroline, Marchioness of Dash."

Caroline reached out and squeezed Lucy's hand. "Good. That is settled, then."

Here was a ripe opportunity to tell Caroline about the midnight thief. Caroline would not think less of her new home, as she already thought poorly of it, and she had heard strange noises in the night. Lucy had also long considered Caroline the soul of generosity.

But a reluctance overcame her, born of her hate of waste and Caroline's news of Dashwood's shocking past. Perhaps she had not been able to think what there could be in Dashwood that impinged on a man's honor because there could be far too many things to choose from.

Perhaps she had not deluded herself into believing that her thief was an honorable man, and not intent on material gain.

Lucy was not certain she liked where such thoughts might tend. They made her feel the contrary pulls of sympathy for her thief and obligation toward Caroline. It was all very confusing.

"I am going to take a long walk, if you do not need me, Caroline. I think I may take my pistol and do some shooting, too. Should I tell the head gardener?"

"Gamekeeper," Caroline said succinctly, putting down her cup of tea. "We are beyond our quiet existence where someone like old Jamieson took care of everything outside. I will have Walters send word round to him. You do not need to track him to ground yourself."

"Thank you."

"Feeling especially restless today?"

"Especially would be too strong. Sufficiently would be better."

Caroline continued to look brightly at her, so Lucy relented and said, "I did not like hearing that there is actually a local highwayman, and not just Captain Sandeford surprising us."

Caroline's mouth creased in sympathy. "I know. Hopefully your brother is out of the country by now, where no one knows his past."

"And he may be judged on his own merits?" Lucy

asked facetiously. She shook her head. "There is nothing to wish for except never hearing of him again. In the meantime, I shall go do some target practice."

"Enjoy."

Lucy left before she would have to fend off more sympathy. She was not as hungry as she had thought.

That morning Ewan decided to search for answers about Miss Lucy Bowes. He dressed as formally as possible, in blue coat and gray breeches, wanting to feel the confines of his clothing about him so he would remember that he was Ewan Sandeford, not Juan the thief. Firmly in hand, he went over to Dashwood to pay her a call, possibly to initiate another game of chess.

But when Lady Dash joined him in the big salon, where he had been cooling his heels the better part of a quarter hour, she said, "My friend has gone for a long walk, Captain Sandeford. I am sorry you are disappointed."

"Who could be disappointed to converse with a lovely woman such as yourself?" he replied.

"You determine your favorite definition of lovely, Captain, and then I shall say thank you."

The remark disconcerted him, given as it was with a little apologetic, but knowing smile, and he stayed only the shortest polite time before bowing himself off. He returned to Barberry Lodge, recognizing his ill humor and resolved to do something about it. If Miss Bowes could take a long walk, so could he. It would clear his head, and he would take his rifle and do some target shooting.

Ewan changed from his stiff visiting clothes into his campaigning regimentals. Faded and patched in the shoulder from the bayonet strike that had made it possible for Charles to once read his name in the casualty lists, the dark green coat across his shoulders felt as snugly secure as he imagined a baby would feel in its swaddling.

He smiled to see that the silver button, which had been loose in Portugal, Spain, and France remained loose now. He had regarded it as something of a lucky charm. So long as that button remained loose, nothing could happen to him. He had instructed his batman never to tighten it.

Ewan paused for a moment before his reflection, registering his smile, and felt amazed that such a simple thing as putting on his old uniform could make him feel so light. He had not felt light in Spain.

He *had* felt invisible, though. There was a reason riflemen wore green to go sneaking and skirmishing through the forests. The 5/60th Royal American Riflemen had learned something from their American cousins.

Would that he were as invisible wearing the black of a thief. Thank God the French had not had Miss Lucy Bowes on their side!

With that amusing but disturbing thought, Ewan thrust all other thoughts away but of sneaking through the countryside undetected, much as a child would pretend to avoid adults.

He spent a half hour in this way, heading northwest toward a ruined abbey, not keeping to any road, but knowing his path. The abbey lay atop a tree-covered rise at the far end of a broad, grassy meadow. Another such meadow spread out on the same elevation as the abbey.

Ewan climbed the rise, picking his way from one covering of grass or stone to another, for the sheer joy of the exercise. How many times in Spain had he wished he had the blond or sandy hair of so many of his compatriots that he might blend better into the sere backdrop of waving grass and sun-drenched sky. Instead he had worked to become better at it, to feel his way with all his senses, rather than relying on his eyes.

Nothing had happened to his reflexes, for he flattened on the ground before he registered his anger at the sudden shot ringing out over the meadow. Another report echoed around him, cutting curiously through the high grasses swishing in the wind. Then another, and another.

Ewan recognized a regularity in their pattern that bespoke one person reloading one pistol. He also realized the shots did not come down the slope, but went beyond him into the next, higher meadow.

Standing and smiling, Ewan tugged down his jacket and brushed off a few stray pieces of grass. Then he hefted his rifle as he had more times than he could count, and quickly but silently approached the ruined abbey.

The southern stone wall hinted at the abbey's past strength, as it would take at least three tall men standing on one anothers' shoulders to scale it. Ewan had explored its overgrown interior courtyard, cells, and church in months past, and skirted around the crumbling wall toward the west, where he could depend on the trees and the wall's morning shadow to provide some cover.

Before rounding the corner, Ewan pressed himself close into the wall. Despite the deep shade, it had shed its nightly clamminess. A late summer haze rose from the meadow before him, but there was nothing unclear about Miss Bowes. She stood, a beacon of yellow in the midst of the tawny grasses, about twenty yards from the abbey's former gates, now weathered into the shape of a broad, toothed saucer.

Her straw hat and the angle at which she stood hid her face from him, but Ewan could tell from any angle the movements of someone reloading a pistol. She had a target made of playing cards set up a far distance away, against a log.

She took careful aim, but unlike a man, she cupped her other hand around the hand holding her pistol. Interesting.

The shot rang out. She lowered her weapon and strode out toward the targets. She plucked up the three cards and replaced them with three fresh.

When she turned to resume her position, Ewan stepped out around the wall into the sunlit meadow. Even with the brim of her hat shading her face, he could tell he had startled her.

"Why, Captain Sandeford," she said, halting. "Fancy meeting you here. With a rifle, no less."

"You and I appear to be thinking alike, Miss Bowes," he replied, amused by how she would force him to come out to her, rather than she to him. He wondered briefly how much Miss Bowes's chess strategies unconsciously mirrored her habits in life.

"Indeed," she said, in that forbidding tone she often adopted with him when he was himself.

"I am sorry if the notion displeases you, ma'am," he said, deciding to go on the offensive before she stole more ground from him.

"I am not displeased—or even surprised—to discover you and I may share similar tastes in shooting, sir. It is merely that I had hoped to do mine in privacy."

"Never tell me you are revealed as a poor shot," he said, and plucked the cards from her hands. All three of her shots had fallen, if not in the direct center, well within the cards' notations. Ewan found himself profoundly grateful he had never called her bluff with her pistol that first night. The second night had been pure luck.

She spluttered indignantly. "Give those to me this instant."

He did. "You shoot well."

"I do not need condescension, sir."

"Who is condescending? I am speaking of facts, no more, no less. Do tell me how I err by speaking of facts?"

She regarded him long, the yellow ribbons of her bonnet whipping about enticingly in the wind. He felt, to his surprise, his heartbeat quicken. Then she said, "There is nothing wrong with your speaking of facts. I apologize if I was less than gracious. I am unused to people sneaking up behind me."

That's right. You sneak up behind them, Ewan thought, and said, "From which I gather you care little for surprises?"

"Lately, sir, they have been none of them good." She rubbed the cards back and forth between her fingers.

"I am sorry to hear that."

She shied away from pursuing the subject, as he expected she would. "Where is your favorite spot for shooting? Does your rifle have different requirements than my pistol?"

"This is no ordinary rifle, ma'am, but a Baker. In the hands of someone trained to use it well, it is accurate to three hundred yards. Sometimes beyond that."

"That qualifies as different requirements," she said and smiled.

The smile, part self-deprecating, part simple enjoyment, softened her features. Despite her gift of mercy the night before, Ewan had not thought of her as gentle in any way. This glimpse of Miss Bowes startled him, and he registered the irony of how little he liked being surprised.

Miss Bowes's smile faded as he did not answer. With a return to her crisp tones, she asked, "So, where is your favorite spot for shooting?"

Ewan berated himself. "I have no favorite spot."

"But you were going to shoot?"

"I had not decided."

"I see," she said smugly and began cleaning her pistol.

"I feel certain you mean something by that remark."

"I did mean something by that remark."

"Then had you not best cease from your restraint?"

She assessed him from under the brim of her straw hat much the same way she had assessed him over the chessboard. "My character sketch of you lacked something, that small detail that illuminates. I have now found it."

Ewan made a little bring-it-on motion.

"You feel unclothed without your rifle. You bring it whether you need it or not, want it or not."

"You do like to provoke, Miss Bowes," Ewan said.

She curtsied.

"There is a flaw to your theory."

"Indeed?"

"I do not always travel with my rifle."

"But you would like to."

Ewan could not deny the truth of her observation. He *had* become so used to having his rifle about him in the Peninsula that he did feel, if not unclothed, at least incomplete without it. He had been back in England over a year, and he had not rid himself of the feeling.

"I must be feeling somewhat dim this morning, Miss Bowes," he said, countering. "I do not understand how this detail illuminates my character."

"It is quite straightforward. You prefer to be armed. Or armored, as it were."

Ewan glanced pointedly at her pistol. "Do not tell me you are the kettle?"

She smiled ruefully. "Perhaps it does take one to know one. Perhaps instead I should leave off my character study and be grateful I have not received some lecture on the inadvisability of women shooting pistols."

Ewan appreciated the ease with which she deflected the conversation, and decided to play along. "I am not of that opinion which claims a man's eyesight as better than a woman's."

"Hurrah for you, sir. Were it only that simple."

"It is not simple?"

"You and I both know the subject revolves around those hazy matters of taste and discretion, not the fact of acumen."

"You also prefer facts."

She raised her brows. "I do, sir."

"Even when the facts describe unpleasant things?"

Her gaze did not so much as flicker. Ewan had to admire her for that. "It is better," she said, "to accustom oneself to unpleasant facts as quickly as possible. That is my armor. Time and custom."

"You would stand first in line to cauterize someone's wound, too, no doubt."

He had meant it as a joke, but she replied fiercely, "If it saved someone's life, yes. You think me cold, sir, but—"

"No, I do not think you cold. In fact, I feel quite the opposite about you. You seem very passionate about your beliefs. If your armor allows you to continue that way, I admire its efficacy."

Her lips compressed, she looked away, over her shoulder, toward the ruined abbey.

He waited for her to say something while the insects droned around them. When she did not, he said, "You were wondering, maybe, whether that was a compliment. It was, and you may say thank you."

"Thank you," she said, her voice neutral.

Another awkward silence descended, while Ewan tried to remember all he wanted to ask her. The trouble was, he thought, she continued to show new and intriguing sides of herself. Intriguing, yes, but he could not quite figure out how best to approach her. Even his sallies had been met with reproofs.

Then it occurred to Ewan that he had never achieved anything without some amount of what others termed daring. He tried it now, although he regretted the risk he took with her fragile goodwill. "I did mean it as a compliment, ma'am. To accept such facts as you must have, well—"

"You know. About my brother, I mean."

An intensity to her gaze pricked at Ewan's conscience. She had not wanted anyone to know whose sister she was. Not that he blamed her. But he had his own brother to think of.

He weighed his options in the time it took a bee to fly past him and land on its next clover. "Yes. I know about your brother. It took me a few days to recollect, nor was I certain until I spoke to your friend Lady Dash. People might whisper, but they do not know for certain. He survived his board of inquiry—"

Miss Bowes laughed. She laughed very hard, one hand over her mouth, the other, the one that held her pistol, clasped around her waist. Shortly she had tears in her eyes.

Concern spun into annoyance, and he found it difficult to remember that she was one of those people who had shown him compassion. Ewan had never appreciated being laughed at. "Would you mind sharing the joke, Miss Bowes?"

She wiped her eyes, dislodging her straw bonnet a little. She righted it, all the while gasping as she sobered. "You do not know about my brother, sir. Forgive me for laughing. I do sometimes forget that what he may have done—likely did do—in Spain caused great consternation there. I have no one who would remind me, you see. Lord and Lady Dash are too kind to mention such things to me."

"I would not have mentioned it either, except that it felt a necessary prelude to saying that he might yet survive his desertion."

"Oh," she said, sobering. "No, sir, do not attempt to be kind about this subject. My brother escaped his board of inquiry but narrowly. As for the other matter, well, he was as wretched a thief as he was a soldier. I hope only that he is making a hash of his life somewhere far from England."

"Good God," Ewan said. "I am amazed that you can speak of it so calmly. Amazed, Miss Bowes, and impressed. I know any number of people who would sooner die than speak of such things at all."

"Perhaps some of my brother's blood flows in my veins, then, sir, for I am too much a coward to do such a thing."

"Do not ever joke about the matter, I beg you," Ewan said, alarmed. He stepped toward her. "I have never found courage in such an act. Despair, yes, but not courage. There is a reason it is a sin."

Her gaze measured the new, closer distance between them. Ewan expected her to step back. Instead she essayed a resigned smile. "Why may I not joke about it, sir? You brought it up."

"I did, didn't I?" Ewan said. He snorted. "You are quite a woman, ma'am."

She tipped her head. "Even though I have a thief and deserter for a brother?"

"We can none of us choose our family."

"True. Of course, they may say the same thing."

"Ma'am?"

"That we let them down in our turn." She looked back toward the abbey. "They had a splendid view from here. They could look out over this wide valley."

Oh, Ewan thought, and let her change of subject stand. "They would never have had rooms overlooking the wall."

"How can you be certain? Almost everything inside has crumbled."

"It has. I trust you took care when you explored it, ma'am."

"I do not look like some missish bit of womanhood to you, do I?"

"No, ma'am. Your pardon." *Missish* had to be the last word he would have ever used to describe her.

"That is as well, then. So, on what do you base your opinion?"

"I have seen my share of forts and garrisons."

"Yes. I suppose you have." She studied him. "I am willing to bet, did I bet, that you were one of the first ones to enter the fray."

"I preferred to cause the fray."

"Do you know, Captain Sandeford, I . . ."

"Ma'am?"

"No. Forgive me. Excuse me, I think I am done shooting." She started back to the fresh cards she had set down.

Although he felt sorely tempted to go with her, Ewan remained where he was. She had revealed much of herself in a short time, and he knew her well enough now to know better than to press her. He told himself it was enough to understand why she had stood so staunchly against his trying to rob Dashwood. She felt, incredibly, responsible for Jack Bowes's thieving and desertion.

Still, his curiosity, indeed, his very will, tormented him with what he did not know, what he wanted most desperately to know: did her compassion for Ewan as Juan the thief arise from her assessment of his character, or from the natural sympathy she retained for her brother?

She had not said she wished her brother caught. She

had said she wished him far from his hunters. Did staunch, fact-loving Miss Bowes have facts she would embrace but not be proud to have others know of?

Thinking that any of her forbearance to him derived from sisterly feeling toward such as one as Jack Bowes made Ewan feel decidedly out of sorts. He and Jack Bowes belonged to an entirely different category of men.

"You are frowning again," Miss Bowes said, returning from retrieving her cards.

"What? Oh, I do apologize."

"Do not trouble yourself, sir."

"It is not trouble, but obligation."

"Obligation?"

"Naturally I should not like causing you distress, ma'am."

"My dear Captain Sandeford, there is nothing natural about it."

"I protest."

"Nothing natural beyond pity, perhaps. I do not need your pity. I shall shift well enough for myself. Though I am plain and outspoken, I am friend to the Marchioness of Dash."

Although Ewan was accustoming himself to sudden swerves in their conversations, this one astounded him. "Good God, ma'am, what prompts such sentiments?"

She turned away to pick up a small satchel she had set down on a flat rock. Then she said, "You are quite right. It is now my turn to apologize. You have shown me much kindness. Perhaps I am unaccustomed to sympathy. Perhaps I did not expect it from you, for which admission I also apologize.

"But, since we both admit our love for fact, I may say with impunity that there are times when I enjoy your company, and then there are times when I find you quite maddening. Nor may you say anything different."

"I should not dare," he said, astonishment deepening into incomprehension.

It was the wrong answer. She compressed her lips. "It grows late, sir." She curtsied and walked briskly away.

"Miss Bowes, do wait."

Her shoulders twitched, but she stopped.

Ewan jogged over to her. "I have no notion right now of what the proper thing to say is, so I will likewise speak of facts. We have not immediately glimpsed those aspects of character in each other that lead to an immediate connection. But that does not mean such aspects of character do not exist. Indeed, I feel I know you much better now, and appreciate the better knowledge. You are quite right when you say you will do very well for yourself. No man could fail to prize your loyalty, for instance."

"Pride, Captain Sandeford, is also a fact, and one of my particular sins. I lied when I said I should do well enough for myself, for I must also admit, in addition to being plain and outspoken, that I have nothing—nothing, do you understand me?—to recommend myself except my connection to the Dashes. Would you, a reasonable gentleman, make an offer to such a one in such a condition?"

"Miss Bowes—" he began, thinking the question remarkably unfair and yet determined to answer it in some positive way.

"No," she said quickly. "No, I am sorry. Truly. I should not have asked you such a question. I beg you to let me leave before I say anything that will embarrass me further." Again she dipped a curtsy, and Ewan could not fail to see how it wobbled.

"Miss Bowes, I *have* come to esteem you."

She sucked in her breath. "Thank you. Good day."

He let her leave, as she had asked, and marveled over their conversation.

He had learned little, and yet he had learned much. Some of it confused him more than he would have liked to admit. That Miss Bowes felt highly conscious of her lack of matrimonial prospects he could not doubt. That she might appeal to him as some sort of gauge boggled the mind.

Ewan could have spent the better part of the afternoon pondering it. He recognized within himself that call of the challenge. Miss Bowes had presented a challenge to his getting into Dashwood. She also presented a challenge to him simply by revealing a complexity to her character he had never encountered in anyone else before. Miss Bowes was unique.

But now was not the time to think about it. What mattered most was that none of what he had learned of her this morning helped him solve the problem of exploring Dashwood. That question remained elusive, and elusive he could not have.

Chapter 10

As she walked along the narrow, twisting wooded path away from the ruined abbey, Lucy's face burned with shame and embarrassment. It did not help her to recognize and understand what she was doing as she was doing it. She had plowed on relentlessly despite all her inner protestations of better sense. She would not rationalize her lack of judgment by trying to persuade herself that Captain Sandeford had caught her unaware.

She was a fool. Learning Captain Sandeford had known the whole of it, she had felt all the fresh pain of Jack's perfidy. How she had writhed to know her brother had stolen from innocent people, had hurt others in its pursuit!

The charges of cowardice had been bad enough to hold her head up through. But at the time when she had first learned of Jack's theft and flight, she wished she could have carried a large sign proclaiming her shameful status and requesting that no pity be given her.

Had she had such a device, she could have maintained her composure much better. She could not even guard her hateful tongue from lashing dear Mrs. Quigley, who had looked at her with commiseration over tea one day.

"Yes," Lucy had said, feeling like she was breaking inside, "my brother did steal that artwork. He is a cowardly deserter on the run from King and Country. What does it matter why he did it? He did it. Do you have any other questions?"

She had treated Captain Sandeford in much the same way, although she had become more inured to the pity. From him, it was the compliments, his saying that she was *quite a woman.* She did not believe it, of course. Had he but kept on as he had begun—stealing her cards and making himself as annoying and supercilious as he had ever been—she would not have bothered poking back at him. She would never have laid so bare her hopes and dreams, or her deplorable lack of expectations. She would certainly never have asked him whether he thought she was any sort of matrimonial prospect.

Lucy blushed more fiercely. How would she ever face him again? How could she stand to have him look at her with pity writ large on his face?

At least there would be no such expression on her midnight thief's face. He did not know she had made such a fool of herself.

Lucy stopped short, discomposed by the thought. That it should matter to her what a thief thought defied all rational expectations she had ever considered herself mistress of.

She turned the pistol over. The metal remained warm from the sun. The butt fit smooth and snug against her hand. She had not intended to trick him last night when she had left her pistol behind. Her argument carried force. It had impressed him. But today she had liked the feel of her pistol in her hand, had appreciated that she could hit a target to within an inch. A small competency in the midst of the chaos of her life did much to lift her spirits.

Stop feeling sorry for yourself, Lucy Bowes, she told herself as she walked on. *Those compliments Captain Sandeford gave you meant little to him. He intended to*

be gallant to put an end to your melancholy mood,
which you had no right to inflict upon him. You might
not like him, but he is an innocent bystander to all that
has happened.

She would act graciously when next she met him. She
would hold her head high, but not so high that she
would feel that need to hit back at the world.

She repeated her litany to herself—that there were far
worse positions to be in. She could be companion to
some hideous old crone who bullied her until Lucy
found herself complaining, even in her own mind, of her
nerves. She could be governess to ten bratty children,
each with his and her own set of devilments. She could
be living in a two-room cottage and wondering whether
she must choose between her next meal or a warm fire.

Thinking about her lack of prospects did little good.
That was a fact as much as they were. She had spent the
better part of a year trying to reconcile herself to them.
Efficacious armor, indeed! For now she would amuse
herself by thinking of her game with her midnight thief.
He was a problem, to be sure, but one that she had
shown herself competent at, and if one could not be in
control, one could at least strive for competence.

Lucy shivered in the warm sunshine.

Ewan had found an unlocked window in the library,
on the main floor. He had seen it by the veriest chance
as he had passed down the hallway the night before. The
wind outside had rustled the mullions, and then he had
spied the green curtains move as though a child were
hiding there.

The library proved itself excessively convenient,
since it fronted onto a hallway that ran behind the main
stair and could enter into the foyer from two different

directions. The hallway to the servants' quarters also emptied onto the hallway, which multiplied the number of ways Miss Bowes might think he had come into the house. Did she know just where, he felt certain she would find a hammer, and, extra nails between her teeth, close off his entrance. Of course, it also multiplied the number of ways some servant could appear.

So Ewan crept stealthily along the hallway to the foyer, having carefully closed the window behind him and congratulating himself on his not giving away anything to Miss Bowes's keen powers of observation. He told himself he needed every advantage, no matter how small. Her conversation with Captain Ewan Sandeford had not gone as she—or he—had expected, but she had never seemed flustered by him when he met her as Juan.

The house was dark as ever, with gleaming stripes of moonlight only appearing in the foyer itself.

Ewan ducked through these, waiting with every heartbeat to hear Miss Bowes say, "*Buenas noches, señor.*"

But she did not. Ewan kept on to the main floor drawing room, found it likewise glazed in moonlight. There lay Miss Bowes in her nightly dark blue dress, asleep on the divan with her head against its side, her feet propped up. Some of her chestnut curls had come loose from their knot and dripped over the side of the cream divan like the hovering shadow of a bird. Sleep smoothed her expression, although Ewan regretted the loss of her keen, sparkling eyes.

Still, she looked unbearably peaceful.

He thought back to their daytime conversation and wondered again what had prompted her to ask him his opinion of her as a prospective wife. He had not, as she had doubtless imagined, considered for half a second that she attempted to sound him out. She barely liked

him. At least as him. Toward Juan he had sensed some
softening, but Juan, he told himself sternly, was not real.

It was sort of too bad. Ewan liked being Juan.

But Juan had a job to do, with opportunity to do it.
Ewan smiled, and the movement tugged at the folds of his
mask. Who would have thought that after all his pondering and strategizing, opportunity would come from Miss
Bowes's being excessively tired? He had never considered
drugging her evening tea. Perhaps he should.

No, he decided. That lay along a coward's path.

He turned away and began—quietly, very quietly—to
pick up the knickknacks and examine them for hidden
compartments. Then he moved on to the backs of pictures, recesses in shelves, finally the intricate carvings
around the mantel. Two and a half hours later, and he
had found nothing.

Disappointment washed over him, leaving behind a
black mood he recognized well from his campaigning
days. He had expected this room to yield the IOU. It had
been his destination these last five days. To have it come
to nothing . . .

Miss Bowes still slept peacefully, and Ewan resented
her for it. If he had to have a wasted night, he could have
at least spent it sparring with her.

He had no other notions of where in the house to
search for such a thing, having exhausted the library and
the marquess's bedchamber his first night. Indeed, the
house, for all its rococo appearance, possessed few of
those interesting nooks and crannies for hiding things
in. What one saw was what one got, however hideously
it grated on one's sensibilities.

He stood at the back of the divan and watched the
moonlight, ruffled by some fine drifting clouds, play
across her face. An odd notion struck him that pushed
his black mood to the far corners of his mind. He no

longer regarded her as plain, as he had the first few times he had met her. Feature by feature, yes, she possessed much to criticize, but he had begun to regard her as a force of will, not as a collection of her features.

Another odd notion presented itself—that Charles had done him a favor by giving him the opportunity to see Miss Bowes this way.

On impulse, he crossed to the desk at the room's far corner, took pen and paper, and wrote a short note. He folded it and laid it carefully in the space between her arm and the divan back. Then, spying a light-colored patterned shawl tossed across a chair, he spread it over her. She sighed and snuggled against it.

Would she snuggle against her eventual husband that way, induce him to wake her from her sleep and make passionate love to her? Miss Bowes could be tender, but she would also be a fierce, ardent lover.

Another impulse pressed at him, surprising in its intensity and direction.

"*Buenas noches, señorita*," he whispered. And he made himself leave.

Lucy had considered burning the note her midnight thief had left for her. Her hand had even directed it, twisted so it would catch quickly and completely, toward the fire in her room. She had drawn her hand back, smoothed the note out, and read it again.

I did not find what I seek, it said in Spanish in a fine but spiky hand. *Do not regret your sleep. I trust you wake refreshed. Yours, J*

She *had* woken refreshed, although disgusted with herself for falling asleep. That her midnight thief had been in the room with her long enough to write her a note, drape her with a shawl, and search the room entirely filled her with impossibly strange feelings.

As a consequence, she had been of little use to Caroline, who had decided to set aside the day to continue their sorting of furniture. Twice Lucy had directed Walters to put a piece in the attics that Caroline wanted moved to another, less formal parlor. The second time Caroline had suggested, in her sweet way, that perhaps Lucy needed a little tea?

Lucy did not know whether Caroline refused any invitations to dine out that night, for Caroline would never embarrass her by inventing some implausible excuse not to go out and thus do what she would consider sparing Lucy the trouble of making conversation with their new neighbors.

They spent the evening reading and, in Caroline's case, catching up on correspondence. Lucy envied her friend her devoted husband, and relived her embarrassment of yesterday, even as she hugged to herself the heady feeling that her thief had cared enough about her to leave her the note and cover her against the night's chill.

She tried not to remember that he had never seen her by daylight.

He had not found what he wanted to find in the drawing room, and there was nothing missing. She could no longer believe him pursuing something for its material value. No, he was looking for something that could be secreted inside a statuette or secret drawer. Lucy had not missed the hungry looks he had given the mantel on their second meeting.

If he had started with the upper stories—and such was his aim—the library was the next logical place for him to look. It was a gamble, but given his successful reconnaissance of the drawing room, she could no longer find a bottleneck he must pass through.

The library it would be.

Still, she could barely contain her surprise at how well she had anticipated him again when she heard the window across the room shudder open. The green velvet curtain parted to reveal a lithe, dark-clad shape.

"*Buenas noches, señor*," she said in a voice that impressed even her with its steadiness.

He swept her an elaborate bow. "*Señorita.*"

"I found your note. Thank you for apprising me of your progress."

"Thank you for sleeping, so I could make some progress."

"My very deepest pleasure."

"You had lovely dreams, I take it?" he asked, leaning against a tall bookcase and folding his arms.

The question smacked of the grossest impertinence. She must not allow him to think for a moment that she had dreamed of him, although she had, and lovely dreams they had been.

No, he was far too dangerous for that. Even in the dark, with half a room separating them, his presence dominated the space. Her perception only, Lucy told herself, but perception possessed force all its own. She had played enough games of chicken as a girl, chess later, to know that.

He was the ultimate game of chicken. Or chess. The ultimate game, period, one she sensed would have repercussions far beyond this sojourn at Dashwood.

"We do not know each other well enough for me to tell you my dreams, *señor*. I am sorry, but there it is."

"You wound me."

"You scoff at me. That makes us equal."

"No, *señorita*, never scoff. You are too fine an adversary for me to scoff at. Tease, perhaps, but never scoff."

His vehemence took her aback.

"Besides," he said in a lighter tone, "you began the exchange by trying to put me firmly in my place."

"Indeed I did not, *señor.* You did with your impertinence."

"What else is a lady to do, is that it?"

"You will have heard such conversations before," Lucy said.

"I have had many conversations with ladies before, yes," he replied. "You sound as if you regret them."

"I have no claim upon you, *señor.*"

"That is a hearty untruth," he said. "Save one other, you have the greatest claim upon me of anyone."

He waits for me to ask him who the other is, Lucy thought with astonished anger. But she would not rise to his gambit by asking. Instead she said, lightly, "I am all astonishment."

"You do not wish to know more?"

"Very well, you may explain yourself," she said promptly.

He laughed then. "You do delight me."

But inspiration had hit Lucy. In her excitement she stood and took a couple of steps toward him. "The other person—you are seeking something for her."

"Him," he said flatly. "Now you know my secret."

"Another Spanish sailor found himself on Albion's shore?"

"You do not believe me? I am being more truthful with you now than ever."

"I must confess you do not inspire me with confidence."

"And what of your protestations of my gentlemanly manner?"

"A gentleman may be a gentleman and still lie."

"Surely only social lies."

"No, *señor.* Through his very teeth."

"Who is the man who has made you feel this way, *señorita*? Give me his address, and I—"

"Will call him out, perhaps? Or would you be better suited to stealing into his house in the middle of the night and causing him consternation?"

He scowled, then shook it off, saying lightly, "The former, obviously."

"And what explanation would you give for your challenge?"

"Am I not a Spaniard, *señorita*? It is well known we need the barest of provocations."

The look he gave her could have kindled the note she retained in her sleeve and sent it up in an instant puff of smoke. Lucy did not need him to draw any map between the provocation of a challenge between men and the provocation a woman might give a man.

She spoke quickly. "But you are the very soul of restraint. Only consider how you have not made the search you would make, that you did make last night, because of me."

"Does it matter what I am, or what people judge me to be?"

This echo of Lucy's own thoughts silenced her.

"Ah," he said, coming closer. "I begin to grasp your difficulties, and maybe I have committed the same sin?"

"What sin?"

"'Friend of the lady of the house,'" he said. "I have marked you for my own convenience."

Lucy smiled. "I cannot think that is all you call me."

"No, indeed it is not."

"Some things considerably less flattering, I am sure."

"Maybe when we first began our game. Now, no."

His voice caressed her skin, drenching her with its liquid seduction. Lucy softened, weakened, wanted to submerge herself in the call of that voice and take another step closer to him. To be nearer him. She resisted, struggled harder than she had against her impulse to lash out at Captain Sandeford yesterday morning.

"Now, despite your pistol and my quest," he said, "I would call you my friend did we meet in the daylight."

"But we can never meet in the daylight," Lucy said.

"Do you never dream of the impossible, *querida*?"

Lucy did not immediately recognize the word. When she did a blush rose through her entire body. "All the time," she said, before she thought.

He chuckled, a low, exciting sound. "Here, then, is something else you would call impossible." He touched her face with a black-gloved hand, traced the line of her jaw, then swept back to brush the curls that framed her face. She trembled as he touched the other side of her face, too, drawing her toward him.

Then his lips grazed hers, and sensation spiraled through her, like confetti caught in a windstorm. And like that, Lucy let go. She stopped trying to manage what happened. She let the sensation take her. Some impulse prompted her to part her lips. With a moan, her midnight thief crushed her against him, plundering her mouth.

Lucy gave what he wanted, took what he offered. Never had she felt so wanton, so right, so in harmony with the world.

Then, as he trailed kisses down her neck—and somehow her head was thrown back to allow it—his silken mask rubbed against her face. Lucy stiffened, inhaled sharply.

What was she doing? What was she thinking? He was a thief. Whatever his motivation, whatever he tried to protect, he was a thief. She had played upon his gentlemanly instincts, but she did not know the extent to which she trusted them.

He was a thief.

She pushed on his shoulder until he met her gaze.

"Yes," he said, understanding clear from the chagrined twist of his delicious lips. "It was impossible, was it not?"

"Could it ever have been otherwise?" she asked, and cringed inwardly because her voice revealed that she asked no rhetorical question.

"I will leave now," he replied. He gave her no time to protest, but threw open the window and swung a leg over the sill. "Good night, *señorita.*"

Lucy followed him to the window, trying to form some protest. He saw her, swung his other leg over, and lost his balance. Lucy leaned over the sill. The ground, covered in gravel, lay some four feet down from the sill, and her thief had fallen, his back to her, against the thicket of ivy that blanketed the house. His hands pulled at something around his face.

"Are you all right?"

"My pride has suffered a mortal injury," he said. He pushed himself away from the ivy. A loud ripping sound made Lucy suck in her breath. There, in the heavier stems of old, old ivy, waved a darker shadow with jagged edges.

But her thief did not curse as she expected him to. Instead he turned around, torn mask covering only the space above his left eye, a scratch down his right cheek, and said in English, "Good evening, Miss Bowes."

It was Captain Sandeford.

Chapter 11

Ewan expected her to be incensed. Indeed, he hoped she would be incensed. He had felt the sharp ivy vine catch under his mask and scratch his cheek, although that was a mere trifle. He told himself he was weighing the options of his getting caught while trying to extricate himself from the gnarled vine. Nor had he needed to turn and show her his face. He could have run off into the far hedges of the garden, the same ones he had not expected to make a few nights ago without a bullet in his back. He could have sacrificed the black silk.

But in that place within himself where he could not lie, he knew he had ripped his mask free so Miss Bowes would know him and be spitting mad.

He had turned, and thus revealed all, because he could not enter Dashwood again, either as Juan or as himself, with Miss Bowes thinking of him as she did. As himself, he would wonder whether any potential starry-eyed moment—and granted, Miss Bowes did not have many of them—was directed at his other self. He writhed to think such things.

But nor could he come into Dashwood as Juan and not kiss her senseless again.

That had set Ewan back on his heels.

Or his mask. The mask had made him do what he had

done. It had to be the mask and the freedom he had given it to give him.

What other explanation could there be? Only one remained: he found Miss Bowes attractive, an object of his desire.

Kissing her had driven all other thoughts from his head. She had tasted sweet, but a spiciness underlay the sweet. That spiciness had driven him on. He needed it, craved it, realized that within it he had found someone who could match him fiber by fiber, step by step, desire by desire. She was unschooled, but if he had learned anything about Miss Bowes, he had learned that she was a quick study.

The notion of his finding his match in a plain, managerial female with a highly defined sense of right and how wrong he was . . . It frightened him as no band of marauding French soldiers had ever done.

In that moment when he could choose how to extricate himself from the ivy, he had succumbed to that fear and revealed all. The fear would pass once Miss Bowes would no longer see him. In the equation of these emotions, no desire on her part equaled no opportunity for fulfillment of desire on his. He would get over his desire. He always had before.

All this he reasoned out while playing with the twisted, tangled ivy, and it had made sense to him.

Or so he thought.

"Good evening, Captain Sandeford," Miss Bowes said calmly, looking down on him from her position above him at the window.

"You knew?" he asked, astounded.

"Of course." She folded her arms. "Why else do you think I put away my pistol? Certainly not for that paltry reason I gave you. I am sorry about the pistol, by the way, but you do understand my position."

He bowed stiffly. "How could I fail to? How?"

"Sir?"

"How did you determine my identity?"

"I noted the similarity in your builds. That does sound awkward, does it not? Perhaps I shall have to come up with an entirely different way of referring to you. I do not suppose you have any suggestions for how such grammatical niceties could be framed? It is something that quite smacks of requiring Latin, although 'twill be quite the mouthful. Captain Sandeford *qua* Captain Sandeford, or Captain Sandeford *qua* Juan." She snorted. "Juan indeed. Why ever did you choose Juan? It feels excessively trite. No, you will claim it made perfect sense, Juan being the Spanish equivalent of your Christian name."

"As it is."

"Do lower your voice, sir. Or do you wish to wake the house?"

Ewan folded his arms, fuming. "What gave me away?"

"Well, I noticed that your shoulders and those of the rude thief occupied roughly the same space. Then there was the gesture that you sometimes make, both as yourself and as Don Juan, that clued me in to your disguise."

"Which gesture?"

"You cup your chin with your fist."

"That was all?"

"On such slight things my suspicions were founded. But your attitude, I must say, contributed the deciding factor for me. How could I help but notice that you as Juan were every bit as rude as you were when I first met you as Captain Sandeford?"

"You did not treat Juan as merely rude," he said in a furious undertone. "You flattered him."

"It was fun," Miss Bowes said with that superior tone he so disliked in her. "I wondered how much you would reveal. How much you would tell me. It was a game, like the chess we played. You said so yourself—and let me tell you, sir, your relish for both games also told against you."

"Your critique means much to me."

One of her eyebrows quirked up, although he could not tell whether that indicated he had struck a blow or that she thought his sarcasm demeaned him. He had the nasty feeling that it was the latter. At least, he felt that way.

"Why did you have to spoil the fun?"

That question astounded him more than her calm response to his revealing his identity. He opened his mouth, but no sound came out. Then he spluttered, "Because."

"Captain Sandeford, 'because' ceased to be sufficient for either of us well before we left our respective schoolrooms."

"I do not need to be lectured at."

"Then I beg you not to be so simple."

"Very well, Miss Bowes, if you seek a reason why I ended our game, as you will have it—"

"And you, sir. And you."

"—you need look no further than the kind of statements you make to me."

"I do beg your pardon?" she inquired coldly.

"You have labeled me as rude. I label you as managing and officious."

Then to his continuing surprise, she smiled and said, "And here I was, thinking you did not like the fact that I had refused your advances."

"Why should I have minded that?" he asked, stung but trying to hide it. "That was wrong of me."

"It did take our game to a new level, did it not?" she asked. "But what other move did you have to get around me?"

Nothing would persuade him to admit he had kissed her because he had yielded to an irresistible impulse. Did Miss Bowes get irresistible impulses? Ewan would have said yes to that question even a quarter hour ago. Now, he had no gauge of what she truly thought or felt, if her interaction with him as Juan had been her performance of her role in a game.

Humiliated, Ewan decided it was time to beat a retreat. "I am glad you had thought through the situation so thoroughly. Truly you have been a worthy adversary. I wonder at Dash's writing to me in the first place. How could he have thought Lady Dash in need of protection when she has you?"

"Why, Captain Sandeford, how kind."

"Now I shall bid you good night."

"Do detach your mask from the ivy before you leave, sir. If someone found it, it would cause awkward questions, do you not think?"

He turned sharply away from her, lest she see how discommoded and out of sorts he was. He struggled with the twisted ivy branch, but finally managed to remove the black silk. He stuffed it into his sleeve.

"I must say, sir, I have especially appreciated your costume."

Ewan gritted his teeth, but sketched her another bow. "Miss Bowes."

"Captain Sandeford." She remained in the window, though, so he had nothing else to do but turn and walk away, his tail between his legs.

Captain Sandeford stalked away. As he approached a short box hedge, he whacked at it with his gloved hand. A moment later he blended into the garden's shadows.

Had Lucy had no other indication, by this she would have known that she had hurt and angered him.

Good, she thought vehemently.

She slid her hands up her arms until she gripped herself about the shoulders and could rest her chin against her crossed forearms. Her façade of calm collection dissolved as an angry tear dripped down her face, quickly followed by half a dozen of its salty friends.

Emotions warred within her for precedence. Anger burned brightest, so it won, and she indulged herself with a fit of temper not even her brother's perfidy had caused.

How dare he do such things? How dare he try to break into Dashwood to toy with her? How dare he make her think that he thought her desirable, a suitable match for his skill? How dare he think that a kiss would so set her back that he could get past her and win the game?

He had chosen incorrectly. She, plain, insignificant little Lucy Bowes, had gotten the upper hand. He would be a fool three times over to try anything with her again.

That thought cheered her, and Lucy congratulated herself on her fooling him into thinking she was not angry at all. That feeling could only be described as darkling sweet, like the bite of molasses. He had expected her to be angry. She had known it, just as she had known how he had tried to maneuver her into asking who he thought he was protecting.

If there really was anyone other than himself he was protecting, she thought, electing to doubt.

So he had tried to provoke her, and she had turned his game on its head. Better, somehow her strategizing brain had separated itself from her roiling emotions and given her the ability to enumerate all those points of similarity between his two personas.

Now that she considered them, she could not help but

wonder at how obvious it all was. Of course Captain Sandeford was the midnight thief. It made perfect sense. A Spanish naval officer making his way inland and discovering that something lay in Dashwood that impinged on his honor . . . Well, it was no more unlikely a story than an English soldier picking up the native tongue in a country where he had resided and fought for four to five years. Lucy knew Dash had done so, although he was an exploring officer who had needed to live off the land and the good graces of the natives.

Whatever Captain Sandeford's position within the Army, he and Dash shared a roving, restless intelligence. Lucy should have thought of him immediately.

The cool night breeze coming in the window chilled her. She sat down, not bothering to force the window closed, letting the curtain shield her from the cold.

She had not wanted to think of him—as Captain Sandeford—that way. It *had* been fun, playing the game with her thief. She had wanted to believe that some man with a noble soul could regard her highly.

Lucy and Captain Sandeford had not liked each other from the first. She found him arrogant, presumptuous, and far too fond of his own opinions. He knew her family's history and likely tried to take advantage of her feeling vulnerable.

Worse, he had seen her in the daylight, and yet had flattered her at night. That made him a liar, not just a storyteller.

Another idea struck her. Had Captain Sandeford challenged her to chess, talked to her about clouds, or met her out shooting that afternoon to better understand how to deal with her at night?

Or had their midnight conversations served as reconnaissance for his daylight dealings?

The question led her back to feelings all too familiar

from her dark days after discovering her brother's second life as a thief. She had wondered who her brother really was. Now she wondered who the real Captain Sandeford was—the correct though ungracious officer by day, or the smooth-tongued thief by night?

God, she thought, that she could call him smooth tongued, even in the privacy of her thoughts! Lucy burned with mortification and some other feeling she did not immediately recognize.

Then she realized she could not put aside the feel of his mouth exploring hers. She had to relive every moment of that bliss and thrum of life along her spine. She imagined his every touch as a bellows stoking her desire until she thought she might have melted and formed into whatever shape he desired.

He must never know she had come so close to that.

She could not desire someone who was a liar. She would not. She would not make any excuses for his behavior.

But she wanted to. Oh, how she wanted to! Even knowing his perfidy, his deceit and his double-dealing, she wanted to make excuses for him.

She could not explain why, and she sat in the dark, staring out a half-curtained window blowing in the breeze, trying out theories and suppositions. What puzzled her most was that through every explanation, she yet felt the strong edge of her anger, although the fury pushing it in hot, pulsing waves had abated.

A recollection brought her up short.

How could she have forgotten the disturbed ivy her very first day at Dashwood? Or the ridiculous story about the marauding polecat? Captain Sandeford had been trying to come into the house before Lucy and Caroline had come to Dashwood.

Lucy could not claim that toying with her had been his sole object.

Something else did draw him into the house.

Her main question now was whether he had made up his ridiculous story of a Spanish thief because he did not want anyone to know that there was something he was after, or because he did not want anyone to know he was the one searching for it.

Or both, Lucy thought dourly. The answer to that main question would send her down any number of branching possibilities.

Which left her with two options. She could either swallow her curiosity, or she could swallow her embarrassment and seek out Captain Sandeford tomorrow.

Chapter 12

The next morning, Lucy attempted to head out the door at the earliest socially acceptable hour. Some of Caroline's neighbors, however, had set their clocks at an earlier hour than even Lucy had deemed acceptable.

Caroline was greeting them as Lucy came down the stairs. She took in Lucy's pelisse and dark blue dress and sensible straw hat—Lucy would have died before she wore anything remotely flirtatious today—with a single bat of her lashes. Lucy could trust Caroline, however, not to ask whom Lucy might want to go visit, and she did not.

Still, Lucy had to consider herself suffering through introductions to the Wilsons—Sir Ronald, Lady Wilson, and Miss Wilson, a shy young woman of about sixteen—whom, under different circumstances, Lucy would have been well pleased to meet.

Nor could Lucy miss the appraising glances Lady Wilson gave the place. Lucy would have enjoyed thinking more elaborately about what suppositions—given the house's reputation for orgies—Lady Wilson might entertain.

But her errand pressed her, so she soon excused herself and set off walking down the road that led in the direction Lieutenant Sandeford had mentioned that Barberry Lodge lay. Lucy did not know what the lodge

looked like, how far it was, or what sort of servants
Captain Sandeford kept.

She consoled her trepidations by reminding herself
that she was both an excellent walker and far past the
point of needing to worry about damaging her prospects
any further. While she could blame her brother's perfidy
for complicating matters, the truth was that she had
never been anyone's ideal in a wife.

As far as eliciting the kind of raw desire that would
impel a man to forget all her imperfections, well . . .
Lucy's lips curled. Juan—Captain Sandeford—had
proved a man would only kiss her to get past her.

Lucy tried to push those dismal thoughts away. She
did not want Captain Sandeford to want her, anyway.
She wanted to know what was going on.

The day warmed dramatically while she walked.
When she had thought she had walked too far, she
chanced upon a laborer. He told her she had passed it,
but only just. She turned back, let him point out the path
to her, and thanked him. As he went on his way with a
tug at his cap, all her trepidations returned. Not want
him to want her she might, but she could not forget how
her body had responded to his kiss.

It did not help that a loud thwacking noise made Lucy
jump. It was not the sound of a pistol or rifle, however.
Lucy reminded herself she was not her brother, who
would have had to give every loud noise its direst interpretation, and started up the heavily treed path.

Up a hill that had Lucy breathing deeply, the path
opened out into a pretty, level clearing, with Barberry
Lodge standing off to the right. A respectably sized
house of probably eight bedrooms, its red and light gray
stone gave an impression of warmth and cheer. Holly-
hocks grew in tall blue, white, and pink profusion
around its front gate, and deep blue morning glories

twined around an arching arbor that shielded some of the front walk from the sun.

Another loud thwack came, much closer than before, accompanied by a flash of light from the left. Lucy walked along the fence.

Wearing only faded gray breeches and a worn white shirt open at the neck, Captain Sandeford was chopping wood. He set a log upon a large stump, sighted it carefully, and hefted his ax. Closer as she was now, Lucy could not mistake the distinctive crack as he brought it down.

She tried to tell herself that it was the noise that made her take in her breath harshly. It was certainly not the sight of him so informally dressed. Had she not seen him dressed almost as informally most of this last week?

Did it matter that those times had been at night, when her eyes might miss details they would hone in on in the daylight? Did it matter that she thrilled to watch all the muscles in his arms and back ripple in his concerted efforts upon the wood? Did it matter that she knew what those muscles felt like under her hands?

He looked sharply over at her. Even with his face flushed from exertion, he managed to redden. He hefted the ax. Lucy wondered if he planned to throw it at her.

He flipped it up to get a better grip and buried it in the stump.

Then he turned and walked away from her, toward the house.

"Captain Sandeford."

He barely checked his stride.

"Captain Sandeford, I do need to speak to you."

He was almost to the house. The back of his shirt flapped loose from his breeches.

She had wondered how their next meeting would go.

Now she knew. "Captain Sandeford, do you really want me to announce why I have come for anyone to hear?"

He looked at her over his shoulder. "I am going inside to make myself suitable for entertaining. You may wait for me in the arbor over there." He indicated an arbor closer to the woods and slammed the door behind him.

"Thank you," Lucy said to the fresh morning air. She compressed her lips, then attempted to locate the best way into the gate and beyond to the arbor, where she could spy several backed wooden benches. It would be through the front arbor.

Lucy walked through it, feeling very much the trespasser and annoyed at Captain Sandeford for making her feel that way. He could have shown her the way in, or failing that, he could have sent someone to show her in. She did not need to be kept outside like a peddler.

But, she decided, the best way to put him off his guard appeared to be to act the way he did not expect, which in this situation would be to not notice his poor manners.

Unless, Lucy thought, discomposed, he began to expect that she would act unexpectedly, in which case . . .

Lucy shook herself from the revolving mental circles she could surely drown within, and looked more closely at Barberry Lodge. Old, but there were signs that the roof had recently been replaced with fresh shingling, the paint freshened, and the gardens seemed very well tended. A vegetable garden stretched along the back of the house, and in the front and side, where Lucy sat, the mixture of greenery and flower, in color, height, and texture, bespoke an eye well in tune with Lucy's own aesthetic sense. Lucy appreciated Dashwood's scale, but also this tidy space for its coziness and simple ability to make the most of itself.

Lace curtains hung in the windows closest to her, pulled back to reveal a dining room with striped yellow and white wallpaper. Cheerful ornaments and plates stood proudly in a sideboard.

How much influence had Captain Sandeford had upon this place? Lucy knew only that he had returned a little over a year ago, not what he had done with himself once he had returned. Could she credit him with balance and taste?

What did it matter if she could? Did it mitigate what he had done?

He returned, dressed now in proper English country gentleman style of buff trousers, correct though simply tied cravat, dark green waistcoat, and brown coat. With his dark hair and flashing eyes, he looked eminently respectable, the very flower of noble British manhood.

How looks could deceive!

When he came up to her he bowed. "You are about betimes."

"As are you, sir." Lucy waved her hand toward the wood. "That is an impressive pile. Have you been working on it long?"

"Long enough. But I cannot take sole credit for it. My laborer usually does the rough work."

"I see," Lucy said.

"You see? What do you think you see?"

"That you are standing very much on your dignity this morning."

"It is all I have left, and not that much of it to begin with."

"No more than I, sir."

"And how do you figure that?"

"Were you not the person who said one can learn much of someone's character by how well they play cards?" Lucy asked. "I am certain you learned more of me than I wished you to know. Before I had determined your identity, that is. You used everything you learned about me, did you not? Either as yourself or as Juan."

He frowned. "Did you come here this morning to re-iterate all the wrongs I have done you? If so, I will beg you to excuse me."

"My dear Captain Sandeford, I do not remember mentioning any wrongs you have done me."

"You are the very model of restraint. My apologies."

"Thank you." By now Lucy had expected him to pace about. Her brother would have. She had seen Dash pace about on any number of occasions. Captain Sandeford's restless personality often caused him to fidget, by rubbing his thumb against his forefinger, tapping his leg, or just looking all about him.

This morning Captain Sandeford stood still, his arms folded. "So. You do not consider yourself wronged in any way?"

"Do not be ridiculous. Of course you have wronged me."

"Oh, well, if it is such a simple matter . . ."

"Do you know, I am finding this conversation very difficult."

"No more difficult than I."

"I have a point to make, so do be silent and let me speak," Lucy said severely, and to her surprise, he did. "It is this. You *have* wronged me. You have also wronged my friend, though she does not full know it yet. You have wronged the person who asked you—trusted you!—to look after his wife."

At that, Captain Sandeford looked away to the wood-pile. For all that the ground was littered with wood chips and splinters, he doubtless wished he could be back there chopping away, instead of having to listen to her.

But listen to her he would.

"Despite all that," Lucy continued, "I believe you

have had a reason, a good reason, a gentlemanly reason."

"Is that why you continued to play?"

"Curiosity will impel me more surely than money. You knew that about me."

"We are back at the point where you threatened to follow me around to see what I searched for."

"Oh," she said, reaching into her reticule and handing him the strap of leather. "You may repair your boot."

He took it, thanked her automatically, then set his mouth in a stubborn line.

"You were reluctant when I said I would follow you, and I understand why. You thought what you found would give away your identity. Now that you know that point is moot, what cavil can you have?"

"Miss Bowes, for all our recent adventures together—and you must understand I say this with much regret—I do not trust you with my business."

"Why?" Lucy asked, stung. "Because I am Jack Bowes's sister?"

"No, because you can play games as complicated as my own."

They stared at each other, and Lucy saw a reflection of her own shock, overlaid with defiance, on his face. Once again, he had shifted the ground beneath her feet.

"That was quite an admission," Lucy said slowly.

"It is not one I am particularly proud of, but it happens to be the truth."

"Do you not see that what makes me . . . troublesome . . . could also be a mark in my favor? That I could be capable of helping you?"

"I could allow it as a possibility, but I have no guarantees." He played with the leather strap, rubbing it between his thumb and forefinger.

"You would not take my word?"

"We return to your ability to dissemble."

Lucy shook her head in exasperation. "As you say, how does it differ from yours?"

He grimaced. "That was unworthy of you, for it was far too easy."

"Indeed that was not my aim, and were you honest with yourself, you would know you asked the question to have me reply in exactly the manner I did." She stood. "I think you want to apologize for what you have done. Why not have done with it, and we may get beyond this issue of your honesty."

He folded his arms. "I certainly do not have any desire to apologize to you. There would have been no need to play any sort of game, or have any sort of deception, had you not been an interfering, managing, officious sort of female."

"You would try to cut me to the very quick," Lucy said, trying not to feel just that way, "but what would you have done if you had been in my place? The very same thing, I do wager. But do not concede the point, I beg you. That might mean you and I would have to have some sympathy for each other, thinking alike as we do."

His mouth twisted a smile. "How did your brother manage to get around you, Miss Bowes?"

"For most of it I was away from home," Lucy said pointedly. "I was visiting my cousins—well, first cousins once removed—then they came back with me, and I realized Jack was acting very oddly. Then I found what he had stolen, and told Caroline, and then—"

"Everything broke loose," he finished for her. "I am sorry."

"You were kind to me before when we discussed this subject. I was not sure if—"

"I was trying to suss out your weak spots."

Lucy had expected this reply, but the quickness with

which he uttered it depressed her. She reminded herself she had an argument to present, and said, striving for calm, "It is a trial, but like all trials, it has its uses. Had I not had this experience, I would not be so peculiarly suited to helping you with your difficulty."

"The two cases have nothing in common."

"Nothing in particulars, maybe, but everything in tone. Does not this something you need impinge on your honor, or the honor of someone you care for? What embarrassments will come to you and yours should it be found?"

"Why do you not argue that your friend Lady Dash would certainly give me whatever I need?"

"I love Caroline like a sister. But you must know what it is like to be beholden to someone."

"I believe I do," he said, as pointedly as she had. "Why do you correct yourself by saying first cousins once removed?"

Lucy blinked. "The remove makes my cousin heir to a baronetcy. It would far too pushing to imply, even by omission, that I or mine were connected in such a way. But that has nothing to do with what we are talking about."

"I believe it does. You are asking me to trust you. How do I know you can be trusted any more than you think I can, when you are likewise deluding your friend? Is that not betrayal?"

"She has much with which to contend. She would change Dashwood's reputation."

"I wish her luck. But how does that change your lie of omission?"

"Have you gotten past me more than that one night?" Lucy asked.

"No."

"Have you taken anything from Dashwood?"

"No."

"Then have I not fulfilled my obligations to my friend, but in my own way?"

His expression lightened. "Was rhetoric your favorite study? I can picture a girl in braids quoting Cicero."

"Do stop being facetious. I came along to help Caroline as best as I could. She can be the veriest pushover does she like someone, and she likes almost everyone."

Captain Sandeford grimaced.

"Just so, sir. Unlike the two of us, who can barely tolerate anyone."

"Now that is a firm basis for trust."

"What is firmer yet is my knowledge that you have a secret. I live in Dashwood right now. I can prevent your entry into it, by day or by night."

"Even if you have to cut up Lady Dash's peace?"

"She may be burdened, but she is not helpless. And while I keep you from the house, I could be looking for your precious secret. The neighbors will also wonder why you are no longer welcome at Dashwood."

"Ah," he said, "finally. The velvet glove recedes to reveal the mailed fist."

"When persuasion fails, do men not resort to force of arms?"

"Yes, frequently," he said, "as I have good reason to know. But you are a woman, as I also have reason to know."

Lucy could not prevent her blush as her body remembered every sensation that had swept through her under his hands and lips. But she pulled herself together, hands on her hips, and said, "Then I fail to understand why you cavil at my mailed fist when you have already tried your own."

"That blow I shall have to take like a gentleman."

"You may take it any way you like, so long," Lucy said,

forcing a smile, "as you again concede that we are more alike than we are different, and that you can trust me."

"I will concede that we make fine opponents."

"You must be the most frustrating person I know, and that includes my brother."

He bowed. "Ma'am. You realize, of course, that we are merely extending our game, although the rules have changed somewhat."

"No, Captain Sandeford, that is where you are wrong. This is our end game. I could play while I waited for you to decide your last way to get around me. Kissing me did that, did it not?"

His expression, Lucy imagined, would have looked exactly the same as it did now when he was taking orders he had little liking for. She had to admire the people who could still give him the order.

"Yes," he said.

"When that failed, too, you thought to appeal to me as a respectable English gentleman. Maybe you thought I would have some sympathy for you because of my brother. If so, you gambled wrong. I can stand the thief I do not know. He is a fact of life. But the thief I know?" She shook her head. "Him I cannot countenance. I will not only prevent your admission to Dashwood, sir. I will denounce you."

"What of your professed hatred of waste?"

"I shall have to hope that by speaking, I will save you from a further life of wickedness. You are a very good thief, sir."

"And I have a taste for it now, is that it?"

Lucy did not answer. She did not trust herself to answer. If he held fast, she would have to carry through on her threat. She did not want to. Her sympathy for him—no, she corrected herself—her attraction for him would make denouncing him the most painful thing she would ever have to do.

He turned away from her and ran his fingers through his luxurious black hair, which glinted in the morning sunshine. Lucy ached to run her fingers through it, as she had not been able to when he had kissed her as Juan. How clever of him, she could not help thinking, to have covered his hair. She could have identified him by that alone.

But such thoughts availed her little. He had kissed her as part of a campaign, not because he had enjoyed the experience. Had he not revealed himself to her within minutes? Did that not mean he found the necessity of kissing her again revolting in the extreme?

She should resent him for it.

But she could not. At least, not entirely. She wanted the experience again. Wanton, crazy, incorrigible, impossible, she could load any number of adjectives upon her desire.

Her desire refused to go away.

"Never tell me you have developed a taste for reticence," he said.

"What else do I have to say, sir?" Lucy asked. "Do I restate the reasons you should trust me in some vain attempt at persuasion? No, I see no cause to do that. You are an excessively stubborn man—"

"Ma'am."

"—so if the logic I have applied does no good, what other appeal should I use?"

"Women have been using other appeals since the dawn of time."

Lucy flushed. She could not fully describe how much she would have liked to try such appeals. Maybe someone like Caroline could have carried them off. Plain Lucy Bowes had no such recourse. "Have we not already concluded that we are not suited to argument on that level?"

He appeared struck by her statement, although for what reason Lucy could not discern. "I suppose I must concede that point."

"So, sir," Lucy said, tugging at her gloves. Her last vestige of hope that he found any small part of her attractive faded away. "What shall it be? Do you tell me what you look for, or do I return to Dashwood and have a long sit-down with Lady Dash?"

Chapter 13

"Is that really a choice?" he asked.

"You made your bed, sir."

"You are a study in contrasts, Miss Bowes. There are times when I do believe you full of everything sympathetic. Then there are the times when you think clouds are a hangman's noose, and you force unpleasant choices upon a man."

Lucy marveled that he yet tried to distract her. "What is your choice, sir?"

"Very well," he said after a long pause of studying her, while she tried not to grow warm and failed miserably. He indicated she should sit back down on a bench. She chose the other one and took obscure pleasure in his grimace before he sat down on the one he had indicated, opposite her. She had won, and she had kept her pride.

"The problem is not me," he said, steadily. "It is with mine." He nodded toward the house. "My brother."

"Then why is he not—"

"You have met my brother several times now. Do you think he could have been Juan?"

Lucy considered Lieutenant Sandeford's jovial, even-handed temper, and had to agree. "No. Does he speak Spanish?"

Captain Sandeford shook his head. "A little French, I think. But even speaking French, you could have recognized his voice easily enough. I had hoped Spanish would be a better disguise. I never knew you spoke it."

"Atrociously, remember?"

"I am unlikely to forget," he said.

Lucy did not know what implication she should take from his neutral tone.

"Where *did* you learn Spanish?" he asked.

"Someone came from Spain to recover the artwork my brother stole. He had to spend some time in my house," Lucy said. She smiled. "I learned the invective first."

"To be sure," he replied.

He had wanted to smile. Lucy had seen it on his face, and yet he had tugged himself into neutrality. Saddened, and angry at him for making her feel that way, she said, "What else could I do, when he would insist on repeating in English everything he had said in Spanish?"

"It is very difficult not to pick it up when so presented. That was the way I learned it too, more or less. Although, I will say, he does sound tiring."

"On the contrary. He was vastly energetic. He spoke twice as quickly so he could say everything twice in about the same time." Lucy tipped her head. "So do say wearisome, rather than tiring."

"As you will. I suppose he was also very young, a mere stripling?"

"About your age. Handsome. He fought with the Spanish Army of the Center."

Captain Sandeford frowned, then twisted his lips derisively.

Lucy did not know what to say to that expression, and the conversation had drifted alarmingly from where she had wanted it to go. "But you, sir, you spoke Spanish only because I caught you. It was not a prerequisite. The person who came into Dashwood did not have to be Juan."

"True."

"But you enjoyed it. I do not know if your brother would have."

"He might have surprised me. And you."

"You will not admit you enjoyed it," Lucy said. "I have a vision of what your commanding officers may have experienced."

Now he did smile, and Lucy felt very much like a girl who had tugged on a dog's tail, only to find it belonged to a wolf.

"So," she said briskly, for she would not have him believe he frightened her, "what are you looking for?"

"A piece of paper only."

"Only. What is written on it?" When he frowned, she decided not to hide her exasperation. "How do you imagine I can help you if I do not know which piece of paper we seek?"

"It is an IOU, given by Charles to Dash. The previous Dash, that is."

"Then it belongs to Dash. Um, doesn't it?"

Captain Sandeford shrugged. "The matter becomes confused. Likely Dash cheated."

"You do mean at cards?" Lucy asked.

"Yes. Then Dash induced Charles to sign away something that did not belong to him."

"How?"

Captain Sandeford compressed his lips, then said, "Charles does not often drink heavily, but that night, he found himself the worse for wear. He does remember trying once to escape his host, and the card game, but not much more than that."

Lucy raised her brows.

"He was neither much ahead nor behind at the time."

"But he did not escape?"

"No."

Lucy chewed this information over. "A moment. This all happened two years ago?"

"Closer to a year and a half."

"But you seek it now?" Lucy asked dubiously.

Captain Sandeford sighed and ran a hand through his hair. "Charles was in the West Indies."

"But you have been here the past year. You could have functioned as your brother's intermediary, no? Dash did not speak to you about it?"

"He did not."

Captain Sandeford's flat, but emphatic tone sent quivers through Lucy and reminded her of how his arm had felt restraining her. She ventured, "Caroline has told me some of her late brother-in-law. What do you edit as unfit for my ears?"

He blinked, snorted, then said, "Charles believes that Dash set him up because of some resentment Dash felt toward me."

"Dash resented you?"

"Charles surmises Dash resented me for years."

"Really?"

He shrugged. "I have no way of knowing. Whatever his feelings toward me were, Dash contrived to get my brother to sign this IOU, and then kept it where it could now be found."

"You do not think Caroline or her Dash would act nicely over the matter?" Lucy asked, carefully, so she would not reveal her disbelief that anyone could think the Dashes would act badly.

"I believe your friend would act as nicely as she could, but I do not know Colonel Lord Dash well enough to judge. He would be the ultimate arbiter. It is entirely likely that he could think—as indeed I thought myself the first time I heard Charles's story—that someone who has once allowed himself to be in such a situation could be lax again. As Major Lord Thomas Dashley, I knew him to be exceptionally stringent with his honor. Yet when I met him here . . ." He shrugged. "People can present different faces to the world."

Lucy did not answer. She knew they both knew that too well.

"I do not wish to make such gambles with my brother's life."

"Or the thing he signed away."

"That, too."

"You gambled instead on getting into Dashwood."

"It seemed the easiest course."

Lucy considered. "Since you introduce the subject yourself, sir, could you tell me why I should aid your brother?"

"I am convinced Dash played him for a fool. How, I am not sure. As I've said, Charles does not remember most of that night and has described it as something that happened in a nightmare. So, although I allow for that other opinion, *I* would sooner put my trust in the person whose character is essentially good and has made a mistake, for such a person is the last person to repeat it."

"You speak from experience, sir."

"I do."

Lucy played with the fringe on her reticule, thinking. She liked Lieutenant Sandeford and could understand how he might have fallen victim to someone's plotting. If his brother trusted him now, she should concede his being worthy of it. Still, Lucy could not help but wonder what experience had made Captain Sandeford capable of such sympathy.

He was watching her play with her fringe, even as his hands continued to toy with the leather strap. She looked away, toward the house, lest he discern her blushing, both from her frustrated desire and her blatant curiosity.

"So," he asked briskly. "Did you have a plan to search Dashwood?"

"I had not given that much thought yet, sir."

"Well, then, Miss Bowes, perhaps we should retire and think."

"Perhaps we should." Lucy stood, and he did the same. She held out her hand. "Please convey my sympathy to your brother, that . . . that he has found himself confounded by this problem."

"I shall certainly do so," he said, taking her hand and bowing over it briefly before letting it go.

"Does he know?"

"Miss Bowes?"

"About us. I mean, about my preventing you from—"

"Yes."

Lucy did not know quite what to say.

"Why?" he asked.

Lucy would have sworn she saw a gleam of devilry in his expression and resented it. "Why," she said breezily, "so that I may know what I may or may not say before him so as not to cause you further embarrassment."

That pricked him. "I shall go tell him this latest development straight away, then."

"Do. May I suggest you call for tea after dinner? By then perhaps I shall have some ideas of how we might proceed."

He bowed stiffly. "Ma'am."

"Good day, then."

He nodded, and Lucy forced herself to walk back along the fence and the path. She did not turn, not even when tears pricked her eyes.

* * *

Ewan laid his arms upon his fence, leaned into it, and thought dark thoughts in the direction of Miss Bowes's retreating back. Never in his life would he have imagined finding himself in the position of having a managerial spinster dictate what he could and could not do. Worse, how he should do it. She would retire and think the matter through, would she? He was to report after dinner, was he?

The nerve of the woman. Did she doubt for a moment why he had spoken in Spanish that first time? Was it fear of being caught? No, it was fear of being caught by her.

Now he was well and goodly snared.

It did not help his morale to reflect upon his own part in his current debacle. Although Ewan had not quite planned to kiss Miss Bowes, he had to admit to himself the temptation had been there for some time. He could date it from the night her rounded bottom had been pressed against him. He had kissed her before his mask had snagged on that damnable piece of ivy.

He could have gotten clean away with it.

Instead he had decided that if he must be caught, he would be caught for maximum effectiveness. He had discarded any notion that Miss Bowes could be of further use.

Yet here she had come, up his walk, into his garden, and coolly appraised his efforts with an ax.

He had no keen sense of why, either. Why did she not just give him away? More to the point, how had Miss Bowes convinced him to tell what he had promised not to tell?

Ewan thought back to their conversation by the ruined abbey. Revealed in the light of her knowledge of his other identity, the conversation's strange directions and tendencies formed some sense. Had she been warning him against trying to fool her anymore as Juan? Her forceful comments about how she had nothing except her connection to the Dashes, how unpleasant facts should be faced immediately, and that she condemned her own brother for his thievery—all could certainly be interpreted as a warning, a manifesto even.

How long would she have allowed him to continue before she had called his bluff? Would she have allowed him to kiss her again in the moonlight?

Ewan did not think so. What had she said? *Have we not already concluded that we are not suited to argument on that level?*

He kicked one of the fence slats, leaving behind a dark smudge. It did not help his mood. *Not suited*, he thought. *Damned if we are not suited too well.* That was the root of the entire problem as far as he could see.

Someone yawned behind him. Ewan did not need to look to know it was Charles.

"Morning," Charles said.

"Closer to afternoon," Ewan said.

"Then you will have breakfasted." Charles leaned into the fence as Ewan did.

Ewan began to feel the weight of the sun prickling on his back, which was considerably more clothed than Charles's. Charles had pulled on a shirt and tucked it into his trousers, but not bothered yet with a cravat.

"I decided to tell Miss Bowes what we seek within Dashwood," Ewan said baldly.

Charles's amazed dismay well satisfied Ewan's need to lash out at his brother. He had not realized he felt such a need until he had said it. But there it was. He had believed his brother had made a mistake for which he was very sorry. Ewan believed everything he had said to Miss Bowes about Charles being more reliable now than someone who had not made such a grievous error. Charles had likewise had almost two more years of service in which to further mature. Ewan had rallied to Charles's cause by breaking into Dashwood, although his actions betrayed the trust placed in him by a fellow officer.

But none of those considerations meant Ewan had to like it.

"You will have a good reason," Charles said, between a question and a statement.

Ewan tried to think of one. "Inevitability."

Charles raised his brows.

"And exigency. Lady Dash plans to take that house apart from top to bottom. It is more than redecorating."

"Yes?"

Ewan grimaced. "Some sort of crusade to change local feeling. Miss Bowes kept me from looking every night and—"

"I trust you," Charles said. "Have I not trusted you?" He sighed.

Shocked, Ewan felt something go out of him with his brother's breath.

Charles surveyed the screen of trees surrounding the house. "I cannot count the number of times I stood against the *Midnight*'s railing and looked out at the sea wondering how I was ever to solve this problem. Now look at me. I'm staring at trees. But I'm a damned sight closer to getting it solved. I'm grateful to you, Ewan, no matter how it comes out."

"Your standards and mine differ greatly."

"You would prefer to have found that damned letter before Lady Dash and Miss Bowes arrived. But when is life so simple? I could not have done what you have done. At the first sight of Miss Bowes, I would have turned and ran and not come back."

"You would have found another way into the house."

Charles shrugged. "Maybe. Who can tell? We are where we are. You do not seem relieved, though."

"You are correct when you say I do not like complications."

"Miss Bowes," Charles said.

"Miss Bowes. She sends you her sympathies."

"She is all that is kind."

"Indeed," Ewan said without conviction.

"Do you not trust her, then?"

Ewan compressed his mouth, then said, "Who can know whether one can trust a puzzle? Unwrap a layer, one finds a fresh labyrinth."

Charles clapped a hand on Ewan's back. "My advice? Bring a long string and beware of bull-headed monsters."

"Thank you."

"What? You did not think I was calling you stubborn, did you?"

"The thought never crossed my mind," Ewan said. If anyone was bullheaded, it was Miss Bowes.

"Good. Maybe your telling Miss Bowes will make things easier."

"Yes, bull-headed monsters are frequently known to show mercy toward their prey."

Charles laughed, and Ewan gave in to its infectiousness. "Come on. Breakfast."

Lucy had worked herself into a welter of bafflement by the time she broached the hill that looked down onto Dashwood. How to go about its searching? Captain Sandeford seemed to have satisfied himself that he had searched the main floor. She counted the windows along the front wall gleaming in the sun. There were twenty on the first floor. Only sixteen on the second, and a mere ten on the third, attic, level. Did she double it to reflect the rear, she would have at least ninety-two other rooms to contemplate.

Bafflement slid into frustration. Had it not been easier to keep "Juan" from the house?

She had committed herself, however.

Someday, Lucy thought sourly, she would learn to leave locked doors locked and prowlers to prowl. Someday. It would not be today, however. Lucy stopped, took a deep breath, and tried to come up with the circumstances that would restrain her. She could not.

With an annoyed shrug, she kept going on toward the house.

Lucy conceded that she understood perfectly why he had done what he had done. She also continued to feel he had treated her very ill. Apart from everything else— laying hands on her, knocking her down, frightening her, making her lose sleep—he had kissed her with false passion. The other aspects of his ill behavior she could understand, even forgive. *That* she could not forgive him.

She had liked it too well.

Lucy passed through the heavy front door.

"Miss Bowes," said Walters.

"Where is John?" Lucy asked, naming the footman who usually watched Dashwood's front foyer. She tugged off her gloves.

"We have exchanged duties for the moment."

"You were waiting for me," Lucy said with some surprise.

"Ma'am," said Walters and bowed. "After Sir Ronald and Lady Wilson left, well . . ."

Lucy blinked, then remembered that Sir Ronald and his family had been calling on Caroline for the first time when she had left for Barberry Lodge. "Well, what?"

"Lady Dash went looking in one of the lesser attics for some furniture to replace the pieces she had removed."

"And?"

Walters looked like he wanted to sink into the floor. "You must understand, ma'am, when we heard you and Lady Dash would come to Dashwood, we—the staff, that is, ma'am—tried to pack up those items which were . . . in particularly poor taste."

"That was kind of you, Walters."

"Yes, ma'am, but the attic she is searching is the one where we put the things we removed."

"Is it?" Lucy asked sharply, a couple of ideas forming. "Is it? Why are you telling me this, Walters?"

Walters ha-hemmed and looked at a point over Lucy's shoulder. "We—the staff that is, ma'am—find Lady Dash a very . . . *genteel* lady. We would like her and my lord to make their home here."

Of course, Lucy thought, amused by his description. The people Caroline could not win over could be counted out on one hand. Lucy knew, however, how much Caroline and Dash had come to love Bonwood House, which Dash had bought when he had first come into her and Caroline's neighborhood. Caroline said she appreciated being close enough to her sister and young half-brother to keep her eye on them, but Lucy suspected she and Dash loved the house because it had been the first place they had made theirs.

But one never knew, Caroline and Dash might well decide to spend some time here, too. "I am glad the staff feels that way," she said carefully, "but you must be more plain with me, Walters."

Walters looked her in the eye. "She will see those things and never want to come back here, ma'am."

"You would be surprised to find that there is a goodly length of steel running through Lady Dash's spine. She knows her brother-in-law's reputation."

"There is a difference, begging your pardon, ma'am, between gazing at a lake and swimming in it."

Lucy resisted the impulse to smile. "You think I can persuade her to desist?"

"Yes, ma'am. *You* could."

"She will want to do something with those . . . items." Goodness, Lucy thought, she was starting to imitate Walters's hesitations. "Having them in the house would offend her sensibilities."

"That I can well appreciate, ma'am. If I may . . ."

Lucy made a go-ahead gesture. She wanted to pull the words from his throat.

"May I suggest that we ask her to permit us to remove them? Permanently."

"I do think that a fine idea."

Walters almost beamed.

Lucy put a finger over her lips and hoped that she had let Walters commit himself far enough so that he would not cavil at answering a question that she really had no business asking. "Has anyone looked through the items in question to know whether the late Lord Dash left anything of importance within them?"

"Ma'am?"

Lucy rolled her hand. "Jewels, heirlooms, papers."

"The late master was not in the habit of leaving such things about for the people who attended his . . . *gatherings* . . . to pick up. He kept his jewels in the safe and all his important papers in the steward's cottage." Walters turned and pointed to the back of the house. "About three hundred yards down the hill."

The steward's cottage! "Yes, I do recall seeing it. It has not been occupied since . . ."

"Indeed not, ma'am. For that we thought to wait for Lord Dash to return from France."

Lucy hoped she contained her interest. "Naturally. But Lady Dash has the keys to it, I assume."

"It is among the keys Mrs. Walters gave her, as it does not involve Mrs. Walters's normal duties."

Lucy kept her internal whoop from reaching her face. "I see. Well, then, I will go up to Lady Dash directly. Which room is it?"

"I will direct you, ma'am."

"Thank you. Oh, Walters, I do not think anything or anyone not announced will be coming into the house anymore."

His expression lightened, became curious, but all he said was, "I see, ma'am."

"On that note, Captain Sandeford, and possibly Lieutenant Sandeford, too, will be coming after dinner for tea."

Chapter 14

Although she could do nothing about a new dress, Lucy nonetheless dressed for dinner with extra care, asking the maid whom Caroline had attending her to arrange her hair in a different style. She felt very daring. The looser style and gentle curls could only be described as coquettish, although it did flatter her face in a way she had never imagined, softening its sharper lines and making her eyes seem more in harmony with the rest of her face.

Would Captain Sandeford notice? Did she care? Should she care?

Lucy thanked the maid, accepted Caroline's sincere compliments, and tried not to feel too exotic. She and Caroline had, after all, been hip-deep in exotic for some quarter hour earlier that afternoon. Every now and again, one of them would smile and catch the other doing it. Then they both would laugh and recount which item had sent them into peals.

"I thought the furniture downstairs . . . *questionable*," Caroline said as they strolled, arm in arm, into the drawing room. "But Thomas will be horribly embarrassed I saw any of *that*. He will be more embarrassed that you did, too."

"Dash will recover," Lucy said briskly. "Although we

shall have to get all references to those things from our minds before he returns. Especially the lamps."

"No," Caroline replied in mock horror, "the books with the pictures of—"

"Do not, I beg you. I shall cry." Lucy had to wipe away a tear of laughter.

"And we must not have that when Captain Sandeford comes to call, I daresay."

If anything could have dimmed Lucy's mirth more readily, she did not know what it was. "Do not be droller than you have to, Caro."

Caroline just smiled and picked up her embroidery hoop. They remained quiet for a few minutes, with Caroline stitching and Lucy wandering aimlessly about, before Caroline said, "I am sorry that you have had to resort to asking Captain Sandeford for a game of chess. You must be lonely here."

Lucy shrugged. "There is nothing to apologize for. With Dash gone, there was really only Mr. Quigley to play with. I would have been lonely for chess there, too."

"Then I am glad Captain Sandeford will oblige. Did his brother not say that he was insufficient challenge as well?"

"Lieutenant Sandeford may have said so." It irked Lucy excessively that Caroline appeared to think she and Captain Sandeford were courting. Perhaps to Caroline, who could have had any man she wanted to fall at her feet, love and marriage were goals she had taken for granted. To Lucy, however? No, one must make allowances for different circumstances, to say nothing of differences in disposition and character.

Any man who would want her had to be a candidate for Bedlam, she reminded herself. And would she want such a man? Lucy smiled wryly. Such a logical circle spun down only into blackness.

Walters came to the door. "Excuse me, my lady, but Captain Sandeford and Lieutenant Sandeford are here."

"Do send them in," Caroline said. Then, as Walters bowed and left, she winked at Lucy.

Both gentlemen had come in uniform and carried their hats under their arms. Lucy could not help but think Captain Sandeford's uniform far handsomer than the lieutenant's, although she insisted on being sufficiently honest with herself to know she gave the uniform more credit for the man who wore it. His perfidy could not deny the fact that he was an attractive man, or that he had shouldered the burden for another.

Caroline exclaimed and fussed over them, more, Lucy thought, to hide how much their appearance in uniform had made her miss Dash than a growing tendency to fuss. Caroline talked one's ear off, true, but her lack of fussing was one of the things Lucy liked best about her. She came on as steady as a gentle trickle of water and wore one down before one knew one should have had one's defenses up from the beginning.

"You have redone your hair, Miss Bowes," Lieutenant Sandeford said. "It looks very nice."

"Thank you, sir," Lucy replied, not missing the nudge he gave his brother. "It was time to try something new."

Captain Sandeford said nothing.

"Lucy set up the chessboard, sir," Caroline said to Captain Sandeford, with perhaps the slightest note of severity, "but I hope you, Lieutenant, will keep me company with some cards or conversation?"

This arrangement surprised no one, and they sorted themselves out. Captain Sandeford's expression as he held Lucy's chair remained forcibly polite.

"Do not—" she began in a low voice, then stopped. "What?"

"Nothing." She would not comment on his lack of

comment. He could have said something about her hair, if he professed to esteem her at all. Maybe, when the matter really came to it, he thought nothing could improve her looks and did not wish to draw attention to it. Facts were facts.

Lucy liked this explanation not at all and took refuge in chiding herself for indulging in vanity she had no business having, and especially not when there were more important points to cover.

"I have found a possibility," she said.

"Let us play," he said, but from the way he lifted his chin and squared his shoulders, she suspected he keenly wanted to know what she had to say.

Captain Sandeford drew white, and they played for almost three quarters of an hour. They did not speak, and Lucy noticed, when she was not studying the board, Captain Sandeford's strong profile, or the dexterous way his hands moved, and that Caroline glanced at them with exasperation.

Doubtless Caroline wanted Lucy to engage him in sparkling, seductive conversation. Did Caroline but know what sparkling, seductive conversation they had already engaged in, she would be crying foul.

That thought depressed Lucy enough to make her careless with her next move. Captain Sandeford glanced up sharply, moved his rook, and said, "Check."

Lucy blushed, muttered an imprecation, and tried to figure out how to extricate her king from his attack.

Raised, excited voices from the hall made everyone look toward the door, where Walters appeared, followed closely by Lord and Lady Grayson, Mrs. Lansing, and Miss Alton.

"My lord," Caroline began.

Even as Lucy and Captain Sandeford stood, Lady Grayson's knees crumpled, and she wobbled against her husband. Mrs. Lansing and Miss Alton looked pale and angry.

"We were attacked," Lord Grayson said, grimly, "not a mile from here. By the highwayman."

"Good heavens," Lady Dash said. "Lieutenant, may I importune you to pour some brandy for Lady Grayson? Ladies, do come in and sit down."

Charles went to the sideboard for the brandy.

"How long ago?" Ewan asked.

Lord Grayson assisted his wife to a divan, took the proffered glass of brandy from Charles, and pressed it into her hand. "Ten minutes, maybe fifteen."

"He took the pearls you gave me, Grayson," said Lady Grayson, fingering her bare neck. She tried a sip of brandy and winced.

"I am going to have a look," Ewan said. "Walters, send round for my horse immediately."

"Very good, sir."

Miss Bowes was studying him sharply. Ewan wondered if she had decided she could now definitely acquit him of being the highwayman. "What do you hope to accomplish, sir?" she asked. "He is long gone by now, and since it has not rained in several days, the ground is too hard to give up tracks."

"Trust my brother," Charles said with quiet authority.

Miss Bowes's gaze flew between Charles and Ewan. She made some internal calculation and nodded.

"I am sorry we cannot finish our game," Ewan said.

Miss Bowes held out her hand. Ewan perforce took it, but as he bowed over it, she whispered, "The steward's cottage, behind the house. Our normal time."

Normal time! Was anything normal between him and Miss Bowes?

He squeezed her fingers in response, bowed to the remaining company, and took off quickly for the stables. The groomsmen had Bella ready for him and looked avidly for information. Doubtless the Graysons' arrival had excited them as much as it had Lady Dash and Miss Bowes.

"Lord Grayson's driver?" Ewan asked the sensible-looking older groomsman who stood by the young groom holding Bella's reins. "Is he about?"

"Yes, sir," the older man said, stepping forward. "Fetch him, Billy." Billy touched his forelock and sprinted off. "I thought, sir, when I heard the order to saddle your mare, that you'd think of speaking to him. His name's Jones, sir, and he's that shaken, although he doesna want to let on. We've given him a tot. Maybe two by now."

Ewan nodded. More likely it was three or four, but the spirits would not have completely befuddled the man yet.

"Here's Jones, sir."

Jones did look shaken. "I've been driving Lord Grayson since he were a boy, sir, and I never had nothing like this happen to me, no, sir, not never."

Ewan held up his hand. "Tell me where it happened, where he waited for you, and what direction he went afterward. Take a deep breath, Jones, and go handsomely."

Jones straightened and pulled himself together. "Yes, sir. 'Twere about a mile away, on the road between Lord Grayson's property and Mr. Montgomery's."

"Along the bend where the river forks?" Ewan asked, picturing the steep drop-off down to the river on the right, the road bending left around a treed hill.

"Yes, sir. There's a rocky notch, sir, almost by the road, in the trees, before you turn the hill. He waited there."

"And where did he go, afterward?"

"The direction we came, sir. I couldn't turn the carriage."

Ewan nodded. It made tactical sense. The question, however, was where the highwayman had cut away from the road: down over the river once the drop-off eased, or over the open fields the other side of the hill.

"Thank you, Jones."

"You're going to go have yourself a look, sir?" Jones asked, glancing at the saddled mare.

"Yes, I am."

"You have a pistol, sir? And a lantern?"

"I have my Baker, and the moon is nearly full."

"Course, sir," Jones said, although he looked dubious and cranky.

"Carry on," Ewan said to the groomsman, and swung onto his horse. He rode off into the balmy night, one hand on his reins, the other holding the Baker. His green rifleman's jacket blended in nicely with the road's shadows, as it ever had in France. He wondered what impulse had prompted both him and Charles to don their uniforms that night. Ewan had tried all day not to think of Miss Bowes as the enemy, but when it came down to it, he had felt excessive comfort in dressing for battle.

Not another soul traveled the road, and, as the bend lay a mile away, Ewan crept up to the place in ten minutes. He looped Bella's reins over a bush on the river side of the road and patted her neck so she would quiet. The moon cast deep shadows from the wood across the road, although as it rose, they would lessen. The highwayman had chosen his spot well, Ewan judged.

He closed his eyes, letting them adjust to deeper darkness before he walked into the shadowy forest. Night sounds surrounded him—crickets, the whisper of wings, the soft stirring of undergrowth, its pattern regular like that of a stout or polecat sneaking through it on its way to the river, and the river itself, which moved with a soft lap and slunk.

The rock provided excellent cover. Even in broad daylight, Ewan would have chosen it.

Were he a highwayman, that is.

And risk Miss Bowes's disapproval? he thought, but could not force himself to stay sardonic. He realized he wanted never to voluntarily provoke Miss Bowes's disapproval again. At least, not in reference to the important things, such as deciding whether he would take to the High Toby. Pricking her here and there could only be considered good for her. She needed to be reminded she did not have all the answers.

As Ewan circled the rock, he found that the forest exposed its back to a gleam of tree-washed moonlight. Likely the moon had moved since the highwayman had lain in wait there. And there, glimmering, at the base of the rock, lay a silver button. Ewan held it up to a brighter shaft of moonlight. Inscribed laurels around the outside embraced a number: 52nd. The person who had worn this button came from the 52nd Regiment of Foot.

Ewan compressed his lips. A former soldier taking to thievery did not surprise him. The abilities one acquired as a good soldier certainly transferred nicely to thievery. Many men had found the peace as bare of possibilities and employment as they had found the war fraught with alternating boredom and misery.

Of course, he did not know how long that button had lain there. It looked clean, uncovered by dirt and bracken, but that in itself proved nothing.

Another notion came to Ewan. Had Mr. Bowes, brother to Miss Bowes and formerly a captain in the 52nd, left this button behind? Had *he* taken to the High Toby?

Ewan pocketed the button and shook his head. That was entirely too far-fetched. Miss Bowes preyed on his mind, that was it. He had not been able to do anything with himself since the night before without chiding himself over whether she would approve him or not.

Nor had his checking himself changed after she had visited Barberry Lodge that morning. If anything, it had intensified.

He had gone into his own dear home, that he had spent the better part of a year not only directing but participating in restoring, and wondered if Miss Bowes would think ill of the wallpaper, the size of the rooms, the way they fit together, the colorful Spanish decorations he had picked up campaigning, or even the selection of books.

He tried to tell himself that she held his interest only as a passing challenge. The thought would fortify him temporarily, so he tried it again and began studying the road on the other side of the most recent carriage tracks. Down the road, on the wooded side, he found a freshly broken branch where the highwayman had pulled his horse's reins away. The road, however, was indeed too dry and hard to make out much in the way of tracks. Ewan followed them, stopped, and looked off the road whenever they appeared to stop. He could find no corresponding tracks off the road for almost a mile.

Resigned, Ewan headed back to Dashwood, where he found his brother and Lord Grayson in sole possession of the drawing room.

"Lady Dash extended the hospitality of the house to the ladies," his brother said.

"My wife and mother-in-law did not wish to travel again this evening," said Lord Grayson.

"Did you find anything?" Charles asked.

"A button, from a regiment of foot drawing from Oxfordshire," Ewan said, strangely reluctant to name the Fifty-second. "But the button alone does not prove anything. Buttons were often traded, and it could have been there for a few days."

"A soldier?" Lord Grayson asked sharply.

"A lot of men have been thrown back on the beaches, my lord," Charles said, sounding for all the world like the officer Ewan had thought he would grow into once this business of the IOU no longer pressed him. "I have seen groups of soldiers and sailors pass through the area looking for work."

His tone impressed Lord Grayson too, at least long enough for the man to harrumph and tug on his lower lip before saying, "Still. This thieving cannot be allowed to continue. I don't care who is responsible."

"Of course not," Charles replied. "Who is the magistrate now, Ewan? Is it still Squire Gordon? Well, my lord, shall we visit him first thing in the morning? I am at your service, and that of Lady Grayson."

"That would be highly satisfactory," Lord Grayson said. "And you, sir?"

Ewan bowed. "There is a militia post in Wells, my lord. I judge it best to alert them to this potential problem."

"A very good thought, sir. Very good."

Miss Bowes appeared in the doorway. Despite her neutral expression, her hunched shoulders suggested she felt harassed. When she turned her attention from Charles and Lord Grayson and saw Ewan, she breathed deeply and her shoulders relaxed. Her shoulders had quite a beautiful line, exposed as they were by the green dress she wore.

The assurance this gesture implied stirred a deep tenderness within Ewan. This feeling—combined with his acknowledged desire for her and his growing realization that he could no longer defend himself by regarding her as "that plain Miss Bowes"—instantly made Ewan feel more uneasy than he could ever remember feeling.

"You are returned, sir," she said.

"As you see."

The line of her shoulders rippled delicately, and Ewan could not decide whether he should consider himself lucky to put her on her guard again so that he should not have to guard himself against his own inexplicable feelings for her.

"Did you accomplish your task?"

"You mean, did I find the highwayman? No, ma'am. I did not."

"Oh," she said, with a tone one bare shade warmer than cold disdain.

Lord Grayson raised his brows. "He thinks it may be a soldier."

"There are enough of them about," Miss Bowes said. "What specifically makes you think so?"

"He found a uniform button."

"May I?" Miss Bowes asked, holding out her hand.

"Best not, ma'am," Ewan said, putting his hands behind his back.

She drew her chin in, startled and annoyed.

Charles, ever the peacemaker, said, "My brother will take it to the militia in—"

"Wells," Miss Bowes said. "Yes, of course."

"You know our county well, ma'am," Lord Grayson. "I thought this your first visit to us."

"It is, my lord."

"I mentioned it once to Miss Bowes, my lord," Ewan said, knowing full well why Miss Bowes would make it her business to know where all local militias might be garrisoned. Again the notion that finding a button from the Fifty-second was a strange coincidence nagged at Ewan. Again he dismissed it. That button could have come from any of a thousand or more coats. "She has an excessively fine recall of such details."

Miss Bowes nodded to him. "I came to tell you, gentlemen, that Lady Dash requests you forgive her her continued absence. She is settling the ladies."

"Lady Dash is all kindness," Lord Grayson said, but although his tone contained no irony, the look he gave Charles suggested they had already conversed about the challenges facing Lady Dash in making anyone of good reputation comfortable in Dashwood.

Well equipped to read such social nuances, Miss Bowes said tartly, "She bids me to make certain that you gentlemen have all you require."

"We do very well, thank you, ma'am," Charles said.

"Would you be available to finish our game, ma'am?" Ewan asked. "Or does the hour grow too late?"

"I would be happy to, sir," she replied. "Let me but reassure Lady Dash."

Ewan bowed, and with a slight curtsy to Charles and Lord Grayson, Miss Bowes left them.

Lord Grayson harrumphed and shook his head in the direction of Miss Bowes's retreat.

"Is something the matter, my lord?" Ewan asked.

"Er, no. Just that those two are unlikely friends, don't you know?"

Ewan wanted to say something terse. Instead he glanced at Charles, realized Charles expected him to say something terse, and remarked, offhandedly, "There is nothing surprising in it to me. They complement each other very well."

Grayson frowned, no doubt wondering what he had missed, and thankfully let the subject drop. Charles steered him into a game of cards.

Miss Bowes returned a few minutes later with Miss Alton accompanying her, Miss Bowes appearing so far from pleased that Ewan wondered if the ladies had exchanged words.

After greeting the gentlemen, Miss Alton said she had come back down because, "How could I miss watching a game Miss Bowes believes she is about to lose in a move or two?"

"Althea," Lord Grayson said, with a look to Ewan, "perhaps that is not quite the correct sentiment."

Miss Alton laughed. "I am so sorry. You misunderstand me entirely. The last time, Miss Bowes won. I shall be cheering her from behind." She dipped a graceful curtsy. "You will forgive me, Captain Sandeford, but we ladies must stick together."

"Miss Alton, I appreciate your solidarity—"

"But, Miss Bowes, you will say that chess is not a group enterprise, just like cloud watching, hm?" Miss Alton asked. "I watched last time."

"True," replied Miss Bowes.

Miss Alton tossed her head. "Tell me, Miss Bowes, what do you *like* to do in company?"

"I play the pianoforte, although very ill."

Miss Alton smirked. "Do you?"

"Yes."

"Then come, Miss Bowes, you are among friends."

Miss Bowes went to the pianoforte. Ewan would have protested, but Miss Bowes's scathing look stilled his tongue. From memory, Miss Bowes played one of Handel's Water Music pieces so laboriously that even Ewan's insensitive musical ear could tell she was wringing the life from it. Her expression, screwed up in concentration, stood starkly at odds with her exuberant posture. She had started having, Ewan decided, far too much fun.

Miss Alton recognized it as well, for her ripe lips puckered dangerously. Until, that is, she caught Ewan glancing at her, and gave a bland smile.

When Miss Bowes finished, Ewan said, dryly, "I tell

you, we should have had no use for drummers to instill fear in the hearts of the French, had we had you and your pianoforte, Miss Bowes."

Miss Bowes dissolved into laughter. Ewan had not expected such a reaction, but then Miss Bowes rarely behaved as Ewan expected. But since she was laughing, Ewan joined her, and Charles jumped in. Even Lord Grayson's lips twitched.

But Miss Alton said coldly, "I think I shall retire. Your arm, brother."

Lord Grayson contained himself, gave his sister his arm, and escorted her from the room.

Miss Bowes wiped streaming eyes, then, before Ewan could say anything, began playing the piece again. This time the melody gamboled happily along. Charles and Ewan drew closer to her. When she had finished, she chuckled again.

"But that was wonderful," Charles said. "You had us believing you were quite unaccomplished."

Miss Bowes tried to look contrite. "I should not have teased her in such a fashion. But I do so resent people who think they may ride roughshod over me."

"You reserve that right for yourself," Ewan said.

Instantly her mien sobered. "Yes, I suppose I do. Generally I can make a fool of myself all by myself. I neither need nor appreciate help. As for the other interpretation I might make from what you said," she said, quickly, to forestall argument, "I do not meddle unless someone either invites me or makes something my problem."

Charles's gaze reproached him.

"Miss Bowes," Ewan said, "I did not mean to—"

"I know, sir," she said quietly. "Lord Grayson is coming back down the stairs. I meant to tell you that we shall now have to postpone our plans for this evening."

She rose from the bench and gestured toward the ceiling. "Too much going on. Tomorrow would be better." She raised her voice. "Good night, gentlemen."

Ewan caught her hand as she started for the door. "Miss Bowes, I—"

"I know, sir." She summoned a smile before freeing her hand from his. She did not look back, but passed from the room with a slight curtsy to Lord Grayson as he entered and murmured a good night to her.

"I say," Lord Grayson said, "did I hear that piece played again and well, or did my ears deceive me?"

Charles made a noncommittal noise, then said, "We are for home, sir."

"Yes," Ewan added.

They made arrangements for Charles to meet Lord Grayson at Squire Gordon's the next morning at ten o'clock. Then Ewan and Charles waited outside in the balmy dark for their horses to be brought to them.

"And to think I used to believe you all charm and no substance," Charles said.

"Button it."

"Right." Charles tapped his toe in the dirt some fifty times before Ewan stopped counting. Then he said, "Maybe I should be the one to make, er, tomorrow's appointment."

"Why?" Ewan demanded.

"Well, it *is* my business, and I *can* be charming—"

"She does not want charming. Or comments about her hair. She wants a challenge."

Charles snorted. "Do your challenges always include hits below the belt?"

"Careful, little brother."

"Take your own advice, then, hm?"

Ewan sighed. "You are right. I am sorry. Miss Bowes provokes me."

"So you do not like challenges."

"Button it," Ewan said again, and tried to ignore Charles's grin.

But he could neither ignore nor dignify with a reply Charles's saying, "Women always appreciate comments about their hair."

Chapter 15

"I do not like Miss Alton," Lucy said to Caroline the next morning as they smiled and waved good-bye to the Grayson ladies' carriage. A balmy day followed the balmy night, although a haze covered the sun. All Lucy's senses seemed a-twitch and on edge, making her suspect there would be a storm by day's end.

Certainly thoughts of Captain Sandeford could not be blamed for all of her nerves.

"Did you really play Handel at half speed?" Caroline asked, taking Lucy's arm and leading her along the path that wound through the garden toward the back of the house.

Lucy shrugged. "Deathly deadly speed. She would insist on insulting me. Worse, she would apologize for the first insult, as though we were all quite stupid and had missed it, then insult me again. I do not understand her. Did we not agree when we came that the Reigning Local Beauty would resent you, not plain little insignificant me?"

Caroline laughed. "You posited and agreed with yourself. I told you that you were an idiot, remember? Or maybe absurd? Anyway, there is nothing either plain or insignificant about you."

Lucy grimaced.

"Do not dismiss my compliment, I beg you. You cannot

truly think yourself insignificant, Lucy. Be honest, do. And the Somersetshire air has agreed with you. I have never seen you in better looks."

"If you insist I take the compliment, I shall smile and say thank you."

"Thank you," Caroline said dryly. "And you're welcome."

"I shall still ascribe Miss Alton's insults to laziness, though."

"Laziness? How do you decide on laziness?"

"To insult you well would be a challenge for her. 'Dear Lady Dash,'" Lucy said, affecting a bored, die-away accent, "'how could you possibly contemplate attending my picnic? You would certainly ruin your beautiful complexion. It must be a sore trial.' You see? It could be nothing but nonsense. The Somersetshire air notwithstanding, I have not your beauty and never will."

"You do not need my beauty. Captain Sandeford fancies you as you are."

"Fustian!" Lucy exclaimed, dropping Caroline's arm. "Where do you get such notions?"

"I am not the only person here who may posit and agree with herself."

Lucy laughed, although she knew its shakiness betrayed her. "You may be as absurd as you like. If Captain Sandeford fancies me at all, it is as someone with whom he may play at chess without fear that anyone would think, for even the barest, briefest moment, that his playing masked a true interest. He could crook his finger at any other woman in the area, Miss Alton included, and she would come running."

Oh, Lord, she thought, *I said "masked." I said "barest."*

"He does not crook his finger at me," Caroline said roguishly.

"He knows Dash would run him through."

"Or speak to Wellington."

"Influence is a dangerous thing."

"Maybe," Lucy said, thinking of how she would have had Dash using his influence, if need be.

"So, do you paint Captain Sandeford as the soul of prudence?"

"No. Prudence is the very last word I would use to describe Captain Sandeford."

"Next you will tell me you may also call him lazy."

They had walked around to the back of the house. The tear in the ivy stood out, although not as starkly. It had been a week, after all. "No," Lucy said. "I cannot call him lazy. Cunning, perhaps, but not lazy."

"You will have it that way, hm?" Caroline asked.

"My will has nothing to do with it. That is the way it is."

"It is too bad you cannot like him."

"Too bad for whom?"

"For you, and for him, of course."

"Caroline, let us be very frank, you and I."

"Oh, dear," Caroline said solemnly, but her eyes were still dancing.

That prompted Lucy to be as harsh with Caroline as she had been with Captain Sandeford, certainly harsher than she had intended, and much harsher than she had promised herself she would be again. "No one in his right mind would want me. I have no money, no looks, no redeeming traits of character, no family connections—"

"Thank goodness you qualified that last," Caroline said, getting annoyed. "For you have connections enough among your friends. And I am blessed if I shall listen to you denigrate yourself any more. You have been my friend forever. Do you think my judgment so poor I cannot recognize an admirable character?"

It was not Caroline's judgment Lucy doubted so much as her trust. But, she thought, this was the first time she had betrayed Caroline's trust. Perhaps she went too far to soothe her own guilty conscience. "You have always been too nice, you know," she said with a light, lilting tone.

"Give over," Caroline said, but she was regaining her sense of humor.

"Very well. And I am sorry, Caro. You have been nothing but decent to me, and I have a difficult time feeling gratitude. It makes me mean. I hereby resolve to feel much less sorry for myself."

"Do not go to extremes, I beg you. Do you become too nice, mayhap Miss Alton will decide she needs to be less lazy."

Lucy laughed. "I will render any small service within my power."

They strolled on again, continuing their circle round the house. Presently they would pass under a canopy of dogwoods.

"Now that I think on it, though, it will do little good," Caroline said.

"Hm?"

"Captain Sandeford will not fancy *her* while *you* are here—for whatever reason you care to supply, my dear!—so I suspect I remain safe from her."

"Marriage has made you very pushing."

Caroline smiled proudly. "Yes, it has, has it not?"

"What news from France?"

"There have been no letters for three days now. But do not worry. I am not despairing. Last night I asked Lieutenant Sandeford about Channel crossings, and he told me they could be quite unpredictable this time of year, 'prevailing winds being against you, don't you know?'"

"Lieutenant Sandeford is a very affable man." Trust-

ing, too, Lucy added. How much trust in his fellow
creatures had Lieutenant Sandeford lost over the incident of his letter and the late Lord Dash? And where had
Captain Sandeford lost his?

The question she had entertained briefly in his garden
the day before struck her poignantly, and she had no
idea why. Never say she was past mere curiosity and had
begun to develop sympathy toward Captain Sandeford!

"Do remind me how Fletcher had said that hole came
to be in the ivy."

"What hole?" Lucy asked, pulling her attention away
from thoughts of Captain Sandeford, including trust,
kisses, and moonlight meetings.

"The one along the wall we just passed."

"Oh. A polecat."

"You were right, then, that it would have had to be
an exceptionally big polecat."

"I hope I never exaggerate," Lucy said, and prayed
Caroline would leave the subject there.

"I wonder what it was, then. I hope it was not that
highwayman."

"He would not be a highwayman, then, Caro," Lucy
said lightly, despite the sudden pounding of her heart.
"He would be a housebreaker."

Caroline smiled. "Trust you to whisk my concerns
away with redefinition."

"Truly, you are not alarmed, are you?"

"This highwayman *has* appeared twice—twice that
we know of, so it could be more—close to Dashwood.
Given Mrs. Walters's nerves, I would be a fool not to
speculate whether they are the result of my late brother-
in-law's demands or some present-day unpleasantness."

Lucy nodded and hoped she appeared thoughtful.
"Captain Sandeford thinks it may be a former soldier.
He goes to Wells today to alert the militia."

"If that is true, it will upset Thomas."

"I think it has already upset Captain Sandeford."

Caroline linked arms again with Lucy. "Well, then, with our neighbors preoccupied with the highwayman and the staff emphatic about our not going through those attics anymore . . ."

"Emphatic states the case too calmly," Lucy said. "I thought Walters's hesitations would turn into outright stuttering."

"Then it does sound as if we may make our own plans for the day. I have some ideas about how we may decorate for my ball. Then there are invitations to go out. It is late notice, I will admit, but—"

"Who would refuse the new Marchioness of Dash? Certainly no one I know, and certainly not I. Let us plan and address away."

"Good. I shall ask Walters to bring us what we need to the west porch. We should take advantage of the pleasant weather while we can. I think it shall storm by evening."

The storm threatened all afternoon, evening, and into the night, until even Caroline complained that if it would storm, it should do so and get it done with. The air felt thick and moist, but it had one great advantage to Lucy. It kept her from becoming comfortable enough to sleep through her midnight appointment with Captain Sandeford.

The wind started up as she prepared to leave, moaning through the trees and causing them to swish and swoosh, odd shadows against the black sky. Umbrella in hand, Lucy crept from the house. She had gone out there once already and knew the cottage lay more than the three hundred yards Walters had advertised.

The first drops of rain spattered upon the patio flagstones as Lucy crossed it. Pleased with her foresight, Lucy put up her umbrella, increased her pace, and proceeded along the garden path. A sudden gust of wind turned her umbrella inside out. The rain shortly doused her with big, splotchy drops.

Lucy abandoned all pretense of pleasure. Tossing her umbrella behind her, toward the patio, she ran for the cottage.

Her skirts were a sodden mess by the time she set foot on its threshold. Panting, brushing her dripping hair from her eyes, and flicking water from her bare arms, she went inside.

"Good God, Miss Bowes, you're drenched." Captain Sandeford emerged from the shadow behind the door on the other side of the front room.

Lucy gasped, although she had half expected him to be there already. She noted he yet wore his regimentals. Had he been all day going to Wells? " 'Tis finally storming," she managed.

"So I see," he said. "And hear." The rain pounded on the roof.

"I had an umbrella. It lost its battle to the wind. Here, help me close the curtains. I left lanterns in the closet."

"I found them," he said. "One went out, but it's an easy thing to relight. Do you always plan so far in advance?"

"Did you bring one of your own, sir?"

"Naturally. Are you cold?"

"No, of course not. It's dreadfully warm in here. And do give me some credit, sir."

He pulled a curtain shut with as much force as the storm raging outside. Lucy winced, held her tongue, and went into the adjoining rooms to close the curtains there. She heard him doing the same in another room before she came back into the front room and removed her lanterns from the closet. She took a thin stick from the fireplace and used it to relight one of her lanterns, Captain Sandeford's lantern, and some candles scattered about.

"A tidy little place," Captain Sandeford said. He seemed to have regained his temper, and gestured toward the cozy collection of dark green chairs and divan, the warm Oriental rug before the hearth.

"Too tidy, was my opinion," Lucy replied. "The furniture is too nice for a steward. It is too nice for Dash's brother, too, if what we found in the attics was any indication of his usual tastes."

"Maybe he came out here to escape from himself."

"If he hid incriminating notes here, sir, maybe he came out here to gloat in private. Who can tell?"

"I should like to tell, Miss Bowes. Do you wish to start in here, or in the other room?"

"I meant we can only speculate on what Lord Dash's motives were. It is more important, surely, to identify his habits."

Captain Sandeford leaned against the door frame, his expression hooded.

When Lucy judged she had not mistaken the noisy rain for some comment of his, she said, "I will take this room, sir."

He instantly disappeared around the corner, leaving Lucy fuming. Why did the cursed man insist on objecting and getting himself worked up into the veriest snit whenever she said the least little thing contrary to his opinions? Could he not allow the mere possibility that she might know something about something?

Lucy collected herself and began looking through a small escritoire in the corner of the room. She found copious stationery with stylishly embossed *D*'s on it, tools for trimming pens, the pens themselves, and behind those, a woman's lace garter. At least, Lucy decided it had belonged to a woman, for it had pink roses embroidered on it.

She left it where it was. She moved over to the mantel and felt around its smooth, painted edges. The storm sounded much louder here, pummeling the flue, and a cold wind blew down the chimney, making her shiver. She found nothing. No secret panel, no buttonlike depression, no hidey-hole.

Lucy stood back and surveyed the room for another likely place to look. Behind the chair cushions? She pulled them up, found nothing, and sighed. She should go beard the lion and ask Captain Sandeford if he had found anything, but as she strode purposefully to the door, her wet skirts stuck uncomfortably to her legs. She stopped and looked down at herself to pluck them away and realized that the rain had soaked through to her petticoat.

Nor had her skirts and hair taken all the damage from the rain. Her dress clung to her like a second skin from shoulder to shin. And although Lucy acknowledged herself plain of face, there was little plain about her figure.

She put a hand over her mouth, realizing what she must have looked like to Captain Sandeford. What had she been thinking, breezing in, dismissing his comment about her being wet through, possibly cold, and ordering him to close the curtains?

He rounded the doorway as she approached it. "Did you find any—" He broke off.

"I did not—I did not realize how wet I was," she said.

"You must be cold now," he said, and although it took him a half a minute to undo the wealth of buttons on his uniform jacket, she could not come up with the protest to make him stop. He settled its warm weight over her shoulders, his fingertips brushing her bare skin above her bodice. They both stiffened, and Lucy heard her own quick intake of breath echoed by his.

She dared to look up to his face and found his expression bemused.

"Do you know, it was easier, being Juan."

"Why is that?" she asked on a breath.

"Juan got to be much closer to you than propriety allows, *señorita*," he said in Spanish.

Everything within her wanted to close the bare inch necessary for their lips to touch. Her body craved it. Her bruised feelings wondered whether she would shortly find out whether he had kissed her that other time only to get past her.

But one little thread of sanity told her that any man would kiss a highly suggestively dressed woman, even a plain one, if he was all alone with her, late at night, in the candlelight, with a storm raging around them.

She had almost lost herself the last time he had kissed her, and likely kissed her for his own purposes. She would lose herself more.

She must refuse him. She must.

A loud thwack at the back of the cottage saved her. Captain Sandeford dropped his hands from the jacket as they both looked back there. Lucy saw nothing amiss except that Captain Sandeford had, in his ill-tempered zeal, pulled a curtain closed so violently that it had gapped on the outer side.

"The storm must have brought down a tree branch," Mr. Sandeford said.

"Did you find anything?" Lucy asked, holding the jacket closed. "I have searched this entire room. Nothing."

Those dark eyes of his studied her, and Lucy both hoped and feared they did not like what conclusion they drew. "I found nothing in what serves as the library. There were precious few books to look in, and the secretary has only twelve drawers."

"There is one other place I thought possible," she

said, and tried to suit actions to words. But since he did not move, she perforce had to walk around him in the small space of the doorway. She headed for the small dining room, where she had noticed a whatnot that stored dishes and was built into the wall. She took a deep, steadying breath, then picked up each dish and found just another smooth porcelain surface gleaming in the candlelight.

Captain Sandeford watched her from the dining-room doorway.

She shook her head at him when she was done. "There must be someplace else. Some strange compartment well hidden."

"It's not here," he said flatly.

"How can you be sure?"

He ran a hand irritably through his crisp dark hair. "A feeling. Because this enterprise has been doomed from its very inception. Damn Dash, anyway."

"But—" Lucy began.

"But nothing," he said. "I should have known nothing good would come of it. The storm is abating. Let us call an end to this farce."

"If you wish it," Lucy said, considering herself wise not to argue.

"I wish it." He blew out the candles in that room, so that shadows fell across his face even as his white shirt gleamed in the light coming from the hallway. To Lucy he looked otherworldly, a new creature entirely, one whose habits and tendencies she did not know and could not anticipate.

"You are staring at me. Am I suddenly possessed of a set of horns?"

Annoyance steadied her as little else could have. "Do you often consider yourself a devil, sir?"

"Devil take it," he replied and stalked off.

Well, then, Lucy thought, *that went well.*

He stomped through the back room and into the library. She went into the front room, where she blew out the candles and lanterns. When she heard him close to the doorway, she scurried over to the front door. Nothing would induce her to be in that doorway with him while he was in this mood.

Nothing should induce you to be there again whatever his mood, she told herself. *He will not be your future.*

He nodded to her, and she cautiously opened the door. The lawn looked slick and inky, ruffled here and there with twigs brought down from the trees above. The air smelled of rain, although a sudden gust of wind brought a cooler, crisper smell in its wake. Thunder growled in the distance, moving away.

"I will walk you back to the house," he whispered at her shoulder.

Lucy started, then recovered herself. "Thank you, sir."

She ignored his dark look, but took his proffered arm. She had not had opportunity to touch him without a coat as Captain Sandeford, and the shock of how thrilling his strong muscle felt distracted her as they picked their way up toward the house.

Thus she squeaked when Captain Sandeford suddenly pulled her against a large tree trunk. He held his hand over her mouth and put a finger over his lips. She nodded, letting him know she understood she must be silent.

He put his face against hers, cheek to cheek, and whispered, "Someone is before us, sneaking about."

His face was rougher than it looked. Lucy whispered back, "One of the groundskeepers?"

"I do not think so."

"Who, then?"

"Likely it is our highwayman."

Lucy sucked in her breath. "How dare he come so close to Dashwood!"

"Shh. He dared to come within a mile of it yesterday, and dared to lift Lady Grayson's pearls."

"Take your jacket. Your shirt gleams."

"No," he said, preventing her by the simple expedient of putting his arm across her. "You will be cold."

"So?" she asked, although she felt the wind pick up and come in rapidly cooling swells.

"I do not wish you to be cold. Besides," he continued, doubtless feeling her bosom swell with her protest, "your dress would show, too. We shall make for the cemetery, the mausoleum. There will be ample shelter there, and we may make for another entry into the house. Gather your skirts together, take my hand, and stay low."

She nodded and did as he asked. He moved them quickly from sheltering tree to sheltering tree, a squeeze on her hand the only signal she would have that he would move again.

It started to rain again, although not the violent, driving rain that had soaked Lucy's dress, and, oddly enough, the moon was peeking out again. Still, the rain fell enough to make Captain Sandeford take them right to the mausoleum. He tried the door, pushed it open without hindrance, led them inside, and closed the door.

Lucy pressed her finger against her nose, lest she sneeze from the still, dusty air. It was darker in there than outside, but not as dark as it might have been. Windows allowed a dim respite from the gloom, and the marble monuments arranged along the walls gleamed with the same faint color as Captain Sandeford's shirt.

"Now what?" she asked in a whisper.

He put a finger on her lips, sat down against the door, and gestured rapidly at her to do the same. Heart pounding, she sat next to him, trying not to huddle.

Less than a minute later, something pushed at the door from the other side. Captain Sandeford had his legs braced and ready, though, and the heavy door did not move.

Lucy did not realize she had gripped Captain Sandeford's arm until he covered her hand with his own. They waited for what seemed to be an hour, listening to the rain slacken again, before he slowly stood and gave her a hand up.

"We go straight for the house. Now," he said in a whisper. "I think they are gone."

"They?"

"Our highwayman may have a friend. I am not certain."

"I trust you."

He gave her hand a squeeze and slowly cracked the mausoleum door. The moon continued its flittering in and out of cloud cover. Again he led her from shelter to shelter, until there was nothing to do but crouch low and make the last, exposed run to the library window where Captain Sandeford had so recently lost his mask in the ivy.

Panting, Lucy pressed herself into the corner while he lifted the window sash.

"I will give you a leg up," he said, lacing his fingers together to make a step.

She took off his jacket and shivered in the sudden cool. "Put this on first, sir." When his lips tightened, she added, "I will be upstairs in dry clothes within minutes."

He still made no move to take it.

"How could I explain having it?"

That argument worked, although why she had had to make it was beyond her. He shrugged the jacket on, although he did not button it. Again he laced his fingers together. She hesitated over her muddy shoe, but decided not to protest.

He propelled her up against the window frame. She

scrambled over the wet sill. Her hands felt the moisture, but the damp barely registered against her clothes. When she could stand in the library and look down at him again, he said, simply, "Good night."

"You will go after him now."

She hoped she had guessed wrong, but he nodded. "I could not, not while you were with me."

"Is it necessary?"

"Yes. Futile, most likely, but necessary."

She knelt, put her arms folded flat along the sill, and rested her head on her hands so she and he would be more of a level. "I wish it were not necessary."

"I wish it were not necessary, too." He looked down briefly. "Miss Bowes, I am sorry I lost my temper with you earlier. The situation is . . . not your fault."

Unsure whether he referred to the search or how close he had come to kissing her, Lucy said, "You are kind, sir."

He nodded, bowed, and left.

Lucy watched until he turned a corner and disappeared from view. Then she removed her muddy shoes, picked up her sodden and dirty skirts, and whispered, "I am sorry, too."

"No need to tell me how it went last night," Charles said next morning as Ewan sat down at the breakfast table. "I can read it in your face. And it was a late night, I surmise, or you would have breakfasted hours ago."

Ewan reached for the coffeepot, poured himself a generous cupful, and added an equally generous amount of sugar. He had found nothing but confused footprints half washed away by the rain. "I remain undecided between whether I am merely in a foul mood, or whether I am in a foul mood and enjoying it."

Charles raised his brows, speared a kipper, then put

down his fork. "Do you think he destroyed it? Have we been plaguing ourselves for nothing?"

"Dash would have sooner died than deprive himself of something as titillating as that. It's there. It's just a question of where, and I do not know where else to look."

"Ewan—"

But the arrival of Ewan's manservant James at the door silenced Charles. "Yes, James?"

"A man, maybe a gentleman, gave this to Higgins by the barn, sir. He said you would want to see him, and he did not want to come into the house."

James held out a silver button, and Ewan did not need to turn it right side up to know it would show a 52 in the center. He passed the button to Charles, saying, "Yes, James, I will see him. Best to keep everyone else away from the barn for a while, eh?"

"Yes, sir."

"I'll go with you," Charles said.

Ewan shook his head. "Best I handle this myself. He sees two of us, he may bolt."

"I'll be watching, from the library window."

Ewan nodded. He strode from the house. The cooler air ushered in by last night's storm made him almost regret not having donned his coat. But anticipation kept him warm enough. Was he indeed going to meet the highwayman who had plagued him the last two nights? Would the man be so foolish as to come here? Or was this merely someone seeking to sell information? Higgins thought he might be a gentleman.

All things were possible.

The man lounged against the shadowy side of the barn. As Ewan approached him, keeping a careful line between the man and the library window, Ewan tried to make him out. He wore nondescript clothes of dark tan and gray, with a soft gray hat pulled low. Not overtall, he yet stood with a certain indolence that implied a confidence not seen among someone who had been a soldier. No, if this one had been in the Fifty-second, he had worn an officer's red sash, too.

The man straightened when Ewan came within ten feet of him, although the hat still shaded his face. "Yes, you're Sandeford all right. Dash it all if I didn't still recognize you, although I had only seen you once, after Badajoz."

"You have the advantage of me, sir," Ewan said, even as the certainty of who stood before him settled upon him like last night's cold, drenching rain.

"You were never known to cut up stiff, Sandeford. Well, it's understandable, I suppose. Permit me to reintroduce myself." The man swept his hat off, causing a shock of long, brown hair to fall forward. He brushed it back, revealing disturbingly familiar features. They were indeed what Miss Bowes might have looked like had she been born a man.

"Jack Bowes," Ewan said.

"At your service, sir."

Chapter 16

"What are you doing here?" Ewan asked flatly.

Bowes smirked. "I had hoped you would be much more impressed."

"With what, specifically? Your theft, your desertion, your evading the law for nine months, or your taking to the High Toby like any commoner?"

"None of those. My ability to keep my mouth shut over what I saw going on in a small cottage at Dashwood, to wit, your almost kissing my sister." He made a tsking sound. "Naughty, naughty. What you see in her, I will never know. All cats are gray in the dark, eh? Too bad for you it wasn't darker, because you had to see something, didn't you? Yes, I thought you would not be pleased. Too bad for you that you had to be caught the first time you used the place to tryst."

Ewan controlled his temper, kept it so tight and close he thought he should not try to breathe lest it rip free. He counted to ten and said, "You have been watching Dashwood."

"Right you are. Damn me, but it's good to deal with someone quick on the uptake. It amazes me that the people I associate with these days can figure out how to steal from anyone . . . except each other."

"You chose the company."

"No," Bowes said tightly. "No, I did not. Dashley—

bleeding Lord Dash—he chose it for me." His voice honeyed, although Ewan could still hear the underlying bitterness and anger. "And my darling sister helped him do it."

Ewan raised his brows.

"You don't believe me? Ask the damned managing interfering female before you kiss her next time. She found the artwork and told her friend, who told Dash."

"A charming story, all. Why were you watching Dashwood? What do you want?"

Bowes tilted his head, folded his arms, and resumed his smirk. "I was hoping to find an opportunity to talk to dear Lucy, of course. I want to leave this godforsaken island for good, and I suspected she'd be the first person willing to help me."

Ewan suspected that Miss Bowes would rather be sorely tempted to hire a ship to sail her brother a league from port and have its crew drop him overboard. Knowing what she knew about Ewan's own brother, Ewan suspected she would not have to go far to find a willing and able assistant.

"Then I thought of a much better idea, about the same time I saw you kissing her. Why try to get into Dashwood when I can ask you for the rest of the blunt?"

"Now why would I do that?"

"Because if you do not, I will not keep silent about what I saw in that cottage."

"Oh, come on," Ewan said, as his mind followed the possibilities down their logical trails. He did not like the scenery. "Who could you tell? You're a fugitive, Bowes, have you forgotten that?"

"There is more than one way to start a rumor, and who knows what rumor I might start?"

"It wouldn't take. Your sister and I are not known to hold each other in esteem."

"No, eh? Oh well, you wouldn't be the first couple who cheerfully disliked each other and progged like rabbits anyway. Just imagine the delicious whispers. Maybe some plucky soul will embroider the tale and hazard a guess that you two played best enemies to hide your improper passions. What fun that would be. Of course you would not have to marry her. Hell, I would not wish marriage to Lucy on Dash even." Bowes snorted. "And how could I possibly contemplate ruining her, hm? Let me tell you, Sandeford, it's damned easy. I feel all light at heart about it, even."

"She's your sister, your blood."

"Had she cared about my blood when she was tattling to Caroline Norcrest—Lady Dash, don't you know—*I* could care a lot more about *hers*. As it is . . ." He shrugged. "Five hundred pounds. That's my price. Five hundred pounds or the whispers start."

"I will have to think about it."

"You're thinking about whether you can catch me while you stall. I know you went to see Wright-Maynard up at Wells yesterday. He's a fool. He couldn't catch his own ass if it were running after him."

Bowes's assessment matched Ewan's. "I would not need Wright-Maynard to catch you if I wanted you caught."

For the first time Bowes looked unsure of himself, but the expression passed quickly. "Come up with the money, Sandeford. Think of it as enlightened self-interest. Then hold on to it. I'll come back as I did today."

"What makes you think I'll let you leave now?"

"The rifle trained on you from the bluff yonder," Bowes said, gesturing with his chin over his shoulder. "The Army and I had our disagreements, but I learned something."

Ewan did not dignify Bowes's statement with a look.

"You dislike me, I know," Bowes said. "I am sorry for that."

"No. You're not."

"No, I'm not. Get me my money, and you can do whatever you like with my sister. Meow." Bowes turned and loped away, toward the bluff.

Ewan watched him go, quivering with rage. Since finding the button, he had dismissed every prickle of intuition that had told him the highwayman could be Jack Bowes. He had never forced down a feeling like that before, had trusted his instincts and intuitions during the war. They had kept him alive on more than one occasion. He had not wanted to think of the complications that could arise if Bowes had been in the area.

But he had not anticipated this complication, nor did he doubt that even as a fugitive Bowes could start a rumor that would certainly ruin his sister. He remembered her poignant words: *"I must also admit, in addition to being plain and outspoken, that I have nothing—nothing, do you understand me?—to recommend myself except my connection to the Dashes."*

What if her friend Lady Dash dropped her over the rumors? It seemed unlikely, but unlikely things happened all the time. What would happen to Miss Bowes then?

Ewan raised his fist to his mouth, rested his lips on his knuckle as her other words came to him. *"Would you, a reasonable gentleman, make an offer to such a one in such a condition?"*

Her conditions were changing by the hour, but only for the worse. Unless . . .

"I'm damned if I'm going to let him get away with it," Ewan said.

"Who, Ewan? Who was that?" Charles asked, Ewan's Baker rifle carried broken over his left arm.

"Someone who thinks he may be thick as thieves with me. Excuse me, I have an urgent errand."

"But, Ewan—"

"I may not be back until much later. Wish me luck. Higgins, saddle my mare."

"Aye, sir."

"Very well," Charles said, baffled. "Good luck."

Ewan stopped in the house long enough to don a maroon jacket over his dove gray waistcoat and darker gray breeches. He ran a comb through his hair, not that he thought it would make much of a difference once he had gone the three miles to Dashwood. Still, he knew he had done what he could.

Bella ate up the three miles in a high-strung trot that took a good part of Ewan's attention to manage. No doubt she sensed his mood, although Ewan did not realize it until he was shown into Dashwood's drawing room.

Lady Dash rose to meet him and accepted his bow with a graceful nod. "Captain Sandeford, what a pleasant surprise."

"My lady. I apologize for coming unannounced."

"Indeed no, sir, I do not mean to upbraid you. It *is* a pleasure."

"Thank you, my lady. I am come looking for Miss Bowes."

"We left your game as you did, sir," she said, although her expression suggested she did not believe for a moment he had come, unannounced, about a chess game. "You will find Lucy out walking the grounds. I do believe she said she wanted to browse by the graveyard."

"Thank you, Lady Dash."

With this assistance, Ewan found Miss Bowes with little trouble. Unnoticed, he observed her inside the mausoleum's hazy indifferent light, reading the inscriptions on the monuments. She wore a simple walking gown of white muslin sprigged with a small pattern in green. Since she looked down, her bonnet obscured half her face, although dark chestnut curls peeked out at the sides and closely decorated her neck.

Could Ewan imagine himself coming upon her thus any time in the coming decades and say, "This is my wife"? Strangely, the notion disturbed him without terrifying him. It would be strange, but novel, to have a wife.

He allowed his boot to slip on the stones, alerting her to his presence. She gasped, then relaxed into semiwelcoming wariness when she saw him.

"You will find this amusing," she said by way of greeting, indicating the monument before her. "Dash had *'Ut fata trahunt'* inscribed here. Then *'Exeat'.*"

"He asks permission to be excused from his fate." Ewan grimaced. "Highly unlikely."

"You assume you know what his fate is. I am not convinced I can presume to know."

"Is there anything ahead of him? No. So, it is nothing difficult to look back. It is looking forward where the whole matter becomes tricky."

She smiled, although wistfully, turned enough away that her hat hid her face, and strolled along the stone walk. "I wanted to see what this place looked like in the daylight."

"You are very keen to see things in the light of day."

"In the *hard* light of day, sir, where one cannot avoid anything."

"No matter how unpleasant."

"No matter," she agreed.

"Is this the place to do it?" he asked, gesturing toward the small windows.

"One makes do with what one has. We certainly know that."

"Do we? You may speak for yourself, of course."

"Thank you," she said over her shoulder.

"Do not assume you speak for me, however."

She turned, hands on hips. "Do you delight in being obscure today, Captain Sandeford? Or is your obscurity due to lack of sleep? Were you very late last night looking for our highwayman?"

Our highwayman, Ewan thought with a pang. Did she but realize how close to the mark that was. "No. I quickly realized I would find nothing. So I am not addled, ma'am."

That made her smile. "I am happy to hear it. I had wondered. So, then, what is your excuse for your obscurity?"

"I was not obscure."

"Indeed?" she asked, still amused.

"Indeed not. I merely disagree with you on your principle that one must always make do with what one has. Sometimes one may choose to make much of what one has."

She sighed. "You do exasperate me, sir. You insist you are not obscure, yet you continue right on."

"Let me put what I say into context for you then, shall I?"

"Do not keep me in suspense, I beg you."

"You would have it that I have had to make do with your help and therefore your person. I would have it that becoming better acquainted with you has prompted me to regard you very highly, irrespective of whatever help you have given me."

Wariness settled over her, and she gauged the distance to the mausoleum door, making Ewan curse inside. "You do not need to apologize to me for what happened last night," she said quickly. "I was to blame. I did not realize how wet I was. I had no right to tease you."

"That has nothing to do with—I mean, it does, but that is not what—"

"Please, do let us leave the matter there," she said, and would have passed by him had he not caught her by the arms.

"I cannot leave the matter there," he said, letting go of her as she swatted at his hands. "Do stop a moment. If you please."

Firmly between him and a clear path to the door, she folded her arms and tossed her head defiantly. "Well, then?"

"I did not intend this conversation to go quite this way," he said. "Truly. Now do stop tapping your toe like that. It will set a very bad precedent. I am trying, in what appears to be a considerably roundabout way, to ask you if you would do me the honor of becoming my wife."

If ever Miss Bowes's reactions had surprised Ewan before, none could as yet compare with her dumb disbelief. She worked her mouth, managed to say, "Why could you ever want to marry me?"

"Maybe," he said, "just to see the look on your face right now. No, Miss Bowes, do not frown. I am teasing you. Badly, it appears. I'm sorry."

"Proposals of marriage do not go over well as jokes, sir. Let us return to the house."

"You misunderstand me. The proposal is not the joke. I do wish to marry you. You are the only person I could make such a joke with. You challenge me at every step."

"Well, that much is for certain."

"I have not felt so awake and alive since I left the Peninsula, despite all the sleep I have lost." It was true, he thought. Amazing, but true, and amazing for being true.

"It must be nice to be compared to a war. I shall attempt to feel flattered." But her lips twitched.

"Do," he replied. He took her right hand, kissed it, then set it upon his shoulder. He did the same with her other hand, then drew her close. She blushed. Gently, very gently, he lowered his mouth to kiss her. Her lips clung to his, and it sent a feeling through him similar to the time he had struck his sword at a French infantryman, hit stone instead of bone, and felt the reverberations all through him. They shocked with their intensity, and he could not deny she felt right and perfect to him.

He deepened the kiss, at first wondering at the chain of events that had led him from their first meeting, when she had pointed her pistol at him, to this moment.

Then Ewan merely lost himself in the heady feeling of her. She gave so freely of herself in her kisses, and since she could be nothing other than the fierce, passionate woman she was, he enjoyed a freedom to indulge his own passion that he could not remember ever doing before.

He almost tipped over the point of return, but recalled himself and drew back gently, nibbling her lower lip. Then he cupped her face in his hands.

When he had first met her, she had looked plain. Later, he had conceded that she no longer looked plain, but like a force of nature. Now she looked like the person who could ignite and fan the flames of his passion and intellect.

She looked beautiful to him.

"Will you?" he asked. "Will you marry me?"

Chapter 17

Lucy could not believe Captain Sandeford wanted to marry her. It boggled her senses and her reason.

Yet he seemed sincere. The question for her, however, was how long he could maintain that sincerity. They shared passion—how they shared passion!—but passion faded. They challenged each other, but how long before challenge led only to irritation?

Lucy liked her world orderly. Captain Sandeford delighted in rash, devil-may-care approaches to his problems. He depended so much on himself and himself alone.

Lucy sympathized. She handled her own problems herself whenever possible, but when she could not handle them herself without breaking the rules, she went to her friends for help. He bent whatever rules he did not like, sometimes broke them entirely. How would he feel about the rules of marriage?

He spoke of passion and challenge, but not love. Lucy imagined herself trying to take up some piece of needlework while contemplating her husband's current mistress and what he might be doing with her. The thought created instant, sharp, driving pain. Without love, her imaginary scene would come into full, bitter reality.

Could she put herself into such a position?

She would be a fool to refuse him, though. What

other offer of marriage lurked around life's next corner?
Going home presented none too happy an option, either.
As the next six years passed before she could declare
Jack legally dead—did the blasted braggart not get himself killed—her house would fall into disrepair, and she
would have to turn away all her servants and learn to
grow vegetables and milk cows. Or accept charity. Certainly she would never enjoy passion.

Captain Sandeford stepped back, although he kept his
hands on her shoulders. "You have the same expression as when your king is in jeopardy and you're
plotting your way out."

"You have surprised me," she said. "Greatly. I do not
know what to think."

"Then I shall assume you do not know what to say, either," he said gravely.

"I know there are three answers."

"Three?"

"Yes, no, and . . . maybe."

"Maybe?"

"We know each other so little," she replied.

His mouth flattened, and he let go her shoulders. "Ap-
parently I believe I know you better than you think you
know me."

"Half the time you were Juan," Lucy said in protest.

"Have you not forgiven me the deception?"

"I can forgive, and yet be confused as to how I feel
about it."

"You were not angry before."

"You did not see it, but when I figured it out, I was
plenty angry."

He grimaced, sighed. "So, maybe?"

"Maybe. I *am* greatly honored by the offer." She
reached out, taking a great liberty, and smoothed back
a dark lock of his hair.

"Be less honored, more accepting," he said, but he smiled briefly before asking, "When?"

"Tomorrow?" she asked. "Come for dinner?"

"Do we have no plans for tonight?"

"Caro and I are promised to the Graysons' tonight. They wish to repay Caro's hospitality. Besides, no other place has suggested itself. Do you know I looked around here?"

He smiled wryly, tucked her arm through his, and guided them out the door and into the blinking noontime sun. "Naturally you did. The light in there did not prevent you from seeing what you wanted to see, did it?"

"No," she said softly. "No, it did not."

Although the rest of the Grayson family had been all that was amiable, Lucy could not pretend she had not noticed Miss Alton's speculative, sly smile directed often toward her. Miss Alton could not know what had transpired in the Dashwood mausoleum, so her air of triumph baffled Lucy in the extreme, although she would not have given any hint of it for the world.

Lucy did not pretend surprise, though, when Miss Alton sought Lucy out after the ladies withdrew. The venue too—against a wall, this one green silk covered—was one of Lucy's favorites for questioning and imparting wisdom to her friends.

"Well, then, Miss Alton, I am in position. Do bend my ear."

Thus deprived of some of her pleasure, Miss Alton wasted no time. "Your brother, whom I understand to be not only a thief but also a deserter and the highwayman who so recently accosted me and my family and stole my sister-in-law's pearls, has met with Captain Sandeford and has asked him for five hundred pounds or he will say what you and Mr. Sandeford were doing in a cottage last night."

Lucy had anticipated she would not like whatever Miss Alton had to say, but this . . . this news shocked her as few things would have. Her heart raced. Jack, here, working the roads as a common highwayman! What could he possibly be thinking?

Money. Of course it was money. He had meant to sidle up to her, the wretch, and ask her for money. He had asked Captain Sandeford instead, because he had seen them in the cottage together.

How?

The crack against the side of the cottage . . . Lucy faced an unpleasant near certainty. Her conniving brother had seen her and Captain Sandeford standing within inches of each other, her dress a wet, clinging invitation. Had he seen their expressions? Had he read desire and believed them lovers?

It should be ridiculous.

It was ridiculous.

Lucy pushed her furiously whirling thoughts into some semblance of calm. "You overheard this meeting?" she asked coolly.

"I did," Miss Alton said, although not as triumphantly, Lucy thought, as she had hoped to be. "I was coming by to ask Captain Sandeford something, and I chanced to overhear them talking by his barn. So, your brother is—"

"When did you overhear this meeting?"

Miss Alton flushed. "Surely that makes no difference."

It made all the difference in the world to Lucy, but she would never let that on to Miss Alton. "As Captain Sandeford spent the better part of the day with me, you will understand that I ask to assure myself of your bona fides."

Miss Alton flushed again, and spluttered. Caroline looked over with concern. She had, Lucy noted, been watching the tête-à-tête between Lucy and Miss Alton, and appeared ready to intervene. Lucy shook her head slightly, and Caroline subsided to wariness.

"You accuse me of lying?"

"I have come to the unhappy conclusion," Lucy said with such forced gentleness that it was ironic, "that not everyone I know tells me the entire truth."

"You must be the most unnatural woman I know."

"Why, thank you, Miss Alton. From you, that is a decided compliment."

Thus pricked, Miss Alton said, "I left for Captain Sandeford's about quarter past ten. That would have put me there about quarter to eleven. There? Does that make you happy?"

Lucy felt as far from happy as she could imagine. She had left for the mausoleum at eleven and been there for some twenty or thirty minutes before Captain Sandeford had come. He had proposed to her after meeting with her brother, likely because of that meeting.

He was being all that was gentlemanly, in the way he preferred. Nor for him any cool denials. No, for Captain Sandeford, nothing would suit but a preemptive offer of marriage.

Whatever his preferred tactic, though, Lucy could not bear being the subject of Captain Sandeford's pity, or being a duty to him, either.

Caroline was at her shoulder. "I think your sister would like you to play something for us, Miss Alton."

Miss Alton curtsied and swept away with triumph and fury mingled on her face.

"She has upset you."

"Jack is here. Miss Alton claims he is the highwayman."

Caroline paled at that, then frowned. "How does she know?"

"She overheard him asking Captain Sandeford for money to flee the country."

"But why should he approach Captain Sandeford?"

Lucy took a breath. "Captain Sandeford went to the militia at Wells. Listen, Caro, when we return to Dashwood, we must have someone patrolling the grounds."

"Yes, I think that would be a good idea. Lucy, I am so sorry."

"Do not be. It's none of your fault." Lucy gestured unobtrusively toward the rest of the party. "We must attend."

Caroline turned back to the others, transforming the concern on her face into amiability with one blink of her lashes. Lucy followed her example, although she found herself not fretting over her brother, but in composing a very necessary, but very painful letter.

Ewan nearly spilled his coffee while breaking open the letter's wax seal. Why had Miss Bowes written him? What could have happened overnight that she had not time to tell him but could trust to paper?

Dear Captain Sandeford,

I must apologize that my brother approached you yesterday. He had no right to involve you in his distressing affairs. I shall deal with him as is appropriate. Therefore, in reference to our conversation yesterday, I must say "No."

I consider what you said as one of the highest compliments ever given me. Do not consider me ungrateful or unmindful of the sacrifice you were prepared to make. It is just that it is no longer necessary. I will, however, request a favor of you. Since I cannot yet anticipate how quickly I can re-

solve the situation, I must ask you to cease all informal visits to Dashwood.
  Yours, very sincerely,
  Lucy Bowes

Waves of unidentified emotion flowed over Ewan, translating themselves into fury. How had Miss Bowes learned of her brother's presence? Bowes could not have approached her yesterday. There would not have been time between when Ewan had left her and her dinner at the Graysons. Ewan had also spent the better part of the evening and night following Bowes around, discreetly, to prevent him from robbing anyone else. Bowes had spent the night drinking and wenching at an exceptionally seedy tavern with exceptionally surly comrades.

Ewan went upstairs into his brother's room. Charles was snoring. "Wake up," Ewan said, nudging his brother with his boot, none too gently.

Charles started awake, shaking his head. "What is it?"

"I did not see you at all yesterday. Where did you go? Who did you see?"

Charles did not appreciate being woken thus, but he rubbed his eyes and said, "You're dashed uncivil in the morning. Probably best you do breakfast before me. Fine, fine. I could go nowhere for a while. Miss Alton arrived not five minutes after you left and—"

"Miss Alton, you say? She came here?"

"She bent my ear for nigh on a quarter hour. If I were you, big brother, I would worry about her. She wants to tuck her pretty claws in you and hold tight. After that I went—"

"She overheard me and Bowes," Ewan said, tasting the bitter certainty of it.

"Bowes?" Charles asked, looking much more awake. "Not *Miss* Bowes?"

Ewan sighed, sat down in the chair next to Charles's bed, and told him about Jack Bowes.

"So it's likely Miss Alton told Miss Bowes about her brother's blackmailing you. I do feel for her. But you did what you could. She is a capable young woman. You have said so many times, and now you are released from obligation."

"I did not wish to be released," Ewan said, which felt like an even more amazing truth than his telling Miss Bowes he had never felt so alive as when he was with her.

But no, it was not. This truth merely existed on the same continuum of feeling. Like the blockhead he was, though, he had not identified it for what it was.

"I am in love with Miss Bowes."

Charles raised his brows, then frowned. "But if you told her that, why is she refusing you? You knew about her blackguard brother before? Well, then, she can't be embarrassed. . . . Oh, you didn't tell her that. It's just like the hair compliment you should have given her. But no, you probably said something about her being a good chess player, and when she found out you'd met with her brother—"

"Do shut up," Ewan said, but without heat, and Charles answered by rising and pulling on a pair of pants, giving Ewan time to think.

"I have to talk to her," Ewan finally said.

"No," Charles said. "You would be wasting your time. She's that mad at you, Ewan. All she'd think is that you're still trying to do your duty by her."

"I do not know how to make this right."

"We're invited to Lady Dash's masquerade two days from now. That is as formal an event as one can have. Give her until then. She'll have calmed down enough to be rational, maybe."

Ewan acknowledged it as a possibility, although an unlikely one.

"In the meantime, do not plan to track down her wretched brother and use him as a whipping post. She won't appreciate it, and it'll cause more talk."

"You're right. You're right. Uncle," Ewan said, holding up both hands.

"I detest being right."

"I have to reply to her letter." Ewan stood. "If Miss Alton chances to call, I'm not at home."

"Understood," Charles said, but Ewan flinched from the worry and the pity in his eyes.

The shriek coming from the drawing room made Lucy pick up her skirts and run back down the stairs, the letter in her hands almost forgotten. Walters and John also came running. The shriek came from Caroline, who had come out of the room with a letter in hand.

"My lady, are you all—" began Walters.

"He's coming," Caroline said, and hugged Lucy. "He'll be here day after tomorrow." She spun the two of them around.

"Dash? Dash is coming?" Lucy asked when she could draw breath.

"His lordship will be here for the ball?" Walters asked.

Caroline regained her composure, although she clung tightly both to her letter and to Lucy, and there were tears in her eyes. "Yes, Walters. Let the staff know immediately."

"Very good, my lady."

"Oh, Lucy, he is coming. He will be here. I cannot wait! Oh, what shall I wear?"

"Your masquerade costume," Lucy said.

"Oh, of course, for the ball, but I meant before, if he

arrives early. Oh, I must find my maid." And she bustled away in a happy haze.

Lucy could not have felt better for her, or more wretched for herself, if only in contrast. She did not need to unfold the letter she held to remember what it said.

> *Dear Miss Bowes,*
>
> *I comprehend your feelings perfectly. It is not unreasonable for you to expect me to storm the castle rather than come under flag of truce.*
>
> *I have never been much for sacrificing.*
>
> *All I wished for was to enjoy the privileged position as your future husband when dealing with our friend, instead of merely "interested party."*
>
> *I shall of course abide by your favor, but if I can be of any assistance, you need ask only once.*
>
> *Your most obedient servant,*
>
> *Ewan Sandeford*

Could she believe him? Could he understand her feelings? She did not know. He was an intelligent man, but a stubborn one. Having decided on a course of action, she would expect him to pursue it to the bitter end. He had it right when he said she doubted he would ever come quietly into any situation. No, the bold, flashy approach was his signature.

Lucy was neither bold nor flashy.

So it was as well, she thought, that she had said no, for all the reasons she had pondered in the mausoleum, and especially for her fear that he would lie to her or hide the truth whenever convenient for him. She did not need more people making decisions for her without her say.

She ignored the tight knot of tearful pain that threatened to choke her, for John had come back, saying, "Fletcher has asked to speak to you outside, Miss Bowes."

Lucy thanked him, took her hat from him, considerate footman that he was, and went to the back. The roof of the steward's cottage, snugly nestled in between braces of trees, mocked her.

Fletcher was in the gardens immediately behind the house, a three-pronged hoe in hand. He straightened. "Sorry, miss. I thought I'd have a moment with these roses."

Lucy shook her head, dismissing it. "Were you able to leave a message?"

"Yes, miss. I found him about where I expected to." Fletcher's tone left no doubt that the place he had found Jack was unsavory. "He said he would meet you tomorrow night. He laughed when I said in the mausoleum. Odd sort of fellow, isn't he, miss? Is he a gentleman?"

"He was born one," Lucy said. "Thank you, Fletcher, very much. I sent you on no pleasant errand."

"No troubles, miss." He stabbed at the dirt beneath the rosebushes and looked askance at her. "There will be some of us out and about tomorrow night, miss. We will be checking the torches for milady's party. You understand, miss?"

"I understand very well, and I know you will do nothing to spook him. Thank you again, Fletcher."

Fletcher compressed his lips and ducked his head. "It's been good around here, miss. Lady Dash, she makes us hold our heads up again. You, too, miss. No more polecats, eh?"

"No. No more polecats."

"I'll have a lantern out there, miss."

Chapter 18

True to his word, Fletcher had left a lantern in the mausoleum. Its glow had helped guide her path in the deepening twilight. Lucy paced about a bit, then suddenly Jack spoke behind her.

"Lucy, my dear, how lovely it is to see you again," Jack said with a purr that turned his words' polite meaning inside out.

Lucy turned, and a tart response rose within her mouth, threatening to choke her. She could not fully comprehend how much she loathed him.

He looked different. He had not shaved in a day or two, and wore his hair in a queue. The Jack she knew had worried excessively about his clothes, making sure they were pressed and polished and perfect. The rumpled gray and brown jacket and trousers he wore now would have caused her eye to pass right over him.

She swallowed and sought composure. "I have worried about you these last nine months."

"I would be willing to bet any amount of money on that. Speaking of money?"

Lucy held out her reticule. "There is one hundred and fifty pounds in there."

"So little?" he asked, snatching it from her.

"I have not had much, since you . . . went away."

One side of his mouth curved up in a spiteful smile.

"I had not thought of that. Oh, that very much makes my day." Then he frowned. "How did you get this, then?"

"I sold Grandmother's brooch. It was the only piece of jewelry I had with me that would bring anything. And I had some money with me for this trip that Caroline has not let me use."

Her brother jumped up onto a carved grave marker and sat astride it. "You are a fool, then. You should have gone to Sandeford for it."

"I see no reason to bring Captain Sandeford into our family difficulties."

"He compromised you," Jack said, for all the world her big brother upbraiding her for some peccadillo she had committed in the ballroom.

Relief washed over Lucy. Jack did not know Captain Sandeford had himself broken into Dashwood. Nor had Jack attempted such an enterprise himself. That served as some measure of the two's relative tolerance for danger, although not deception.

The smile bubbling up inside her deflated. "We both found ourselves taking shelter from the storm. He was about to give me his jacket. I was wet."

"And what were you both doing out there, eh?"

"I could not sleep. The heat, remember? As for him, I think he may have been looking for you."

"Sandeford went to the militia, too," Jack said, considering. Jack was not stupid, although his plans tended to favor the cowardly and venal.

"You left a button behind, when you waylaid the Graysons' carriage the other night."

"The who?"

"Pearl necklace."

"Oh." He tipped his head, considering. "Didn't fetch much. Sandeford would have paid more."

"You believe that?"

Jack smirked.

"Jack, he did not compromise me. Besides, if you are the only person who saw us, it counts as nothing."

"And how do you figure that?"

She almost said that he was an outlaw, but realized he would likely take such a comment badly. "Because my secrets are safe with you, just as yours are safe with me."

Jack snorted, making Lucy realize she was unlikely to convince him.

"Do you have enough to safely leave the country now?" she asked.

He jumped down from the marker, took her chin in his hand, and wagged her head with it. He had done that since their childhood, and Lucy had never grown to like it. "Do you worry about me, dear Lucy?"

"Once I got over the surprise of your being here," Lucy said. "I have never liked surprises, as you well know. Besides, Dash will be back here tomorrow night."

"Dash?" Jack asked, pulling back and clutching the reticule.

"He sent word to Caroline that he returns tomorrow night. Hopefully in time for her ball. What would he do, Jack, to apprehend you if he thought you in the area?" Lucy asked. "Ask for more than one local militia, I have no doubt. And he would get them."

"You would like that, wouldn't you?"

"No," Lucy said, and almost meant it. "You have been a very big nuisance, Jack, that I will not deny. But I do not wish you to come to such an ill end. Just go. There is nothing here for you. Go, and start a new life for yourself. The United States, perhaps. Land is cheap there, and they have not yet found the end of it."

"And have the chance to be murdered by a savage."

But he did not sound so much bitter as resigned that he must be bitter.

"Here they will certainly hang you."

"You are full of pleasantries this evening."

"Can you not believe that I wish only—for both of us—to go on with our lives as happily as we can? I promise, I will do what I can to keep our house from falling down around my ears, and maybe some day you will have a son who may come back and inherit it."

He turned away from her and said, "You are a sentimental fool."

"There is nothing sentimental about me. Shall I lay it out plainly for you? It is no pleasant existence as the sister of a thief, but it would be infinitely worse to be the sister of a hanged criminal. No, there is nothing sentimental about me, for when I think of the harm you did to so many people, some large part of me rejoices in your punishment. But you are my brother, and I will do my duty by you."

"Your duty?" he demanded, turning around. "Your duty was to keep quiet about what you had found."

"I told only Caroline, so she could ask her sister about the artwork. How was I to know you would attack that cursed Spaniard and leave him in the woods for Dash to find him?"

"So Don Alessandro led you a merry dance, did he?"

"He stayed for months," Lucy said through gritted teeth, "and drank a lot of claret."

"Any left?"

"Some. Between gulps, he muttered in Spanish."

Jack smirked. "I would wager you are leading Sandeford a merry dance yourself."

"Since you would be wagering with my money . . ." Lucy checked herself, furious she had let her temper run away with her.

"Only with your money, dear sister. That is one thing about thieves, they steal, and the easiest pickings are one's fellow thieves." His mouth hardened.

"Then I am sorry for you. Take it. Go. Leave your 'friends' tonight, so it will stay entire. Do something with yourself that you can be proud of. It is not too late."

"Too late for what? For you to cozy up to Sandeford?"

"Captain Sandeford is nothing to me. Must I always repeat myself to you? We found ourselves both seeking shelter from the storm. That is all."

Jack flicked his finger on her cheek, and would have again taken her chin had she not jerked her head back. "He may be nothing to you, but you are something to him. It does amuse me."

"Go," Lucy said, and some of her loathing leaked into her voice. "Go, I beg you."

Shoulders suddenly slumping, he looked away, toward the open mausoleum door, where night poured in its darkness. "I will write you and let you know where I have settled."

"Don't," Lucy said, as gently as she could.

His mouth tightened, and he walked away from her into the night.

Lucy covered her mouth with her hand and washed it with a sudden gush and gulp of tears. She stood there a long time, trying to recover herself, but she could not find anything to center herself on, one thought that would give her solace. That her brother could say her pain amused him struck her as more heinous than his attempt to steal artwork.

He was truly gone for her, as good as dead. He had been absent for the last nine months, but she had not mourned him as lost. Lucy discovered, all out of reason, that although she hated him for what he had done, she mourned something and was without the ability to identify it.

She had no one she could talk to. She could not pull Caroline from her happiness, and she had given away the right to share such troubles with Captain Sandeford.

Lucy tried not to feel desolate about that and wiped her tears with the edge of her shawl. Her handkerchief had been in her reticule, gone with Jack and her last good piece of jewelry, her small connection with history and her favorite grandmother.

That, she realized, was what she mourned. Change, and the facing of ever more unpleasant facts, with little true happiness to anticipate.

Lucy picked up the lantern, blowing it out when she stepped outside the mausoleum. To the sides of the house, torches winked on and off as the garden staff called out to each other. Lucy hoped they had given Jack quite a fright.

She had no trouble getting to the house. Once there, though, she stopped and stared at the blackness of the ivy, the blacker hole where it had yet to regrow.

In the cool night air, she forced herself to say the words out loud, so they would be binding. Still, all she could manage was a whisper. "I will leave after the ball. I will give Caroline and Dash time together. I will give Captain Sandeford time to get over his madness. And I will get over loving him."

Chapter 19

Lucy continued to turn that thought over in her mind. Thinking "I love Captain Sandeford" kept her awake that night, woke her early the next morning, and preoccupied her over breakfast and into lunch.

She wished she could feel all the wonder and joy Caroline had told her she had felt when she discovered she loved Dash. But for Lucy, the revelation merely worried at her like the reminder of a task that she had no idea how to perform or a bill she knew she could not pay.

Finally Caroline found her and set her hands to overseeing some of the last-minute preparations for the ball. Then it became time to dress and, since Dash had not yet arrived, time to utter many soothing words to Caroline, who looked to jump from her beautiful Aphrodite costume and walk the roads, the sooner to meet him.

When Lucy had spare moments, she chided herself for wondering what Captain Sandeford would wear to the masquerade. He looked thrilling in whatever he wore, but would she recognize him right away? Would he recognize her?

Caroline had wanted her to attend in some grand, impressive costume. Lucy would have preferred to go as a shepherdess, or some other unpretentious, conventional, unalluring creature. Instead Caroline and Lucy had compromised. Lucy would attend as a dryad.

A week ago, when Caroline had begun planning the party, she had insisted Lucy accept a gown of pale green in similar draping lines to the beautiful Grecian cut of Caroline's own. When Lucy set her mouth stubbornly, Caroline persuaded her by saying how unlikely it would ever be that Lucy would wear such a dress again.

"So it is not charity, Lucy. It is a loan, which you will do me great pleasure to accept, since neither you nor I had any idea you would be required to wear a costume on our sojourn to Somersetshire."

Lucy had agreed to this assessment, but she had also taken excessive pleasure in the costume. Four-inch-long feathers dyed green and clustered as ash leaves formed the headdress, and shorter ones covered the mask, obscuring her features. A rope of ivy looped gently over her left shoulder from below the bodice and continued down the train. A week ago ivy alone could have decided Lucy, but tonight she could not look on it without pain.

"We look very well," Caroline said, pulling Lucy up to stand next to her in the cheval glass. She tipped her head and tapped a finger against her lips. "But there is something missing. What is it? What *is* it? Ah, I know. You have no jewels, Lucy. It does make sense that you not wear your dear grandmama's brooch, for it does not go with the green. I have nothing that would go except these diamonds I am wearing."

They were magnificent diamonds, too, Lucy thought, with earbobs to match. A wedding present from Dash.

"Let us see if we can find you something from the Dashley collection," Caroline said, and before Lucy could protest, Caroline called for her maid to summon Mrs. Walters with the keys to the Dashley family safebox.

"I do not need jewels," Lucy said.

"Nonsense. Everyone needs jewels from time to time. Do please let me treat you, Lucy. I do not know what I should have done here without you. Truly, so do not smile at me as if you would humor me like any simpleton. As much as I have enjoyed setting up my own households, every now and again I wish I could turn to my sister and ask how she would have done it. Your good sense has balanced me instead. And I know there have been occurrences in the house that have been odd, and that you have handled them."

"Caroline, what do you think has been going on?"

Caroline smiled, suddenly very much Lady Dash. "I have no idea, just that Walters has told me you have reassured him."

"You do not want to know?"

"Only if you want to tell me."

"You are entirely too trusting, you know."

"To me, it is a question of whom I trust, not that I am too trusting."

Lucy just shook her head.

Caroline's maid entered, bearing a large, highly polished wooden box. Caroline signaled her to open it, and all three women drew in their breath at the jewels within it. Gold, silver, sapphires, rubies, pearls, and emeralds, as well as garnets and topaz gleamed on what looked like the top drawer of a nested set.

Caroline lifted out an emerald pendant necklace and an emerald bracelet. "These two, certainly, and do not open your mouth for a single protest, Lucy Bowes. But there are no earbobs. You must have earbobs."

While Lucy leaned forward to admire the warm jewels around her neck in the dressing-table mirror, Caroline lifted up the top drawer.

"But what's this here?" Caroline grinned. "Do look at what Dash liked to do. He has wound up his reminders in his rings. Not the best method, I must say."

"What?" Lucy asked, peering over Caroline's shoulder. The drawer contained ring after ring, all set in rather higgledy-piggledy, as each ring contained a piece of paper wound up inside it. "Oh, my God."

"What is it?" Caroline asked.

But Lucy picked up the rings, heart beating fast, and began removing the papers. She glanced at several and tossed them aside.

Then she found one in a gold ring with a large, flat topaz atop. Perhaps three inches by five, the note had been folded and was very crumpled, as though it had suffered through being unfolded and rolled out and rolled back several times.

Lucy pressed the top corners of it flat and read,

> *To his Lordship, George Dashley,*
> *Marquess of Dash,*
> *I hereby promise the sum of £2,000, for which*
> *I offer the property of Barberry Lodge,*
> *which adjoins Dashwood, in Somersetshire.*
> *Signed, this 7ᵗʰ of June, 1813,*
> *Charles Sandeford*
> *Third Lieutenant, HMS* Midnight

"It's an IOU," Caroline said. "Dash held his IOUs here."

Lucy put her hand over the signature. The rolling paper had obscured all but the first three lines from Caroline, since she could not look directly down upon it.

Barberry Lodge. Lieutenant Sandeford had somehow signed away his brother's house. "Little wonder he wanted it back," Lucy muttered.

"What was that?" Caroline asked. She picked up the ring the note had come from and turned it around in her hand. "Who wanted it back?"

"The person who signed this travesty."

"But this *is* an IOU given to my brother-in-law?" Caroline asked.

"This is an IOU written in what I think is your brother-in-law's hand and signed by a drunken fool."

"Is this one of those matters you have handled for me?" Caroline asked, expression keen. Her hands worried at the ring, turning it over and over.

"Sort of," Lucy replied. She grimaced. "Very ill, truth be told, but could I ask you to trust me about this until after I speak to someone?"

Caroline hesitated, then she said, "Thomas is not yet home, so all decisions still rest with me. But I may have to mention it to him."

Lucy swallowed and tucked the IOU into her glove. The paper bulged, wanting to keep in its roll, but Lucy patted it down. "Fair enough, and I do—"

"Ow!" Caroline exclaimed, and put her finger to her mouth, only to withdraw it immediately. "Ugh."

"What is it? What did you do?" Lucy asked, stepping closer to Caroline.

A drop of blood oozed from Caroline's finger. "The ring. I think the setting is loose." She picked up a handkerchief and wound it around her finger. "What a thing to happen, tonight of all nights."

"It will stop soon."

"It left a vile taste on my finger." Caroline held up the ring. "Do look! The stone is on a hinge. And that is . . ."

"What?" Lucy asked.

"Opium," Caroline said, blanching, with anger as much as with shock.

Opium! Lucy thought furiously. She now knew how the late Dash had convinced Lieutenant Sandeford to sign such a strange IOU. She had had trouble acquitting him of signing it when his only excuse was too much liquor. A gentleman should be capable of holding his liquor or having the sense to stop drinking. But opium? Opium made fools of many a fine person.

What sort of opium could take away the pain she felt now that she knew what had been at stake in Captain Sandeford's search? He had proposed marriage to her out of duty, but he had not trusted her. Somehow, despite all, he had not thought she deserved his trust.

"I do dislike this house," Caroline said. "In how many other strange places will I find nasty things?"

"Hush, Caro," Lucy said soothingly, "it is but a small thing, and was easily overlooked. I am certain the Walterses found everything else. Who would have thought to look here?"

Who, indeed?

Caroline bit her lip. "Likely you are right." She sighed. "I am sorry. I have been abysmally distracted. I shall throw off all my gloomy thoughts this instant. Promise."

"Were my husband coming home tonight in the midst of an enormous ball I was planning, I would be distracted, too."

"It will all come out right, won't it. Thomas will be home soon, and you will see Captain Sandeford. It is unpardonable that he has left you by yourself for three days. There, I put down the nasty thing, and yes, here are the earbobs that go with your necklace. Put them on, and we shall see how nice they look."

Lucy schooled her face, lest she weep from Caroline's assumptions, assumptions that could have all been true had he not proposed for the wrong reasons and Lucy not refused him.

"Thank you," Lucy said, and then some sprite within her added, "You assume I wish to see Captain Sandeford without a chessboard handy despite our earlier conversation."

"Which one? Oh, you mean when I said he fancied you and you pretended not to be pleased?"

"Caroline," Lucy began in protest, hating the feeling of her cheeks heating.

"Very well, I shall not tease you. Can you at least tell me what Captain Sandeford's costume is to be?"

"I do not know."

"We shall find out what our neighbors wear very soon. If I am not mistaken, the commotion outside is three or four carriages pulling up at once." She sighed a combination of anticipation and disappointment. "I so wish Thomas would have been here from the outset. Dratted man."

Lucy had to laugh.

"Our masks, Laramie," she said to her maid. "Quick." Then to Lucy, "I may love the man desperately, but that does not mean I am not allowed to be frustrated by him from time to time."

"Where would the limits of your frustration be, Caro?" Lucy asked, trying to keep her voice light.

Laramie began fixing Caroline's mask, and Caroline replied, equally lightly, but without a trace of teasing. "Probably the basic simple ones: a break in either fidelity or honor. I have not given it much thought, for Thomas must be the most faithful, honorable man I know. On these I base respect for someone. Without respect, for me, there can be no love. That is my character."

"And for me," Lucy said, as Laramie fixed her mask on. "What is my basis for respect?"

"Thank you, Laramie," Caroline said, and the two women gazed at their masked reflections in the mirror. "As for you, Lucy, you are a more complex creature than I, so I would add that you must be able to pull with your equal and constantly strive for that equality. It would not be at all comfortable for me. I am happy to be someone's complement."

Caroline's assessment struck Lucy deeply. "You are as complex a creature as anything, otherwise you could not be as dear to me as you are."

Caroline smiled. "Very well. We will allow my character complexity, but not competitiveness."

"Competitiveness is not an attractive trait in a female."

"It is for those gentlemen who need that balance as well. I suspect they are rare, but then again, gentlemen with highly developed senses of honor and faithfulness are as well." Caroline turned them to the mirror. "We look positively stunning. Let us go tantalize some hearts for a few hours."

Lucy laughed and did her best to emulate her friend by shrugging off her blue megrims. She looked as well as she ever could, Jack was on his way out of her life, and she had found Captain Sandeford's IOU.

Even if I must feel pain, Lucy thought, *I will indulge in no more hysteria.*

She and Caroline went downstairs together and greeted the guests, who began as a trickle, then turned into a positive torrent. Soon the house hummed with excited chatter and dance music.

As the line thinned, there was no sign of either Captain Sandeford or Lieutenant Sandeford. A lone gentleman in a black domino approached Lucy and Caroline and bowed low. "May I make myself known to the lady of the house?"

"Thomas!" Caroline exclaimed, and fell into his outstretched arms, regardless of the people around them. Fortunately, the indulgent glances outnumbered the indignant. Caroline hugged her husband so tightly her knuckles showed taut through her gloves.

Dash kissed her long, then set her arm firmly upon

his. "So, I surmise there is a party. Well done, sweetheart."

Caroline merely smiled.

"Dash, your powers of observation do you proud," Lucy said facetiously.

"Do not overlook my ability to blend in, either," he replied, sweeping the cape of his domino back to reveal popular black evening clothes rather than regimentals. "Lucy, my dear, how are you?"

Lucy accepted a kiss on the cheek. "We are glad you are back and in one piece."

"I was likelier to die of tedium. Has Captain Sandeford been looking after you?"

Lucy wondered if Dash's gaze lingered on her more than it should. Caroline had, after all, been writing to her husband. So Lucy managed a smile and a noncommittal nod.

"Where is he, then? I should thank him straightaway."

"We have not greeted him," Caroline said. "Besides, he has elected to keep his costume a deep, dark secret."

"He did have a reputation for being a fair rogue," Dash said admiringly.

"Let me introduce you to a few of our closer neighbors," Caroline said. "Let us start with—"

"Miss Alton," Lucy said with her. The two friends chuckled. "I shall let you make the introductions, Caro. I might be tempted not to do it properly."

Caroline and Dash both gave her such identical looks of anticipation and easy friendship that they made Lucy's heart ache with bittersweet happiness. They turned away, Caroline guiding her husband, leaving Lucy wanting to be like them, one part of a couple which understood the other so well and moved through the world in harmony.

Lucy wandered through the ballroom. Walters and the rest of the staff looked to have the event well in hand.

Lucy took a glass of wine from John, but had to put it down immediately as a cavalier bowed low and asked her to dance. He was not Captain Sandeford, nor even Lieutenant Sandeford. His slender, wiry build told Lucy that much, but she enjoyed her witty, flirtatious conversation with him so much she recklessly agreed not only to a second dance with him, but also a third.

After that, he took her toward the patio so they might catch some fresh air, and bade her rest while he secured them wine. Lucy stepped outside, humming the music to the next dance and breathing in the cool, crisp air. Then she gasped as a shadow separated itself from the ivied wall.

"Juan."

Chapter 20

Even though she whispered, he bowed low. He had added a long black cape to his ensemble. It swished around him.

"*Señorita.*" In a trice, he swept her off her feet, carried her around the corner of the house, and set her down with her back to the ivy. His eyes glittered behind the mask, and he breathed deeply with excitement, his mouth an inch from hers.

"What are you doing?" she asked, trying to sound repressive, but not succeeding. His heat and eagerness called to her, demanding she answer him in kind.

"My lady Dryad? My lady? Oh, I do beg your pardon, did you see a woman dressed as a dryad?" It was her cavalier, asking others on the patio.

Captain Sandeford covered her dress with his cape, merging her into his shadow. "I saw you dancing with him," he whispered in his dark, liquid Spanish. "He looks a pleasant fellow. He would flatter and adore you the rest of your life. Give me a push. Your slightest push will send me away."

Lucy closed her eyes, inhaled his wild, turbulent scent, and thought she would die of longing. Her body and heart told her to give in, and her mind steadfastly refused. She also knew that her mind eventually had the last word, for better or for worse.

She had to look, and judge. As she opened her eyes, the sweet languor of her desire bound her gaze powerfully to Captain Sandeford's. If the cavalier came round their dark corner, Lucy neither saw him nor he them.

One word from her would have ended it, but, she realized, it was not yet time for that one word.

"Look inside," some unknown male voice answered the cavalier. "She is not here." The man laughed, mocking the cavalier, and only strains of cheerful music reached Lucy's ears after that.

"You do not push," Captain Sandeford said, his breath stirring the fine curls near her face.

Sanity seemed to be fading all around her. She moved her arm up, intending to stroke his face. She loved his face, its strong, handsome planes, even its fierce hauteur. Then the paper crinkled in her glove against her arm. With a gasp, she recalled herself. "I have something for you. I found it."

Tension entered every line of his body, and he stepped away from her. Lucy pulled the letter from her glove and handed it to him with shaking fingers. "It promises your house," she said, amazed her voice did not break.

"Yes," he said, soberly.

"You did not trust me," Lucy said. Abruptly the night air seemed less sweet, the music less cheerful.

"It did start out that way," he said.

"It is about to end that way, too."

"What are you talking about?"

"You have what you need. There is no other business between us."

"You would refuse to see me now? Why? Because you think I did not trust you?"

"Did you trust me? Did you tell me about my brother?"

"I wished to spare you pain. As for my house, I knew you struggled with your loyalties—"

"I have not have struggled over this," Lucy said, distressed. "Not since you were prepared to deter my brother. For the rest of your life. But this closes our account. I think . . . I think Caroline will not be long here. I do not anticipate our meeting much, in future."

Captain Sandeford stiffened. "You will insist on considering my proposal a sacrifice."

"How else can I consider it? You neither trust me nor—"

Caroline's voice on the patio silenced Lucy. "Maybe she is out here, Thomas. Lucy? Lucy?"

Lucy pursed her lips and walked around him, into the light pouring from the open ballroom doors. "Here I am. But Caroline, what's wrong?"

"Sir?" Dash said, looking over Lucy's shoulder. "Perhaps you would be so kind as to excuse us?"

"It's Sandeford, my lord," he said. He had stepped up right behind her. She could not decide whether his presence made her feel better. Caroline was biting her lip. Something had happened.

"Sandeford. Good to see you again. Thank you for making yourself available to my wife and her friend. From all accounts, you have made a fine job of it."

"It was my pleasure."

"There is something I must speak to Miss Bowes about. You do understand, sir?"

"If Miss Bowes wishes me to leave, I will."

The two gentlemen inspected each other, making Lucy's nerves stretch to the breaking point. "What is your news, Dash?" Lucy asked.

"Your brother has been arrested," Dash said, very grave, "attempting to rob a coach on its way here. The head of the local militia just informed me."

"Lucy, I'm so sorry," Caroline said.

Although she had expected something like this, Lucy felt the way she had when Jack had punched her in the stomach as a child. She wrapped her arms around herself, and Captain Sandeford's arm drew her in close to him.

"Did you need to tell her like that, my lord?"

Lucy flinched and stepped a little away from Captain Sandeford's protective arm. She had no right to stand under it. He had given what he could. *This closes our account.* It could not possibly matter that she wanted more.

"It is best to have it out and done with. Thank you, Dash, for finding me right away. You will . . . do what we talked about before?"

"Of course. Their major told me I could speak to him about it tomorrow."

"Thank you. That does relieve my mind considerably. If you do not object, I would excuse myself for a few minutes." And before anyone could object, Lucy picked up her skirt and hurried away. She needed to take her mask off before she wet it irreparably.

Ewan marveled at her composure even as he ached for her.

"I shall go after her," Lady Dash said.

"She wants to be alone," Ewan said.

"No, she doesn't. She planned in case this happened, but it is still hard to plan one's feelings when the thing comes to pass. Excuse me, sir." Lady Dash dropped Ewan a curtsy, glanced significantly at her husband, and swept away.

Ewan watched her thread her way through the crowd and said, "What did Miss Bowes mean, when she asked you if you would do what you agreed on?"

"I cannot say it is your business, sir," Dash said, pleasantly enough, but with more than a hint of steel. It left Ewan curiously in mind of the Dash who had written to him, telling him he was audacious rather than reckless.

Whatever Ewan's impression of Dash from last summer had been, here was a man to be respected, and likely trusted. But embarrassed before—no, Ewan would not like that.

Such thoughts availed nothing, though. The IOU was safe in his sleeve, safe from question or comment. *She* had done that for him.

Nothing could be embarrassing, though, about saying to Lord Dash, "I have asked Miss Bowes to marry me."

"Just now?" Dash asked, astonished. "Dressed like a thief? Knowing what her brother is?"

"No, not just now, and I—have my reasons," Ewan said. His reasons sounded thin, even within his own mind. He had wanted to be Juan again, to experience that freedom, to remind Miss Bowes of every exciting, thrilling night they had spent, for Ewan knew she had enjoyed it as much as he had.

Dash's question, however, led Ewan to wonder if, in his zeal, he had not given enough weight to her other feelings. He should have realized the position he had put her in by appearing, before the Dashes at such a time, as her *other* thief. Could she have felt more threatened, more vulnerable?

Yet Ewan knew that despite whatever she might be feeling, she had kept his and Charles's secret. She deserved more from him, maybe more than love, even. Maybe understanding. And honesty.

Dash raised his brows. "She asked if I would intercede for her brother, request that he be transported, rather than hung. I think she wanted to ask me straightaway, but she waited until she was sure of me. She worried, I believe, that my history with Bowes might prevent me from even contemplating such a course of action."

Ewan thought darkly about his conversation with Bowes. "He does not deserve her attention, or her sympathy."

Dash shrugged. "I agree with you, but, as you have personal experience, for the honorable, it's not easy to snuff feelings of duty and loyalty. She had made the plan, proposed it, and if I have learned anything about Miss Bowes, it is that she rarely wastes her time planning about something or someone for whom she cares not a straw."

Miss Bowes had certainly planned ways to prevent him from stealing around and from Dashwood. But Ewan's perennial question remained: had she done that out of loyalty and love for her friend, or any feeling for him? Had her planning started out as one thing, and changed to another?

A reckless man would have hied off to question Miss Bowes that very instant. Indeed, Ewan felt the allure of that urge. A thoughtful man, who successfully carried out daring plans, however, would accept Dash's offer to "Accompany me back into the mêlée, Sandeford?"

So Ewan counted to ten and said, "Thank you, I would." His estimation of Dash rose when he found he did not have to ignore any smothered smiles or askance looks.

They moved through the party effortlessly, two tall men who had commanded others, Ewan thinking furiously.

Over glasses of champagne, they spoke of war and soldiering and the state of the peace. Ewan could not ask, although he wanted to, whether it had been seeing Waterloo or meeting and marrying Lady Dash that had so changed Dash from the distracted, dissolute-looking man Ewan had seen last summer.

Lady Dash found them, and although she smiled gracefully, Ewan had learned enough of her to think she was worried.

A rowdy jester jostled her, almost knocking her down. Lord Dash put a steadying, protective arm about his wife.

Ewan grabbed the jester and whispered fiercely, "Act like a gentleman," before letting the startled man go.

"Lucy did not go to her room," Lady Dash said as the jester scurried away.

Ewan forced down his fear that Miss Bowes would do something rash. She did not have the constitution of someone who acted well when she acted rashly, but she did have that pistol. How far had Miss Bowes planned, and could her request to Dash have been a feint?

Ewan could check another possibility first, though. "Does the party continue into the drawing room? To the library?"

"No."

Ewan bowed. "I will look for her."

He navigated the crowd with little trouble, caught a glimpse of the jester, who quickly went the other way, and left the main hubbub for the library. A fire in the large fireplace illuminated the room.

Miss Bowes's light green costume gleamed other-worldly in the soft glow. She stood next to the window he had used to enter and exit Dashwood. Ewan did not know exactly why he had thought she might be here, but he could not deny the pulse of satisfaction he felt at being proved right.

Nor could he deny his relief at finding her safe and sound, with no pistol in her hand. "Thank God I found you."

Her shoulder flinched, but she did not turn. "Please go away."

"I cannot."

"Is something restraining you?"

"Yes."

Now she turned and passed a none-too-friendly eye over him. "I see no shackles." She winced, and Ewan surmised she had imagined her brother in them.

"Not all restraints must be onerous."

"Are we about to begin another metaphysical conversation, Captain Sandeford? If so I must beg you to excuse me. I am not currently up to the task." She turned back around, but now he could glimpse her reflection in the window. Her forlorn expression wrung his heart.

"When have we ever spoken of metaphysics?"

Her brows quirked. "It is true we have never engaged in the subject directly. Instead we have danced about it—have we not?—with such conversations about whether clouds are nooses or wedges of wretched cheese, or whether thieves are really thieves."

"What am I?" he asked.

"A housebreaker," she replied. "And overqualified for the position."

He moved closer to her. "Is that a compliment or a criticism?"

"You can best answer that, sir."

"Do you know, I have not lost my amazement at how you do turn everything I say or do upside down."

"May I continue to entertain," she said.

Their gazes tangled in the window's reflection, but she still shivered when he laid his hands on her shoulders. "You do not entertain me, per se, Miss Bowes. You delight me."

"You give a distinction looking for a difference."

"Then let us move into less contestable territory, that of fact."

"By all means. You have come to tell me Caroline is looking for me."

"She is, but that is not what I came to tell you."

"There is more bad news?"

"Only if you will consider that I love you bad news."

Chapter 21

Lucy thought she stopped breathing. For several frantic beats of her heart she wanted to believe it so badly she did believe it.

But whatever her feelings, it could not be so. He had proposed to her before to prevent her brother from creating scandal.

Now that she had refused him and her brother had been caught, Captain Sandeford likely feared what Jack might say. Lucy conceded that Captain Sandeford's desire to protect her stemmed from all good and noble sources, but good and noble sources could not sustain one forever without other, less agreeable emotions creeping in and creating its own surly admixture.

Lucy turned to face him. The mirroring window felt too intimate, almost magical. Captain Sandeford had it right when he said it was time to deal in facts.

"That is no news at all," Lucy said.

"I beg your pardon?" he said, then shook himself. "I mean—no, I mean I beg your pardon. How can you say so? I have not said it."

"To be news, something must be of relevant interest." Although she spoke in as neutral a tone as she could muster, and although most of his face was masked, she could tell her words pained him. She added, "I have refused your offer of marriage already.

Surely that fact is sufficient to render this conversation moot."

"On its surface, I would have to agree with you."

Lucy released a pent-up breath and felt a deep depression settle over her. "Very well, then." She tried to step around him.

He blocked her way. "I believe I said 'on its surface.'"

"You claim depth?"

"I do indeed."

Lucy folded her arms. "How?"

"When I proposed to you, I did not mention that I loved you."

"True."

"You noted it?"

"I did."

"I feared as much. I should have. Just as I should have complimented you on your hair."

"My hair is neither here nor there."

"You looked very well," he said stubbornly, and looked like he would stroke a silky curl right then. Then he either collected himself or correctly gauged her mood. He sighed. "Regardless, I apologize. I did the thing very ill."

"You *did the thing* to prevent us being embroiled in scandal, and for that and all compliments on my hair I continue grateful, but—"

"Lucy Bowes, I do not want your gratitude."

"Very well. I withdraw the gratitude. Entirely. I feel no gratitude toward you whatsoever." She whisked her palms together as though wiping away crumbs.

"You are the most frustrating woman," he said between clenched teeth.

"Which is why it makes no difference that you say you love me. Soon enough, I would frustrate you right out of love, and then where would we be?" Lucy asked, and she regretted it. He might be deluded, but he was no fool. He would register the fierceness of her emotion and how she had betrayed herself.

"Ah," he said, smiling. "You *have* thought this through and come to the very worst conclusion. Now we find the true depths of the matter."

Yes, he was no fool. "Whatever do you think you are talking about?" Lucy asked, seeking refuge in annoyed bravado.

"Sweetheart, I love you because you frustrate me. This I know I said before: you make me feel more alive than any person I know."

"We are back to the war."

"No. We are not, and you may not retreat that way."

He was waiting for her to attack, and attack she did. "It is impossible and incomprehensible that any man should love a woman because she frustrates him."

"I am not any man. What, do you now equate me with such dull, respectable worthies as Lord Grayson or Sir Ronald? You have accused me of recklessness before. It is no new epithet and may have been deserved at one point or another. But if it rose, it rose from either trying to think my way from boredom or by being convinced I could accomplish what others failed to do conventionally."

Lucy frowned. "I do not follow you."

"I crave the challenge you provide me."

"I do not recall my efforts slowing you down much."

He pointed to his sleeve. "You gave this to me. I could not find it."

"That was a vagary of the late Dash's. And, Captain Sandeford, there was opium in the ring it was wound in."

"Opium. Indeed. That does explain a few things, doesn't it?"

"I thought so."

"Would I have had the chance to look where you found this?"

But Lucy shied away from the question.

He lifted her chin, again giving her no place to retreat. "You will insist you have nothing to recommend you, but your cavalier asked you for three dances."

"I was masked," Lucy said, furious. "He neither saw my face nor my lack of funds."

"He found you charming, interesting. Just as I do. Your face is as dear to me as anyone's could be. You may not admit that as a possibility, but I declare it a truth." His hand stroked first her forehead, then trailed to her heated cheeks and wound down her neck to graze the open, creamy expanse above her bosom, leaving a trail of fiery, shivery sensation behind. "And then there is the rest of you, sweet Lucy."

When he bent his head to kiss her, it felt as natural as breathing, although breathing had never tasted as sweet. She craved more, wanted to be as closely connected to him as the ivy that twined thickly on the walls outside. It frightened her, how much she wanted him, how deep she wanted him to sink roots into her, and she into him.

Could they grow old together, so twined, or . . . ?

"You want to tell me," he said, between nuzzling kisses along her neck, "that passion too will fade. But I tell you, I will want to love you until I am in my grave."

Lucy scraped together her reason. "You have lied to me before to follow your honor."

He became very still, his hands heavy weights upon her shoulders. "That resembled retreat not at all. Remind me to kiss you thoroughly the next time I want your true opinion."

She tried to pull away, but he wrapped her hands in his. "I am sorry, sweetheart. I did not mean to make light. You are correct in all you say. It would be all too easy to believe that in thrall to my sense of having done you injury, or out of sheer pity, I am proposing to you and using whatever argument might work to convince you that you should say yes."

Lucy did not know how to respond. She had given him little credit to his face, but she could not bear to leave her question about his honesty unanswered.

"It would be easy to believe, and if you do believe it, I will go immediately to Dash and admit that I have trespassed in his house and broken faith with him despite his enjoinder to me to watch out for Lady Dash and her good friend Miss Bowes."

"You would not," Lucy said, startled.

"I would not like to, no. Ah, I have it," he said, smiling. "Should you ever become dissatisfied with me, you may go to Dash, tell him what I was about way back when, and the threat of that embarrassment will send me right back to true."

"That is absurd."

"No more absurd than your insisting I cannot love you."

Lucy put her palms on his chest, felt the warmth and stimulating solidity of him, and dared to hope. "Did I marry you, I would have to work very hard all the time to keep doing things well."

He laughed. "I beg you, go easier on me than that. All you need do is be yourself and you challenge me sufficiently. Did you work at it, I shudder to think what might happen."

"People will wonder why you married me," Lucy said.

"Let them say it is for your money," he replied.

She half frowned, half smiled.

"One way or another," he said with a touch of grimness, "you will be your brother's heir."

She had almost forgotten. "True."

"I am glad I had proposed to you once already, before you had any hint of inheritance."

Lucy held her hands palms up and moved them like scales. "Scandal, inheritance, scandal, inheritance."

Again he took her hands. "That is what you may say to those creatures like Miss Alton, who would not understand that the person within illuminates and drives the person without. Had I succumbed to an attraction to thieving, for instance, what would I be now?"

They both knew the answer to that question.

"Did thieving hold an attraction?" Lucy asked.

"It was the chase," he replied, setting her hands back upon his chest and encircling her waist. "The trying to get past you. Like playing chess."

"The Dashes will be our neighbors either place."

"I would be honored to call them friends and have them call me friend, as they do to you, if . . ."

"If what?" Lucy asked.

"If you would but say that you will certainly marry me."

"I have not?"

"You have not."

"Yes, Captain Sandeford, I will marry you."

"Does that possibly mean you care some little bit for me? An amount that could fit into your littlest finger would do."

Lucy blushed but rallied. "Do you know, when I first met you, I thought you positively meek?"

"You what?" he asked, astonished.

She smiled. "There, then, you must take as well as give."

"You do make me want to wring your pretty neck."

"Well, I love you too."

"That satisfies," he said wryly.

Lucy twined her hands behind his neck, found the knot where he had tied the mask, and drew it off. "Promise me we will shoot pistols together?" She stood on tiptoe, brushed his lips with hers, and then, greatly daring, nibbled his earlobe.

He inhaled sharply, but said, "And play a lot of chess. A garment of clothing for every piece taken. One cannot always count on rain."

"And travel to interesting places?"

"Where you may practice your Spanish."

Lucy laughed. "Maybe I can learn Italian and speak it with a Spanish accent."

"That I should like to hear."

"And never let you be bored."

"Nor you. No matter what." He kissed her again, thoroughly, intoxicatingly, and Lucy felt all her doubts and fears wash away. She loved him and accepted that however impossible such a notion was, he loved her.

Captain Sandeford gently clasped Lucy's face and brushed back some stray curls. "We must reassure your friends that you are quite all right."

"They sent you to look for me?"

"I volunteered."

"Are you not nice?" She strained forward so she could kiss him again. "Um, very nice."

"Witch."

"Thief."

"Oh, no," he said, smiling. "I never stole anything, remember?"

"Well, if you must insist on technicalities, then I am not a witch."

"Very well. Not-witch."

"Thief." She raised her brows. "I have thought of something you did steal."

He traced an *X* on the bare skin of her cleavage. She shivered deliciously but said, "You did not steal my heart, dear sir. No, that I gave to you. You stole my unhappy notions, and for that loss, I will be forever grateful. I shall become an advertisement for your alternative kind of thievery."

"Thank God," he said, with some irony, "that I wanted someone unconventional."

"Oh!" Miss Alton exclaimed from the library entrance. "Oh!" She turned and ran down the hall.

"We have shocked and appalled her," Lucy said, attempting gravity.

"We are not kind," he agreed, his eyes dancing.

"We should go find Caro and Dash, before Miss Alton fills their ears with unpleasantness."

"Likely for the best, but do kiss me again before we go."

"That is an entirely easy request. Have you nothing more difficult?"

"I shall get to work on that straightaway."

"Do."

More Regency Romance
From Zebra